# OXFORD LETTERS

# OXFORD LETTERS

Veronica Stallwood

headline

First published in 2005
by HEADLINE BOOK PUBLISHING

1

Cataloguing in Publication Data is available from the British Library

ISBN 0 7553 2639 3

Typeset in Times by Avon Dataset Ltd,
Bidford-on-Avon, Warwickshire

Printed and bound in Great Britain by
Clays Ltd, St Ives plc

Headline's policy is to use papers that are natural, renewable and
recyclable products and made from wood grown in sustainable forests.
The logging and manufacturing processes are expected to conform to the
environmental regulations of the country of origin.

HEADLINE BOOK PUBLISHING
A division of Hodder Headline
338 Euston Road
London NW1 3BH

www.headline.co.uk
www.hodderheadline.com

For Diana

# 1

Spring had at last reached Oxford and was now tiptoeing down the Cowley Road.

As the early mist lifted, a greasy film of mud spread across the pavements, ignoring spring's arrival. But away from the traffic, in the side roads, trees were showing the first hint of leaf, the sky above the slate roofs was a promising blue, and daffodils nodded their brazen heads in window-boxes and front gardens. Soon baskets of petunias and lobelia would hang from every lamp-post, and dusty windows would creak upwards to let in the warm air and allow the pounding music within to escape and join the cacophony of traffic below.

To greet the new season, house-owners were checking on the rise in the value of their property since the previous autumn. If they noticed the daffodils at all, it was only in terms of their kerb appeal, and as for the petunias in the hanging baskets, they hoped they would indicate to potential buyers that this was an up-and-coming area in which to invest. As the sun disappeared behind a bank of cloud and a light drizzle fell, couples day-dreamed of exchanging East Oxford for the lavender fields in Provence or olive groves on Zakinthos. The advent of spring would tempt buyers out from their winter hibernation, they told each other.

Raphael Brown, estate agent, turned the sign on his door to 'Open' and looked forward with confidence to a day filled with restless home-owners hoping to sell their properties.

He switched on his computer and admired the smart logo on the opening page for a moment before downloading his emails. Fifty-two new messages, and forty-eight of them spam. He had just dealt with one of the enquiries when the door opened and a couple entered. Raphael (known to everyone except his mother as Rafe) rose from his desk and crossed the floor to greet them, since Jenny, his assistant, was out of the office, measuring up a new property for sale. This particular couple had the purposeful air of genuine buyers.

'We're looking for a property to buy,' said the man, on cue.

Yes, they appeared ideal. The man was tall, probably in his fifties, but fit-looking, with no sign of a paunch. Face tanned, hinting at time spent enjoying warm sunshine during cold winter months. Suit expensive, but tweedy enough for the country. His hair was silver, cut in a short, modern style that made him look more youthful than he was. In fact, the man looked as though he had just stepped out of an advertisement in *Country Life*.

Rafe was being judged in his turn, he realised, feeling the man's grey eyes taking in every detail of his appearance and focusing on the centre of his forehead, as though attempting to read Rafe's mind. Rafe looked away, glancing out of the window at the clean, new-looking car parked on the single yellow line. A Beamer.

'Your car?' he asked.

The man smiled his assent.

'Better keep an eye out for the traffic wardens. They're like vultures round here,' Rafe said. But the man made a dismissive gesture: apparently a parking fine meant no more to him than a bus ticket, and Rafe felt he shouldn't have brought it up.

His wife was about the same age as her husband, with a

soft hairstyle that made the most of her round, forgettable face. 'It's so kind of you to mention it,' she said in a voice that was as comforting as a goose-feather duvet on a cold night. 'Marcus would be furious if he collected another parking ticket and somehow – wouldn't you just know it! – it would be all my fault.' She twinkled at him conspiratorially and leant towards him in a friendly way.

'May I offer you a coffee?' he asked her. 'I think I might even manage to find some biscuits, too.'

'No thank you,' she said gently. 'I think that Marcus is eager to get on with our house-hunting mission.' And then she smiled at him. It was such a sweet, motherly smile, crinkling the corners of her forget-me-not-blue eyes, that he saw that she must be a very nice lady indeed. If you had a problem, she was just the person you would confide in. She would sit and listen to you with that attentive, caring expression on her face, tilting her head to one side, and you would tell her everything, even the despair you had felt that morning in December when you watched Trish drive away from your marriage in the old Volvo, the children's pale, mournful faces pressed against the rear windows. He quickly stopped himself from following that memory any further down the road and turned his attention back to the buyers.

He stood up a little straighter, proffered his hand to the husband and said: 'Rafe Brown.'

'Marcus Freeman,' came the reply. Freeman's hand-shake was firm and confident. 'And this is my wife, Ayesha.'

Rafe pulled chairs into a circle round a low table, inviting the Freemans to sit down, and fetched his laptop. He switched on and watched his logo swim reassuringly into view, and then opened a New Client page and prepared to take down their details.

As he filled in their names, Ayesha said apologetically,

3

'Officially my name is Sheila, so it might be as well to put me down as that.'

'But Ayesha suits you much better,' said Rafe gallantly.

'We've already sold our property in Kent,' said Marcus. 'And now we want to start afresh in a town that holds no unhappy memories for us.' Some family tragedy had prompted them to relocate to a different part of the country, Rafe inferred from his expression.

'Oxford is such a pleasant, cultured city, don't you think?' added Ayesha.

'It certainly enjoys a rich cultural life, Mrs Freeman.'

'Do call me Ayesha,' and once more she treated him to her warm smile.

'And in spite of the current climate, I hear it has a buoyant property market,' said Marcus.

Rafe was able to confirm his good opinion of Oxford. Then he asked, 'So, would you be cash purchasers?'

'We are,' agreed Marcus.

'You won't regret investing your money in Oxford,' Rafe said. 'There will always be a demand for property here, what with the universities – Brookes, you know, as well as the dreaming spires. And then there are the hospitals, of course.'

'We've had a little look around to get an idea of the town and see which areas might suit us,' said Ayesha.

'North Oxford seemed an obvious place to start. Or Headington,' said Marcus. 'But you'll be able to tell us which other neighbourhoods we should consider.'

'Yes, Rafe,' said Ayesha. 'What do you suggest?'

'Grandpont's very desirable,' said Rafe. 'And Jericho, of course.'

'I thought the properties in Jericho were crowded too closely together. And it's still rather shabby in places, isn't it?' said Ayesha.

'And Grandpont's on the wrong side of town,' said Marcus.

They'd obviously done their homework, thought Rafe, even if he didn't agree with their conclusions.

'Have you thought of village properties at all?' he asked.

'Too parochial,' said Marcus.

'Too isolated,' said Ayesha. 'The villages are full of commuters and weekenders, aren't they? They must be silent and empty most of the time. I don't think we'd like that.'

'Headington and North Oxford it is, then,' said Rafe.

'We're looking for a place with no motorbikes, no teenagers hanging around the street corners,' Marcus explained. They also required at least three bedrooms and two reception rooms, all generously sized, plus some kind of studio or office, he told Rafe.

'So you'll be working from home?' asked Rafe, curious to know what kind of business had generated Marcus Freeman's apparent wealth.

'I may have retired from full-time work, but I don't see myself sitting idle all day,' said Marcus Freeman, failing to provide Rafe with any clue. Rafe found himself watching the man's hands, which were large and well formed, with carefully manicured nails. Freeman emphasised his words with gestures that were, to Rafe's eyes, almost priestly in their formality, bringing back memories of his years as an altar boy. Come to think of it, Freeman's sonorous voice, too, was that of a professional persuader. Rafe didn't think that a clergyman made enough money to buy himself a three- or four-bedroomed property in one of the best parts of Oxford when he retired, though, and he didn't quite see Freeman as a retired vicar. There was something a little too worldly about the man for that.

Ayesha Freeman gazed at her husband placidly, apparently admiring his energy without wishing to emulate it. She had settled herself into the egg-shaped chair as though in her own home, reminding Rafe of a pedigree cat – relaxed and decorative – though he still thought she'd make a sympathetic listener.

'But don't forget, darling, we must have somewhere with a garden,' she was saying to her husband, and her words conjured up a warm summer's day, the humming of insects, a hammock beneath an apple tree and a misted glass of lemonade. Rafe pictured himself sitting beside her, confiding the secrets of his life.

'I can't live without flowering plants around me,' she added. 'Foliage and the rustling of leaves in the breeze create a place of great spiritual tranquillity, don't you agree?'

Rafe was saved from replying by Marcus saying briskly, 'And we'll need a double garage, as well as room for our friends to park their cars when they visit.'

Rafe typed in the details of their requirements and tapped a key decisively to call up a screenful of information.

'Just searching the database,' he said. 'It will take a few seconds.' The Freemans waited. 'Let's see how many matches there are, shall we?' Rafe scanned down the lines of print on the screen, then looked up, feeling pleased. 'Here we are. I believe—'

But at this moment the street door crashed open, breaking his concentration, spoiling the intimacy of the agent–client relationship. He looked round, momentarily forgetting to wear his professional smile. Ah, yes. Roz Ivory and Mrs Fordham. It was Roz who had thrown open the door in that ebullient manner. He half rose from his chair, not wanting to abandon the Freemans, yet reminding himself that Fordham and Ivory were regular, reliable clients, and therefore to be treated with respect. He readjusted his expression to one of friendly welcome.

'Have a seat, ladies. And why don't you pour yourselves a cup of coffee? You know where to find it, don't you, Mrs Fordham.'

'Property developers,' he explained quietly to the Freemans. 'And they could well be working on a house you'd be interested in. Let me have a quick word with them – you could get to view it before anyone else has a chance.'

'We can see you're busy, Rafe. Don't worry about us, we have errands to run. We can easily come back later.' Roz Ivory, red hair pinned up, wearing paint-spattered blue jeans, looked ready for work.

'Why don't we come back in twenty minutes?' That was Mrs Fordham, always so precise. She was as neat as ever, too, managing to look smart and businesslike even though she too was wearing denim and plaid. She'd probably feel more comfortable in something formal, unlike Roz, who, given half a chance he felt, would wander round in bare feet and a sarong, with her red hair hanging down her back. He'd fallen naturally into the habit of calling her by her first name, although she was a fair bit older than him, but when it came to Mrs Fordham it was hard to imagine anyone ever calling her Avril.

'I brought you this, Rafe.' It was Roz, leaning over his chair, placing something on the table in front of him: a terracotta pot filled with paper-white narcissi. Damp compost scattered in an arc across the table while the light from the window struck sparks from the diamonds on her fingers: a hoop of five large stones set in platinum as well as a solitaire that would gladden the heart of a footballer's wife. Trust Roz Ivory to wear rocks like that for a morning's painting and decorating! Either the property business was more buoyant than he had thought or else she had formerly enjoyed the admiration of a very rich man.

'What a beautiful scent,' said Ayesha Freeman, leaning

back with her eyes half closed. 'I can feel it soothing my nerves and bringing joy to my spirit. And how delightful the flowers are.'

'It's just a small reminder that spring is here at last,' said Roz. 'And if the daffodils are in bloom, then long, sunlit days can only be a week or two away, I always think.'

Outside, the rain was falling more heavily than before and a chill wind rattled the door, but Roz Ivory was ever the optimist.

'Thanks so much, Roz. This is really thoughtful of you,' said Rafe, brushing at the spilt compost with his handker-chief. 'How's the North Oxford project going, by the way? It must be nearly completed by now.'

'That's what we came to see you about. We want to show you around and convince you that we have another winning property on our hands. You're going to love it!'

'But we don't want to interrupt you when you're with clients,' said Mrs Fordham.

'And we want to know what new properties you have to show us,' continued Roz. 'We're itching to find our next project as soon as possible. What have you got on your books, Rafe? We're on a roll!'

'That might take a little time to sort out. But I can't wait to see the one you've just finished, ladies. I don't suppose you have any photos on you, by any chance?'

'I'm afraid not,' said Roz.

'Why don't I meet you there in an hour's time? I'll bring my camera with me.' Rafe wasn't going to let such a large potential commission slip through his fingers. He turned back to the Freemans. 'From what I've heard, I think this might be just the place you're looking for, and you can bet it will be snapped up as soon as it's on the market.'

'If you're that sure, why don't we come with you?' asked Marcus.

'It's not quite ready to view,' said Avril. 'We haven't dressed it yet, have we, Roz?'

Marcus gave Roz no time to reply. 'Let me introduce myself. Marcus Freeman. And this is my wife, Ayesha.'

Roz and Avril gave their names and the two women shook hands with Marcus while Ayesha watched.

'I don't suppose it would do any harm to show Mr and Mrs Freeman round, Avril,' said Roz.

'Marcus, please.'

'And do call me Ayesha.'

'Why don't we make a firm appointment for three days' time?' said Avril. 'We can promise you that no other buyers will see it before then.'

It was no good trying to convince Mrs Fordham that she should be less cautious and grab the chance of a quick sale, Rafe knew, but Roz's flair for presentation could well add a good few thousand to the price, so he wasn't going to quibble.

'I expect we can wait three days, Marcus,' said Ayesha comfortably. 'And we're not going to buy the first house we see. We need to get a good idea of what's available, and I'm sure that Rafe will look after us beautifully.'

Sensible woman, thought Rafe.

'We'll be on our way, then,' said Roz. 'And we'll see you in North Oxford in an hour or so, Rafe?'

'Jenny should be back soon,' he said. 'So I'll be free to join you. Let me see you out, ladies.'

Just outside the door he told them what good clients he thought the Freemans were – and such a charming couple, too.

'It won't hurt to make them wait a couple of days,' said Avril.

'They'll be all the keener,' said Roz cheerfully, knowing that their house would sell as soon as they put it on the market.

Rafe watched them climb into their van and pull away, then turned back to the clients waiting patiently inside.

'Very competent property developers,' he told them. 'Always a high-quality finish to their work, and well-thought-out designs. Roz Ivory has real talent when it comes to the design. They've been at it for three years or more and they know their market. Of course,' he added quickly, 'it would be a good idea to look at other properties, too.'

'Yes, I agree that we need to get the feel of the local market. But I'm very interested in what those two have to offer. Perhaps you'd confirm that we'd like an appointment to view as soon as they can manage it.'

Rafe printed out details of substantial houses for the Freemans to look through, and gave them the number of his mobile so that they could get in touch at any time. 'I'll make the appointments for you and take you round,' he said. 'We could set aside tomorrow morning, if you like.'

'You've been very helpful,' said Marcus, standing up.

'I know you're going to find us something really special, Rafe,' said Ayesha, joining him.

Rafe accompanied them to the pavement. From the right, a small, weasel-faced man in a yellow-banded cap and walking with the hurried gait of a fanatic was closing in on the Freemans' BMW, notebook in hand.

'Get in the car.' Marcus Freeman spoke quite sharply to his wife, and there was no mistaking the fact that he was used to being obeyed. Ayesha waved farewell to Rafe from the passenger window as Marcus accelerated away.

Rafe re-entered his office, closing the door behind him. The phone was ringing and he crossed the room to answer it. 'Rafe Brown,' he said into the receiver. 'How may I help you?'

As he answered the routine enquiry, he was still thinking about the couple who had just left. Even if the Freemans didn't buy Ivory and Fordham's property, he was sure that he would find them something suitably expensive in one of the best parts of town. He and Ayesha had hit it off, he knew.

Yes, those two were serious about buying, and he was the man to find the right house for them.

He fetched a saucer and placed it under the pot of narcissi, then brushed away the spilt compost. Roz was right: spring was here, and good selling days lay ahead.

# 2

According to its official diary, the New Year at Oxford starts not in January but in October. This is when the old year's memories are reviewed and edited before being tidied away, together with the mistakes of the past twelve months. Then the new diary is taken out and plans are made to fill lengthening evenings and damp, misty mornings with novel pursuits and fresh ideas.

And quite right too, agreed Kate Ivory as she picked out a rather good photograph of a Norwegian fjord sparkling under an August sun, and attached it to the grey cartridge paper of her holiday journal. When she had finished writing up the notes on her recent holiday, and illustrated them with the photographs she had taken, she could take stock of the past year and dream about what she would do in the new one.

She turned the page, and from the heap of photographs she selected a view of a glacier tumbling down towards a turquoise lake. In the foreground stood a sun-bronzed figure with short brown hair and a long, thin face, smiling into the camera lens: Jon Kenrick. In that place, on that morning, he had lost his usual preoccupied, defensive expression – and shed about ten years from his age in the process.

She remembered the first time they had met, in her friend Camilla's house, when her safety was at stake and he had needed her to help in one of his own investigations. Not that he was a policeman, he'd told her, but a member of NCIS, the National Criminal Intelligence Service, gathering inform-ation on serious and organised crime. Their relationship had developed slowly. Oxford and London are only fifty miles apart, but the distance prevented them from meeting on impulse: they met for the weekend at his place or hers, and occasionally spent a couple of days on his boat, but this was the first time they had taken a longer holiday together. They'd never discussed it, they'd just silently agreed that they were both people who needed their own space.

Yes, he was really a very attractive man. Certainly the blonde woman who had been staying at the same hotel in Balestrand had thought so. She and her husband had joined their table for breakfast one morning, and she had found Jon so amusing, leaning across to hear what he was saying, resting her hand on his arm, that she had suggested that the four of them should hire a boat and explore the fjord. Luckily Jon's reaction had been all Kate could have hoped for. He made their excuses and then, when they were alone had said, 'Let's get off early tomorrow morning, just in case they want to join us again.'

'Don't you like them?' Kate had said.

'They're pleasant enough. But we have little enough time alone together as it is. I don't want to share you with other people just yet.' And she had marked that as a step forward in their relationship.

In the next picture, she and Jon stood together, his arm round her shoulders, both of them looking fit and tanned and happy to be together. It was good to think that, if she wanted, she need never spend another weekend on her own. But that was the problem: she liked to know that, if she wanted, she could do exactly that.

The phone rang, destroying the sun-drenched memories.

'Bother!' She looked on the display for the name of the person calling, but there was a number only, and not one that she recognised. 'Hello?'

'Hello, this is Avril Fordham speaking.' The voice was

precise and belonged to her mother's business partner. 'We don't know each other very well, Kate, but I felt I had to talk to someone, and I couldn't think who else to contact.'

Kate remembered when she had met Avril for the first time: a well-preserved woman in her sixties sitting on the bead-sewn cushions of Roz's crimson sofa, drinking Earl Grey while Kate and Roz eyed the bottle of rioja Kate had brought with her, wondering whether they could pour themselves a glass. 'A sensible woman' was how Kate would describe her.

'It's about your mother,' said Avril.

What had Roz done this time? Had she once more involved herself in some ill-judged money-making scheme? Kate had thought that Avril had been a calming influence on her and that she and Roz had been making a comfortable living from their property dealings. Or had Roz fallen in with an unsuitable man? Surely she was getting too old for that sort of thing. Or would she still be attracting flashy, unreliable men even as Kate wheeled her into the Twilight Home for Incurable Romantics? All too likely.

'I've tried to talk sense into her, but she just won't listen,' continued Avril.

'What's wrong with her? What's she been up to?' She was sure that all her fears were about to be confirmed.

'Oh dear, this is very awkward. Look, don't think I'm criticising at all, but I gather you haven't seen her for a while,' said Avril delicately.

'I saw her only the other week,' Kate began, then she stopped. 'No, you're right. I've been back from holiday for over a fortnight, and it could well have been a couple of weeks before I flew to Norway when I last went over there. So that would be, well, six weeks or so ago. She'd hate it if I was round there every other day, though, and I did send her a postcard.'

'I'm sure you did,' said Avril. 'And I know you're both independent people with busy lives to live. It's just that I'm worried about her, and I thought you ought to know what's happening. She hasn't told you anything about it, has she? That's just so typical of her.'

'About what? You'll have to fill me in right from the beginning.'

'Where to start?' Avril sighed. 'I'm very fond of your mother, and we do mesh together really well when we're working. But I have to admit that I don't always see eye to eye with her over, well, people.'

'What is it this time? A shady, unsuitable man? Some loopy woman she met while travelling in a yak caravan across the desert, who's just turned up on her doorstep, seeking asylum?' Anyone would think it was a teenager Kate was talking about instead of a woman old enough to have a daughter in her thirties.

'I don't think they have yaks in the desert,' said Avril doubtfully. 'And it's not nearly as irrational as you're suggesting. These friends of hers are a married couple and seem quite respectable, though I can't say that I took to them, but that's my problem, not hers – I wouldn't be ringing you if that were all. It's to do with her health, and it's that I'm worried about, Kate.'

'But she was blooming last time I saw her...' Kate's voice trailed away to silence. Was this true? Had she even bothered to notice whether Roz was well or not? She'd been so full of the plans for her holiday with Jon that she'd breezed in and out of Roz's East Oxford house without noticing anything at all. Roz could have been pining away from some fatal disease for all she'd cared.

'These things are so insidious, aren't they?' Avril was saying. 'And I'm sure that an outsider notices signs that a family member wouldn't, because the changes are so gradual. You only see what you expect when it's one of your own, don't you? It comes as such a shock when they're suddenly whisked into hospital.'

'Hospital?'

'Oh, no. I didn't mean that *Roz*—'

'I should have spotted that something was wrong. I was too wrapped up in my own affairs, that's the trouble. But please tell me: what exactly *is* wrong with Roz?'

'She's lost weight.' Avril's voice was businesslike again. 'And she's lost her usual energy, too. You know what she's like, Kate. She'll work on site all day and then, just when I want to put my feet up and relax in front of some undemanding television programme, Roz is ready to go out for the evening.'

'That sounds familiar!'

'But these days she apologises for being so feeble, then packs up to go home for a rest at three in the afternoon. And I look at her white face and the hollowness round her eyes and I know that bed's the best place for her. Now, is that the Roz we both know?'

'I see what you mean,' said Kate slowly. 'It certainly isn't like her: I've never known Roz to sleep in the daytime. What does her doctor say?'

'That's what I meant about people. She hasn't seen a doctor at all as far as I can make out. She welcomes these friends of hers – they're called Freeman – into her house every day and follows all their ridiculous suggestions, but she won't take five minutes off to visit a real doctor. Quacks and charlatans, she calls them. And hospitals are dangerous places, according to Roz. Well, of course, I see what she means when it comes to this dreadful MRSA, but mostly they do more good than harm.'

Kate sighed. She understood that Roz had been at her most irritating. She'd probably been dosing herself with some alternative remedy, egged on by these batty new friends of hers, and if Avril tried to argue with her she'd just grow more stubborn.

'I'd better get straight round to her place. It's odd she hasn't rung me, though, if she's not been well. I could at least have done some shopping or a little light dusting for her.'

'That's the other thing,' said Avril. 'That's where the Freemans come into the picture. They're hanging around all the time, it seems to me: running errands, cooking meals. Roz and I are in partnership, as you know, and I can't seem to get any sense out of her at the moment. Between us, we have a lot of money at stake – I'm sure Roz won't mind my mentioning this. But as soon as she and I start to talk business, there they are, pushing in and preventing any sensible discussion. In fact, you'd think it was Marcus Freeman's property we were discussing rather than mine and Roz's.'

Whatever else she might get up to from time to time, Kate had found that Roz had been completely committed when it came to her work.

'Haven't they got jobs to go to?' asked Kate.

'Not that I've noticed. They're obviously not short of a bob or two, so I suppose they can spend their days minding other people's business. I'm sure they're well-meaning, Kate, but I do wish they wouldn't interfere.'

'I'd better pop round to Roz's house and suss out the situation, and then I'll get back to you.'

'Oh, would you? That would be such a worry off my mind.' Avril appeared to have greater confidence in Kate's ability to influence her mother than Kate herself did. 'This week we should be searching for a new property to renovate, but Roz keeps making excuses and leaving the decisions to me.'

'You're right. That isn't like her at all. She must be ill. And what about these Freemans? Do you know anything about them?'

'Not very much. They use a lot of words without imparting any sensible information. All I know is that they came here from Kent a few months ago. Apparently we met them at the estate agent's, back in the early spring, but they didn't make a lasting impression on me. Rafe brought them to look at one of our developments, and they were very complimentary about it, but it wasn't quite large enough for them.'

'But they kept in touch with Roz, you say. I wonder why.'

'She's a convivial person, don't you think? Perhaps it's just that they like her. If they've moved here from Kent, they must be wanting to make new friends.'

When she had replaced the receiver, Kate tidied away the record of her holiday with Jon. The two denim-clad figures, glowing with robust health, still smiled up at her as she tucked them into the album, but now they appeared self-absorbed and uncaring.

She picked up the first jacket she found on the hook in the hall and left the house. Roz must be really under the weather, but if she phoned her now she could imagine her mother fobbing her off with protests about being fine, really, and so it would be better to call unannounced.

The days were growing shorter and the afternoon sun was low in the sky, but it was a fine autumn day and Kate decided to walk across to East Oxford rather than drive and join the traffic crawling through the town centre. She would pass through the covered market on her way and pick up a little gourmet something or other. Roz enjoyed good food, and she wasn't averse to a bottle of Australian red, either.

\* \* \*

19

Kate emerged from the market swinging a plastic bag stuffed with goodies from the deli, and turned right into the Turl. She was forced to step into a college gateway to allow a group of chirruping tourists to pass and she stood for a moment admiring the mellow old buildings and perfect green lawn of the quadrangle. Creeper-hung walls caught the afternoon sun, blazing in gold and scarlet. An arched gateway in the opposite corner lay in shadow and promised to take her not just into another tree-shaded grove, but backwards in time as well. And then the pavement cleared and Kate walked on through the twenty-first century before another group of visitors could impede her progress.

# 3

Kate rang the bell and waited. No familiar footsteps pounded down the stairs and approached the door. Behind her at the kerb stood Roz's car – no longer the old egg-yolk-yellow Beetle which her mother had been driving when she dropped back into Kate's life some five years ago, but a pristine silver Peugeot – so it seemed likely that her mother was at home. She took a couple of steps backwards and looked up at the bedroom window. The curtains were half drawn as though the occupant hadn't quite made up her mind whether to get up that morning or retire back to bed with a plateful of warm croissants and a jug of coffee. Kate rang again, and this time she detected a slight movement inside the house and the sound of unwilling feet approaching the door. She expected it to be flung wide in Roz's usual exuberant manner and her mother to make some excuse for keeping her waiting, but when the door finally opened it was only halfway, and Roz just stood there, looking at her, saying nothing.

'May I come in?' asked Kate.

'Yes, of course,' and Roz stood back for her daughter to pass through into the living room. She sounded tired and her voice lacked animation.

Roz looked different too, and Kate was cross with herself for not having taken the trouble to notice this before Avril's prompting. Her face was much thinner; she wore no make-up, and her skin had a yellowish tinge; there were strands of grey in her red hair that Kate had never seen before; even her shoulders had taken on a slight stoop. Her mother, she realised, looked old. And the thought, in relation to Roz, was so unexpected as to be disturbing.

'Shall I make us both some tea?' Kate asked solicitously.

'I thought that this was the time of day when you were in the habit of pouring yourself a glass of cold white wine,' replied Roz with her customary acerbity, Kate was relieved to hear. 'Why don't you get us both one? You'll find a bottle already open in the fridge.'

That was more like the old Roz. Maybe there wasn't much wrong with her after all. Just a virus. This was just the time of year for such a thing. There must be dozens of them floating around in the damp Oxford air.

'I've brought you a few things from the deli,' said Kate. 'And a bottle of red, in case you need building up. Shall I put them away for you?'

'I think I'm still capable of doing that for myself.' Her mother obviously didn't appreciate the reference to 'building up'. 'Just leave them on the kitchen table.' But Kate was glad to see that she sniffed appreciatively at the Belgian ham and the French cheese and read the wine label before placing the bottle in the rack. 'Thank you for all this. But why the sudden visit, and bearing gifts, to boot?'

'I haven't seen you for ages,' replied Kate. 'And since I was passing through the covered market I thought I'd see what was on offer.'

Roz's stare was as sharp and sceptical as ever, but all she said was, 'I loved the postcard with the polar bear. Why don't you get out the glasses and I'll pour the wine?'

They took their drinks through to the sitting room and settled themselves on Roz's comfortable, cushion-strewn sofas. Looking around her, Kate was aware that the room looked different somehow. She was not one to run her finger along a shelf to see if it needed dusting, or even to care if it did, but it struck her that the house was getting a little unkempt. Out in the kitchen, too, there had been more dirty dishes stacked up next to the sink than she had ever seen before in Roz's house.

'Why don't you put your feet up, if you're feeling tired?' said Kate.

'Do stop fussing, Kate. It isn't like you. You're reminding me of Avril. Ah . . .' She paused and stared suspiciously at her daughter. 'Avril's been in touch with you, pouring her worries about my imminent demise into your receptive ear. That's why you've come rushing round with wholesome, health-giving food and drink, enquiring after my well-being. I'm right, aren't I?'

'Why wouldn't I do that without prompting from Avril? And anyway, I wouldn't call red wine, jambon d'Ardennes and Vignotte particularly healthy nosh.'

'Of course it is! Look at the French! And Avril's a wonderful woman, but a terrible one for fussing over nothing,' said Roz firmly.

'She struck me as unusually level-headed and sensible,' said Kate, deciding against pointing out that the ham was Belgian and the wine Australian.

They glared at one another. There was no point in arguing with Roz when she was in one of her pig-headed moods. Kate decided to get straight to the point.

'Avril phoned me because she was worried, and it's at least a couple of months since I've been round to see you. Tell me honestly, how have you been keeping?'

Roz stared at her daughter over the rim of her glass. 'I've told you, I'm fine.'

Kate tried again. 'You're not looking yourself. Have you had your flu jab?'

'I have no intention of going down to the surgery for an injection of poison. You're more likely to pick up some

23

infection when you visit the doctor's than prevent one, I've always found. I steer well clear of that place.'

'It might just be a good idea—'

'You know how I feel about doctors, Kate. Quacks and charlatans the lot of them! Did I ever take you to the surgery when you were a child?'

'Not that I remember.'

'Exactly. And look at you: a fine, strong, healthy specimen of womanhood!'

'I'm not sure you can put that down entirely to an avoidance of doctors,' said Kate, remembering her recent pleasurable holiday. How could she steer the conversation back to Roz's health rather than her own? Her mother seemed determined to deny that anything was wrong with her.

As Kate was considering what approach to take, she heard a key turning in the front door lock.

'Roz dear!' called a female voice.

'It's only us!' added a male one.

'In the living room,' called back Roz, and Kate wondered who was on such intimate terms with her mother that they possessed the key to her front door. She certainly hadn't been trusted with one herself, and she didn't think anyone else had before this, either.

# 4

'My friends, the Freemans,' announced Roz, and from her lack of surprise, Kate sensed that they were expected. Perhaps they arrived at this time every day. She felt the same jolt of resentment that Avril must have felt when they walked in on her business discussions.

Marcus Freeman strode into the room, followed a step or so behind by his wife. They reminded Kate of actors, the way they immediately filled the room with their personalities. Keep an open mind, Kate, she reminded herself, and don't be swayed by any preconceptions. It wasn't that she was possessive about her mother, she told herself, but couldn't they have been a little more reluctant to interrupt a private conversation?

'Marcus and Ayesha,' said Roz.

'And this must be the daughter we've heard so much about,' said Ayesha, while Marcus beamed at Kate in a welcoming manner.

If she had expected 'Ayesha' to be an exotic beauty, she would have been disappointed. This woman was probably in her early fifties, and had dishwater hair, pale blue eyes and a formless, pale face. She wasn't quite as tall as Kate, and was dressed in flowing, vaguely ethnic clothes that made her look shorter and wider than she was in reality. Kate recognised the fabric, striped in shades of cinnamon, Prussian blue and aubergine, from the display in the window of one of the expensive dress shops in the High Street. So, not short of a bob or two, as Avril had put it.

25

'Dear Kate. How lovely to meet you,' said Ayesha, grasping one of Kate's hands in both hers and gazing into her eyes. 'I can see that we're going to be friends.'

'You can?' Kate wondered how she could see this so clearly on a thirty-second acquaintance. 'I'm not sure—'

Ayesha laughed. 'You don't agree! You think I'm just an irritating old woman, don't you?'

'No, no, of course not!' exclaimed Kate, disarmed by Ayesha's candour.

'But we have a lot in common, you and I, and I know we're going to get along. Trust me. I have an instinct for these things,' said Ayesha. She took a step backwards and looked Kate over critically. 'I can't see much of your mother in you, though. You're not at all like her, are you?'

'I think we have a certain strong-willed, stubborn streak in common,' said Kate, retrieving her hand, but warming towards Ayesha.

'What she means is that she's pig-headed, just like her father,' put in Roz.

'Ah, such a cruel loss!'

'I think I'm probably over it by now,' said Kate. She didn't like strangers – or even her friends, if it came to that – invading such delicate areas of her past.

'He wasn't exactly a memorable man,' put in Roz. 'If you were going to lose a parent, Kate, it was just as well that it was him and not me. You'd have turned into a really boring person without your mother to shock you out of your tendency towards conventional behaviour.'

'Don't worry, Kate. Your mother never says such unkind things about you when you're not here. She's always very complimentary, and Marcus and I are thrilled to meet a successful author,' said Ayesha soothingly.

'Well . . .' said Kate, charmed by her flattery, and relieved to have left a painful subject.

26

'I believe it's a first for us,' said Marcus enthusiastically. 'We've never met a popular novelist before, not to talk to like this. Will we find your books in Blackwell's or Borders?'

'I believe they do have one or two of my titles,' said Kate, striving to look modest about her achievements.

'We'll have to get straight down there tomorrow morning. And tell me, are you working on something at the moment?'

'It's a never-ending process, isn't it, Kate?' said Roz drily.

'More or less. I have to earn a living, after all.'

'You make it sound so mundane!' exclaimed Ayesha. 'I'm sure that you sit there waiting for inspiration to strike some mornings. So tell me, what do you do for spiritual refreshment?'

'Well, I, er . . .' She didn't feel she knew the Freemans well enough yet to give them a description of her weekends with Jon, and looked across at Roz for help. But Roz was leaning back with her eyes closed, probably enjoying Kate's discomfiture. 'I find that a long walk, or a run along the canal and through the woods can work wonders,' she said.

'Communing with Nature,' commented Ayesha, nodding her head in approval. 'The source of all inspiration.'

'It helps me to think,' said Kate flatly, not liking to investigate the sources of her inspiration too closely in case they disappeared. 'It's something to do with the silence and the physical exercise, though scrubbing a floor can work just as well.'

'Come and sit over here next to me, Ayesha,' said Roz, who had opened her eyes and was sitting up, looking alert once more. She moved to one end of the sofa and patted the cushion next to her, reminding Kate of her own actions when persuading Susanna, her marmalade cat, to join her when she watched television. Come to think of it, Ayesha did resemble a cat. A large, fluffy cat, entirely convinced of

27

her own unique merit and waiting for some well-behaved human to pour the cream into her bowl. It was this self-absorption that Kate admired about cats.

In a whisper of jewel-bright silk, Ayesha crossed the room and sat down next to Roz, beginning a conversation in a low murmur, excluding the other two. Kate turned to Marcus Freeman. He was perhaps a year or so older than his wife, with silver hair cut severely short, a face tanned much more deeply than Kate's own, and a way of standing that demonstrated that he was admirably at ease inside his own skin. His clothes looked as though they all had designer labels inside them.

'Don't let Ayesha put you off,' he said, laying a hand on Kate's arm and smiling down at her. 'She's a creature of impulse, you'll find, but utterly sincere, and if she says that you and she are going to be friends, you can depend on it that it will be true one of these days.' His hand was warm and heavy, exerting control, and Kate wished that he would remove it. As though sensing her dislike of the contact, after a few seconds he did so.

'Why don't you two sit down and make yourselves comfortable,' suggested Roz, breaking off her conversation with Ayesha. Marcus's eyes fell on the glasses of wine and for a moment Kate thought she saw a small frown.

'Can I pour you some wine?' she asked.

'It's a little early in the evening for us, thank you dear,' said Ayesha, with a smile, but just the hint of a reproach in her voice. 'But a small glass of organic apple juice would be very nice.'

'I nearly forgot, Roz,' said Marcus. I've brought a few things for our supper. Just a light and nutritious snack, nothing too demanding for the digestion. I'd better put them in the fridge, hadn't I?'

'And don't forget the supplements,' added Ayesha.

'Of course. I'll pour the apple juice while I'm out there. Would you like some too, Roz?'

'Not at the moment,' Roz replied, adding, 'And Marcus, you really must let me write you a cheque for the food and supplements this time.'

'When you feel up to it,' said Marcus. He turned a concerned face to Kate. 'I'm so very sorry. I hadn't realised we'd be enjoying the pleasure of your company too, Kate, or I'd have catered a little more generously.' He made an expansive gesture with a well-shaped hand.

'Don't worry. I'm not staying long,' she replied quickly. 'I only popped in to say hello after my holiday.'

'Roz tells us that you lead such a busy life,' said Ayesha. 'Well, of course, as a successful author it must be difficult for you to find the time to visit your mother at all regularly. We quite understand, and no one would dream of blaming you.'

'Well, I'm not sure that Roz—'

'Not that you have any need to worry about her being lonely,' said Marcus.

'I wasn't going—'

'Not while Ayesha and I are here,' he added in explanation. 'Roz explained to us that you and she are quite separate people, with separate lives, and with only the most casual contact from one year's end to the next. But I think you'll find that in your absence we've introduced your dear mother to a number of small, healthful improvements to her lifestyle and I'm sure you'll soon see some beneficent results in her physical being.'

Roz was allowing the conversation to wash over her, but taking no part in it.

'That's reassuring to know,' said Kate, wishing that her mother would open her eyes and tell the Freemans to stop fussing and let her enjoy her wine – not to mention a slice of jambon d'Ardennes or a little ripe Vignotte. 'And I hadn't realised that her lifestyle needed much improvement.'

The Freemans continued to smile, but Ayesha said softly, 'Oh, but I think we all know that there remains much to accomplish in that area.'

'I can see that you have her welfare at heart, but don't you think you should persuade her to visit her GP?' Kate blurted out. The Freemans both laughed indulgently.

'Western medicine treats the symptoms. We know that we have to treat the whole person, don't we?' responded Marcus patiently. 'The body has its own wisdom when it comes to healing.'

Kate looked across at her mother, expecting her to protest at Marcus's patronising tone, but Roz still said nothing.

'I'm very lucky in my friends, Kate,' said Roz. 'You and I don't need to be in and out of one another's houses every day – you'd hate that, and so would I – and I'm sure you won't resent the fact that I have good friends who keep an eye on me now and then. After all, we spent a long time when we hardly said hello from one year to the next.'

Kate could have pointed out that that was hardly her choice. It was Roz who had disappeared into the blue for years without so much as a postcard to tell Kate where she was. 'I didn't realise you needed looking after,' said Kate stiffly. 'I'd have come round straightaway if I'd known.'

'That's the trouble, isn't it, Kate?' said Marcus reasonably. 'We just don't see the problems faced by those who are nearest to us.'

As an expectant silence appeared to have settled over the room, Kate said eventually, 'Yes, well, I suppose I'd better be on my way and leave you to enjoy your meal.'

'That's right, Kate,' said Roz, opening her eyes again. 'And don't worry about me. I'm absolutely fine.'

'Oh, good, I'm so pleased you're better,' said Kate, as though giving in. 'Why don't you see me to the door?'

As Roz pushed herself up and off the sofa and crossed the room, the Freemans looked as though they might leap forward to prevent her from joining her daughter. Kate took her arm, closed the door of the sitting room behind them and steered her mother towards the front door.

'You can come home with me if you like,' she said. 'All you have to do is sneak away and leave them to it. I've another bottle of wine and some decent food in the fridge, a pristine toothbrush in the bathroom cabinet and a spare room waiting for its first customer.'

'Why on earth would I want to leave my own house?'

'They're taking over your life.'

'Don't be ridiculous.'

'I can see that they're kind, warm-hearted people and that they're doing everything they can to be helpful, but is that really what you want?'

'If I didn't, I could ask them to leave,' said Roz reasonably.

'And why have they got their own doorkey?'

'Now you're just sounding childish and jealous!'

'Maybe, but I'd like to know, all the same.'

'They were very kind when I wasn't feeling well. You've probably noticed that they've done little bits of shopping for me. And Ayesha didn't want to bring me down from the bedroom when I was resting, so I gave her a key.'

'I just wish I could help in some way,' Kate said. She wished, too, that she and Roz hadn't spent so many years apart. It seemed the right moment to give her a hug, or at least to put an arm round her shoulders, but there was something in Roz that stopped her from doing so. Her gesture would be rejected, in the nicest possible way.

But when Roz spoke, her tone was more conciliatory, as though she knew what Kate was thinking.

'You are right: I have been a bit off-colour recently. It's probably a virus of some kind and nothing to worry about. My mother always said that illness showed a lack of moral fibre and that I should just snap out of it. It's not a bad way to behave, you know – better than whingeing all the time and taking every little ache and pain so seriously. And the Freemans have been giving me a hand when I haven't felt up to going out to the shops and so on. I don't have to agree with all their funny ideas, you know, but their hearts are in the right place. And there's a lot in what they say about Western medicine: I've never been very keen on it myself. And Kate, they're very kind people.'

'I can see that. I can see why you like Ayesha, at least. But can't I—'

'Just go home, Kate, and stop worrying about me.'

There was nothing more to say, for Ayesha had appeared at Roz's shoulder. 'Why don't you go and sit down, Roz dear. You look like you could do with a little rest after all the excitement. I'll wave Kate goodbye for you.'

Roz made her way back into the sitting room, and Kate was turning to leave when Ayesha stopped her with a hand on her arm.

'You must forgive me for what I said a little while ago,' she said.

'What was that?'

'I mentioned your father, and I could see straight away that I'd touched on a painful subject. I'm sorry, Kate, for bringing it up.'

'Well, you weren't to know, Ayesha.'

'But I do generally know these things,' she said. 'I feel them. Here,' and she pressed a padded fist against her bosom. 'And I wanted you to know that I recognised your hurt. Tell me, dear, do you remember very much about him?'

'He wasn't a very noticeable person. Not like Roz. But I

32

have got a few photographs, so I know what he looked like.'

'But you must be searching for his emotional likeness too, surely?'

'I'm not sure what you mean.'

'I've offended you again, haven't I? I shouldn't speak to you like this when we've only just met. Forget I said anything at all.'

'Don't worry about it, Ayesha. Just try to . . .' She wanted to tell Ayesha to look after Roz, but she couldn't bring herself to say it.

At last Ayesha removed her hand from Kate's arm, and a few seconds later she found herself outside in the street, the front door closed firmly behind her. As she walked away, she heard the three voices in the front room raised in animated conversation, as though they had only been waiting for her to leave in order to enjoy themselves.

A mist had fallen while she was in Roz's place, and it thickened as she crossed the town centre and walked towards the canal. Buildings appeared suddenly out of the haze, distorted and unrecognisable; street lamps, switching themselves on earlier than usual in the false dusk, cast pallid circles of light that reached no more than a yard into the obscurity. Even knowing these streets as well as she did, she might easily lose her way.

Marcus and Ayesha left Roz's house only half an hour or so after Kate. Marcus drove slowly through the thickening mist.

'Well, what did you think of the daughter?' he asked his wife.

'Not at all what I was expecting.'

'No. Roz gave me the impression that they hardly ever saw one another and their lives were quite separate. I wasn't expecting to meet her there this evening: she hasn't been around for months.'

'She does care about her mother, doesn't she? Especially now she's noticed that Roz isn't well.'

'She didn't look happy about the supplements we'd brought over. I hope Kate doesn't think you're feeding her mother poisonous herbs and potions!'

'Don't joke about it. Those are high-potency products from a most reputable source, and I don't want Kate suggesting to Roz that they're anything else.'

'OK. Point taken. I don't suppose we'll see her again in any case.'

'Getting back to what we were talking about this morning,' said Ayesha, changing the subject. 'What shall we do about the cleaner?'

Marcus waited to turn right at the traffic lights in the High Street. He looked at his wife. 'Maria? You don't still want to get rid of her, do you?'

'I told you. She's too nosy. I'm sure she's been going through my desk.'

'You're imagining it. She can hardly read her own language, let alone English.'

'You only want her to stay because she's pretty,' said Ayesha petulantly.

The lights changed and Marcus turned into Longwall. 'Don't be ridiculous! I want her to stay because she keeps the house clean. Do you want to waste your time on dusting and hoovering?'

'We could find someone else.'

'She might not work as hard. I should give Maria another chance.'

'Very well. But if I catch her trying on my clothes, she's fired on the spot.'

Marcus drew up at another set of lights. 'Fair enough,' he said.

# 5

That night, before retiring to bed, Roz Ivory unlocked her desk drawer and stood for a while looking at the mass of letters crammed inside: an ocean of blue paper, covered with words, threatening to drown her. She lifted one out at random, but she didn't need to read it, she couldn't forget the phrases, however hard she tried.

*I do want you to read this very carefully indeed.*

She should have thrown away the first letter instead of replying to it, she could see that now. Kate would tell her that she had spent too long in California, drinking in woolly New Age superstitions and using enough alcohol and weed to kill off useful brain cells, so that now she was taken in by such nonsense.

'Don't be silly, Roz. No rational person would fall for this,' Kate would say. And now she wished she had shown that first letter to Kate, but it had seemed harmless enough to send off the cheque for twenty pounds instead.

*I do not want your money. This is not a confidence trick. My services are completely free. All I ask is that you send me a small sum – most people believe that twenty pounds is reasonable – just to cover my expenses, so that I can continue to help those, like yourself, who are standing on the brink of disaster.*

It had been curiosity more than anything else that had made her do it, rather like stepping into the fortune teller's booth at the fair. And twenty pounds was a modest sum.

*You will find my address on the reverse of this letter.*

But when she posted off her cheque, she hadn't realised that this would be only the beginning.

*I urge you to listen to what I am saying. Believe me, I have your very best interests at heart.*

There had been a swift response to her cheque. A whole flood of letters had arrived, warning her of the dangers that surrounded her. They hadn't even come from the same source, she realised, when she looked at the return addresses, but this time they urged her to send her credit card details – so much more convenient than writing out a cheque.

*I see a dark presence standing at your shoulder. I should like to tell you more about the danger you are in.*

Perhaps she would have laughed it all off, just as Kate would have done, if she had been feeling herself. But it was about then – April or May it must have been – that she started to feel so tired. It had seemed easier just to let these people, whoever they were, charge her credit card each month. Let someone else take away the dark shadows from her loved ones. From her daughter, Kate, for example.

*I urge you to beware of the one who is standing close to you. Reply at once and I will tell you more about the danger at your shoulder.*

It had been one afternoon at the end of May that Ayesha had called round and found her lying, exhausted, on the sofa. And then Roz had told her all about it. The story, and her worries, had just poured out. It was such a relief to let someone else into the secret, and Ayesha was such a good listener. She hadn't told Roz what a fool she had been, or even asked her how much she had spent – not that she would have been able to tell her, not to within a thousand pounds or so.

Ayesha had understood immediately why Roz had done it, and just how frightened she had been by the overwhelming tide of warnings.

She had told her to go to bed for a good rest and then had brought her up a cup of soothing herb tea.

'Don't open another of these letters, Roz. Just hand them all over to me to deal with.'

But Roz had known that she wouldn't be able to see a blue envelope without opening it; the temptation was too great to resist.

'It's a human failing, isn't?' said Ayesha sympathetically. 'If someone says "Don't look!" we just have to take a peek.' And so Roz had told her where to find the spare key and Ayesha had put it into her handbag. She had told Kate a white lie about the key, but she didn't want to go into the story about the letters and admit to Kate how much she had spent.

'What time does the post arrive?' Ayesha had asked.

'About ten to ten, usually.'

'I'll be here at five to and remove all the unwanted mail.'

'How will you know which to take?' But to tell the truth, at that moment Roz really didn't care if Ayesha took away everything, important or not.

'I'll remove anything in a blue envelope!' And Ayesha left, promising to call in again the next morning.

There was one more message, in a white envelope so that Ayesha missed it, which arrived a couple of days later.

*Beware false friends. You must contact me urgently. I need to tell you more. If you ignore this you risk the loss of something that is very precious to you.*

She had handed it to Ayesha the next time she saw her, and her friend had helped her to laugh at it, but still it left a nasty taste behind.

And then, some time the next week, the prophecy had come true, just the way the letter had predicted it, and all her old fears returned.

The ring had disappeared. It wasn't a ring that she ever

wore, so she couldn't be sure exactly when it happened. And it wasn't a particularly valuable ring, not like the diamonds that she had bought for herself in the past year or two. But over the years she had taken it out of its worn leather box from time to time and looked at it before putting it away again in her ebony and mother-of-pearl chest.

She could still see the ring quite clearly in her mind's eye: red gold, set with garnets, because she had always loved them – and John had at all times tried to give her what she wanted. It wasn't his fault that she had finally found him painfully dull. And not his fault, either, that he had died, barely forty, leaving her with a young daughter to bring up on her own. She and Kate rarely talked about Roz's husband, Kate's father, John. Perhaps they should have done. Oh, husbands! How troublesome they were! But she had intended to pass the ring on to Kate one day. Now she would have to give her the peridots instead, which had come from a man who was also dear to her, but was not Kate's father.

Yes, the garnet ring had gone missing, and she felt bad about it. There was no way she could have mislaid it. And no way, either, that someone could have stolen it. No strangers had been in her house. And how would they even know that she possessed it? If thieves came after her jewellery it would be her diamonds they took if they had any sense at all.

It left her with what she could only describe as a sense of foreboding. She and Ayesha talked about it, and her friend tried to calm her fears. It was her health that was out of kilter. She needed vitamins and minerals and various herbs that Ayesha and Marcus swore by.

Marcus and Ayesha were right in saying that Eastern philosophies had so much to teach us about ourselves and our relationship with the world, both visible and hidden. When they talked like that they reminded Roz of old friends of hers in North Africa and California, two places where people were open to ideas and beliefs that Avril Fordham and Kate, too, would find laughable.

*I see a dark shadow hanging over someone very close to you, someone that you love.*

That warning, too, had escaped Ayesha's vigilance. And Roz hadn't shown it to her since it could only refer to Ayesha herself, or to Kate. But she was waiting for the second blow to fall now, sure, too, that this would be more serious than the loss of a garnet ring.

With sudden violence she pushed the drawer closed so that the letters were hidden from view. But even when they were out of sight, a feeling of unease was creeping over her.

Her bedroom was dark, almost gloomy, with its fringed hangings, its oriental rugs and figured duvet cover. Usually she liked its mysterious corners and the soft gleam of brass lamps. But tonight she wished she could get rid of all the encroaching shadows. She must paint the walls cream, the woodwork white, and choose fresh, light curtains and bedding, so that it looked just like one of the bright, airy rooms in one of the properties that she and Avril developed so successfully. Until now she had never wanted anything like that for herself. She preferred the mixture of textures and colours, the patterns that complemented each other without matching, the *objets trouvés* that crowded every horizontal surface, gathering a light patina of dust over the years.

And now she wanted to throw it all out. Someone or something had come into this room, had opened the small drawer in the ebony cabinet and taken out her jewel box to remove the ring. The feeling of evil still hung in the air, like the mist outside in the street.

She would start redecorating tomorrow. If only she didn't feel so tired all the time.

# 6

Back in her own house, Kate poured herself a large glass of cold white wine. She took it into the sitting room and made herself comfortable on the sofa. Susanna, sensing her mood, came to join her, draping herself across one of Kate's knees.

'Thank you, Susanna. You're just what I need at this moment.' There was something particularly soothing about the close presence of a cat, especially when it purred with satisfaction at the simple fact of being with you. In a moment she would go and prepare their supper: something out of a tin for Susanna; something finely sliced and cooked in a wok with a selection of chopped vegetables for herself.

She had thought that the walk across Oxford would help her sort out her impressions of the Freemans and Roz, but it hadn't. The couple who had invaded her mother's house weren't her type: she would find their presence stifling if they invaded her own house like that. But she saw no reason to doubt their good intentions. She had the feeling that Roz herself would find them wearing to her patience if she were in her usual robust health.

And that was another thing: she didn't agree with their ideas about the treatment of illness, either. And again, Roz did – she always had thought along those lines, as Kate remembered.

When it came down to it, it was a question of taste. Avril disliked the couple; Kate herself liked Ayesha better than Marcus; and Roz plainly found both of them agreeable.

41

She drank some more wine and absently stroked the cat, who appeared to be unmoved by her inattention. She had a nasty suspicion that her slight antipathy to the Freemans, and Marcus in particular, might be put down to jealousy.

Perhaps she would be more inclined to align herself with Avril if the Freemans hadn't been so very kind about her work as a writer. But had she just fallen for the most obvious kind of flattery? No, she was sure that they were genuinely impressed by her profession. Well, if it came to that, she was proud of it herself.

As she finished her glass of wine she reflected that there was one aspect of the problem she had ignored so far in her deliberations: there was a large elephant sitting in the centre of the room, and she was pretending it wasn't there.

Roz's health. She had never known her mother to be ill before, but now there was clearly something seriously wrong with her.

She wished that she would see a doctor. She was used to Roz's tirades against the medical profession. She felt that they were part of her mother's image of herself as someone unconventional and free-spirited, but she usually gave in in the end and behaved like a normal, sensible person. And if the Freemans were really the friends they professed to be, why were they encouraging her in her batty ideas? Anyone could see that Roz was ill, really ill.

She gently pushed the cat off her knee. It was time to make their supper.

As she chopped a couple of spring onions, she found herself still worrying about her mother. She looked up at the clock. It wasn't late. She could phone Avril when she had eaten. She thought she could rely on her level-headedness, but she was beginning to think that Avril herself was suffering from prejudice.

'Do you think I'll be as mad as Roz one of these days?' she asked Susanna. 'Or am I more like my father, do you think?'

Susanna made it plain that she was more interested in cat food than in Kate's questions, so Kate stopped her aggressive chopping and fetched the cat's bowl and a pouch of chicken pellets.

'Hello, Avril. I've been to see Roz, and met the Freemans, and I agree with you that Roz is obviously unwell, and the Freemans are . . . well, I'll just say that they're not my type, but I can't say I'm as anti them as you are. I'm certainly not convinced that they're bad people. Misguided perhaps, but I think their intentions are good.'

'Evil or misguided, they're a bad influence on Roz,' said Avril, concise as ever. 'But I'm glad that you agree with me about her health. Roz is so dismissive of my fears that I was starting to think it was all in my imagination.'

'Definitely not. The thing is, what's our next move?'

'We have to get Roz to a doctor and the Freemans out of her house,' said Avril. 'We can hardly frogmarch her round to the surgery against her will, though, unfortunately.'

'I think you can forget about getting rid of the Freemans, at least for the present. We'll probably have to wait until Roz gets bored with them. They are a bit overpowering, aren't they? I don't think I could stand having them around the place every day, but I think we have to concede that they're a fixture in Roz's life at the moment – at least until she starts on her next enthusiasm.'

'If only we could make her see that odious couple for what they really are!'

'She will, in time,' said Kate soothingly. Privately she thought that 'odious' was too strong and that Roz was more likely to get tired of them if she and Avril ignored them.

There was a contrary streak in Roz that would make her automatically want to hang on to friends whom her daughter and the conventional Avril wanted to get rid of. 'You mentioned that you and Roz met them at the estate agent's. I wouldn't have thought that was a promising start to a close friendship.'

'Apparently they bumped into Roz again a couple of weeks later at the supermarket and they all went off for a coffee together when they'd finished their shopping. And I'm getting so suspicious of them that I can't believe their meeting in Tesco's was as accidental as it appears. I think they engineered it in some way.'

'That's going a bit far, isn't it? Why would they go to all that trouble?'

'It struck me that they could be after her money.'

'Roz isn't rich!'

'Have you calculated the value of her property portfolio recently?'

'Not really. I thought you bought a house, did it up and sold it on, making a few thousand profit. A reasonable amount of money for an enormous amount of hard work. That can't add up to a fortune, can it?'

'We don't sell them all. Anything that's suitable for letting, we let. We make a very small profit that way as the market's glutted with rental property at the moment and interest rates have risen, but the capital value of our investment is still increasing every year.'

'I thought that house prices were slowing down.'

'Just a little, but they'll pick up again in a year or two, I'm sure. There will always be people looking for somewhere to live in Oxford, after all. Roz will be worth a tidy sum eventually, you know.'

It all seemed far-fetched to Kate. Why would the Freemans take up with Roz on such a casual acquaintance? Even Kate

44

hadn't known much about Roz's property business, so why should they?

'Do we know if they've bought a house, and if so, where?' she asked.

'I suppose they must have done, but I don't know the address.'

'If it was close to the Cowley Road it would explain why they use the same supermarket, but from what I saw of them I wouldn't have thought they'd be attracted to the area.'

'I believe they were interested in North Oxford, or Headington perhaps,' said Avril.

'Well they can hardly be after her money, then! They must have a fortune of their own!'

Avril muttered something about people not always being what they seemed.

'And do you know anything about their background?'

'Apart from the fact that they're supposed to have moved here from Kent, nothing. They've certainly not confided in me, and Roz steers away from the subject of the Freemans because she knows I don't like them. Actually, I stay clear of the subject mostly too, as I don't want to cause ill feeling between us.'

'Yes, it must be awkward for you. What do you want me to do, Avril?'

'This may sound crass, Kate, but my concern is that they could be planning to swindle Roz out of a large sum of money, and then our partnership might be in jeopardy. Could you ask a few questions about them, do you think? Or find out something about their past life? I can tell that you're not suspicious of them, but it's for your mother's sake I'm asking as well as my own. And I gather from Roz that you're quite good at this kind of research.'

'Is that what she says?' asked Kate, feeling pleased.

'Where to start, though?' she mused. 'Kent's a large county, isn't it?'

'If they're even telling the truth.'

'I suppose I could try again with Roz. If I approached her in a conciliatory and friendly manner, showing interest in her fascinating new friends, that might work.'

Avril laughed. 'I think that Roz would see straight through you,' she said.

As Kate went to make herself a cup of coffee, she found that the Freemans' faces kept intruding into her preparations and their voices echoed in her ears. Ayesha's smile was no longer sweet and caring, though. There was a mocking edge to it now, and Marcus's voice was bullying rather than firm and resonant.

This was ridiculous: she was being influenced by what Avril had been saying, and she was sure that Avril was exaggerating.

The crux of the matter was: what was in it for the Freemans? Were they really as disinterested as they made out? It could do no harm to enquire a little further into their background. Any daughter might do the same for her mother, after all.

She went to her computer. If she had wanted to find out something about a new acquaintance she would probably start by Googling them. If the four of them had met at the estate agent's, would they have exchanged names? She thought it was unlikely. And Roz and Avril, she knew, went around in jeans and old shirts when they were working, so their appearance wouldn't have shouted money at someone meeting them casually. But was Roz wearing the flashy diamond rings she'd acquired this last year? All too likely, thought Kate. And then she remembered that Roz and Avril had bought themselves a new van back in the spring: very smart, and with their names and phone numbers written large and clear along the side.

She typed Avril's and Roz's names into the box, clicked 'UK only' and watched to see what would appear. To her surprise, she found that they even had a website – something else that Roz hadn't bothered to mention.

Very nice. Professionally designed. And it gave out the message that Roz and Avril had a very substantial business. If the Freemans had been house-hunting in Oxford they must know that Roz and Avril had a lot of money to invest. Certainly, if they were looking to swindle someone, these two would be worth investigating.

Oh, come on! she told herself. Avril Fordham had disliked the Freemans on sight and now had some bee in her bonnet about their being rogues and thieves. Kate would find out just how innocuous they were and she and Avril could forget about them. At least they could if Roz wasn't taking too much notice of their loopy advice over her health.

Jon would be ringing her soon. She could tell him all about it and ask for his advice: it would be such a relief to rely on someone else for a change. But Jon would give her only sensible suggestions about allowing Roz to make her own decisions and form her own friendships. If Roz were really ill, he would say, she'd visit the doctor: she's an intelligent woman. He and Roz got on surprisingly well, considering how different they were, and in an argument he might well take Roz's side against her. And if she told him how she intended to find out more about the Freemans he would be horrified – well, disapproving, at the least. She should mind her own business, he would say.

It wasn't worth falling out with Jon by telling him that what she really hoped was that she'd find some huge scandal in the Freemans' past, present Roz with the evidence and her mother would show them the door. Then Roz would start to pay proper attention once more to what her daughter was saying.

No, she'd ask him for advice only if she found out something really serious in the Freemans' past. When he rang this evening they would reminisce about their holiday and make plans for the future. She wouldn't even mention the subject of her mother.

'You're sounding distracted,' Jon said, when they had been talking for a while. 'Is anything the matter?'

'I'm worried about Roz.' And so much for her good resolutions about keeping her concerns about her mother to herself.

'What's up?'

'Oh, you know what she can be like. I think – and her sensible business partner, Avril, agrees with me – that she's not at all well, but we can't persuade her to see a doctor.' There, that sounded quite rational, she thought.

'What makes you think she's ill?'

'She's lost her energy. Her colour's awful. She's looking thinner and greyer. She just isn't herself.'

'Maybe her age is catching up with her at last.'

'She's not all that old. I don't think she's seventy yet. That's no age these days, is it? And it's come on so suddenly – just over the past three or four months.'

'Why don't I come down to Oxford this weekend? I could call in to see her and find out what's wrong.'

'That sounds like a good idea,' said Kate dubiously. 'But I went round there earlier today and she wouldn't listen to me. I'm not sure that you'd fare any better.'

'Look, I know that you and Roz have had your ups and downs. I expect you just put it to her in the wrong way. She thought you were interfering in her life, or else she was just feeling contrary. I'm sure I can get through to her.'

'She'll think I put you up to it.'

'Well, she'd be right. But it's worth a try.'

'Friday evening, then?'

'Better make it Saturday morning. There's a lot going on at this end, with all the talk about the reorganisation of the unit, and I'm not sure how soon I can get away.'

When she'd hung up, Kate found she was feeling a lot happier. Jon would sort things out. Roz would listen to him.

# 7

In a boardroom at the top of a concrete block in the commercial district of Porto, five men were holding a meeting to review the achievements and failures of the past month. All five were Portuguese, but to a casual observer they appeared to come from two separate backgrounds.

At the head of the table was António Filipe Soares da Silva, still handsome in his early seventies, and wearing a formal dark suit. On his right sat Carlos Costa, some twenty years his junior, also formally dressed, and with the same air of authority as the older man. The other three were technicians, perhaps, or clerks. The youngest of these, Jorge, was a strong-looking, fresh-faced lad in his early twenties.

Outside, the sun was shining from a cloudless blue sky and a cool breeze blew in off the Atlantic. The air-conditioning had been turned off at the request of da Silva, who disliked its constant humming, and so instead they listened to the shrieking of seagulls through the open window.

'The response percentage has risen this month,' commented da Silva. 'I believe that this is due to the improvement in the text of the letters, so we congratulate you, Carlos.'

'You will notice, too,' said Carlos, 'that we are taking in a greater amount, over a period of three months, than we were doing at this time last year. I believe that this, too, is because we have refined and improved the content of the letters.'

'Sales of our mailing lists to other interested parties have now more than covered the cost to us of the original lists that we purchased. And we thank our young colleagues for their hard work on the demographic analysis contributing to this part of the operation,' said da Silva. 'We are concentrating our efforts not only on people who are known to respond to unsolicited requests for money, but on those who are most vulnerable to the content of our messages. Well done.'

The younger men smiled in return.

'I think that Pires and Oliviera can leave us now,' said Carlos. 'And they will, of course, receive bonus payments in their week's wages.'

When the two had left the room, the atmosphere felt at once more relaxed, and yet with a certain edge of menace.

'We now turn to the question of these English interlopers,' said da Silva. 'Remind me, Carlos, how much we had received from Mrs Ivory.'

'Fourteen thousand seven hundred and twenty pounds sterling,' said Carlos, reading from the printout in front of him. 'We were just getting into our stride, and there was plenty more we might have expected from this source.'

'So we must do something about it,' said da Silva.

'Are you sure it's worthwhile?' asked Carlos. 'Promising as this source was, it would have dried up eventually. Wouldn't we do better to keep sending messages to new targets and just write the account off?'

'But this is personal,' said da Silva. 'Mrs Ivory, as she calls herself, and I are very old friends and adversaries. I hadn't realised that she had been caught in our scheme until you showed me this list of cancelled subscriptions, Carlos. Perhaps I would have erased her name from the list if I had known beforehand, I don't know. I might even have returned the money myself with a graceful note of apology. But what

I will not accept is that someone else is taking her money. It's a question of honour.'

'Are you sure that she is the victim of some other fraud?'

Da Silva winced at the word. 'The letter from da Gama makes it quite clear. He is living in the same part of the town of Oxford as Mrs Ivory and he has reported the daily visits of a couple called Freeman who appear to have influenced her.'

'Perhaps they're simply friends who have persuaded her to cease responding to our appeals,' suggested Carlos.

'Da Gama doesn't think so. He believes that they have their own agenda, and they may even have used one or two of our letters for their own purposes.'

'But da Gama's own operation has nothing to do with the letters,' objected Carlos. 'He is concerned only with the placing of our unofficial immigrant clients in paid employment. How can he know so much about Mrs Ivory?'

'It is true that the usual employment found for our clients is menial: there is a shortage in Oxford of domestic staff willing to accept low wages, and da Gama and his people do useful work in filling this need,' said da Silva. 'Their employers imagine that their foreign cleaners understand no English, but they are mistaken. What our clients learn, they pass on. We need to find out more, of course, before we act.'

'I assume that this is where Jorge comes in,' said Carlos, seeing that da Silva was not to be persuaded.

'Your English is still good, Jorge, after your year as a waiter in London?' asked da Silva.

'I believe so,' said Jorge respectfully.

'In that case, you will go to England and gather as much information as possible about this couple, the Freemans. Here is a folder containing all that we have learnt to date, including their address and telephone number. Pires and

Oliviera are using their electronic data collection skills to find out more. But what we have gathered so far is enough for me to be sure that we are dealing with criminals.'

On Saturday evening Jon drove Kate out to a pub on the south side of Oxford. It was an old stone-built inn, with beams and a log fire, which had been unobtrusively modernised and now served excellent food.

'I think I'm going to have a glass of wine,' said Jon, who usually kept to mineral water when he was driving. He'd been unforthcoming so far about his visit to Roz Ivory's house that afternoon, but now they settled themselves in chairs by the fire while they studied the menu, and Kate hoped that he would tell her what had happened. The waitress poured them each a glass of wine from the bottle he'd ordered, and after a minute or two he started to talk.

'You were right,' he said. 'First of all she invited me in, as usual, and offered me a choice of herb teas – not so usual. When I enquired about her health – just casually, you know – she accused me of being put up to it by you. To be specific, she said, "Kate sent you round, didn't she?" in a very accusing tone of voice.'

'You'd been expecting her to say that, though.'

'Yes. I told her that I'd been concerned when you told me that she wasn't well and, just in case you were exaggerating—'

'What!'

'Don't try to deny that you do, sometimes, exaggerate, just a little, Kate.'

'I'll try to forget you said that.'

Before he could continue, the waitress arrived to take their order, and they quickly decided what they were going to eat, without taking much notice of what they were choosing.

'Now, go on,' urged Kate when the waitress had disappeared again.

'She started by saying that it was nothing, just the after-
effects of flu. But eventually she admitted that she'd been
feeling exhausted after a morning's work, which was
quite unlike her, and she was afraid that she'd lost her enthusiasm for renovating houses, or for doing anything else if it
came to that. And you were right, she didn't look herself at
all.'

'She's looking older, isn't she?' said Kate sadly.

'Yes, I'm afraid she is. But it's come on too suddenly for
it to be a case of her age catching up with her at last. I asked
her what advice her doctor had given her, and she admitted
that she hadn't seen him recently. I really thought we were
getting somewhere. She seemed to be listening to what I
was saying, but—'

Again they were interrupted as the waitress came to tell
them that their table was ready. She showed them into the
adjoining restaurant and brought them their starters. The
tables were small, but widely spaced, so they could carry on
talking in reasonable privacy. Jon poured a second glass of
wine for Kate and a tumbler of water for himself. Kate
started on her Thai fishcake while Jon took up his story
again.

'Then there was the sound of a key opening the front
door – no ring at the bell or anything first – and this couple
came barging in. The woman even trilled, "It's only us!" as
they came into the room.'

'The Freemans,' said Kate with resignation, putting down
her fork.

'They came in so exactly on cue that it even crossed my
mind that they had the place bugged!'

'I gather that you didn't take to them.'

' "Unctuous" is the term that occurred to me to describe

55

Marcus Freeman. And his wife was all touchy-feely and dressed up like the Queen of the Night.'

'I can see that they weren't your kind of people, but I didn't think they were that bad!'

'Is everything all right?' It was the waitress again.

'Fine!' replied Jon, so emphatically that she hurried away and left them to their own devices.

'I suppose we'd better eat up,' said Kate, 'or she'll come and check up on us in another couple of minutes.'

They concentrated on their food for a while, then waited for the plates to be cleared and their main course to arrive before talking again.

'So what are your conclusions?' asked Kate. 'What do you think I should do?'

'I'm not sure there's much you *can* do. Your mother's a free agent: she can go to the doctor or not, as she pleases, and she can choose her own friends. I wouldn't want them hanging around my house all the time, but Roz does have different ideas from you and me. What do we have against them, after all?'

'Marcus has large hands and an unctuous voice.'

'Ayesha has an improbable name, awful dress sense and disapproves of wine.'

'I can see that it might not be enough to take out a restraining order,' said Kate, taking the hint and drinking the rest of her second glass of sauvignon blanc.

'You could talk to your mother again, but I think it might be counterproductive. If she thinks you're putting pressure on her she'll resist it, whether she agrees with you or not.'

'Maybe you could have a second try. She did listen to you, didn't she?'

'I'm not sure I'll have the time. I think I mentioned the reorganisation at work?'

'Yes. I saw something about it on the news. But does it affect you?'

'It affects us all. You'll have seen that they're forming a new serious organised crime agency, rather like the FBI in the States, and absorbing us and the National Crime Squad into it. I have to decide what I want to do: join the new agency, or try something different. I need to be in London, at least for the next couple of weeks.'

'Oh. I hadn't realised it was such a fundamental change. We won't see each other for a while, then.'

'You can come and stay with me, can't you?'

'Yes. Of course.' But could she happily leave Roz to the care of the Freemans while she was away?

'I'm sorry I can't come up with a solution to your problem with Roz. But it comes down to the simple fact that if you don't like her friends, you can't change that, and if she doesn't want to see a doctor, you can't make her.'

'Until one day she collapses in the street and someone calls an ambulance, I suppose.'

'I'm sure it won't come to that.'

'Next you'll say that all she needs is a tonic!'

'Don't let's quarrel over it. We're in agreement, aren't we?'

But while Jon was content to leave the situation as it was, Kate was determined to do something to change it if she could.


Kate left it a couple of days before contacting her mother again. She had wondered whether to call round bearing gifts, this time of food and drink from the organic section of a distant Waitrose. Or should she drop into Lush and buy something sweet-smelling and chemical-free to raise her mother's spirits? A bunch of flowers, maybe? Chocolates? Mothers were supposed to like chocolate, but Roz had never adhered to the stereotype. And at their last meeting Kate hadn't been much good at knowing what Roz wanted. In the end she chose a book that she thought Roz would enjoy, and left it in its plastic bag to show that this was merely a casual visit.

In fact, when Roz opened her door it was obvious that she was just leaving the house. She was wearing a long jacket over her jeans and had put on some make-up so that at first Kate thought she was looking a lot better.

'I'm off to meet Avril. We have a house to look at,' she said briskly. 'Sorry I can't stop to chat.' Then, as Kate handed over the small package, 'What's this? The latest William Trevor? Oh, good. I look forward to reading it.'

Kate brightened. Her mother was on the mend. Then she noticed the colour applied to her cheeks and the dark circles beneath her eyes that she had been unable to disguise. Roz was putting a good face on it, but nothing had actually changed.

Kate spent two days trying to find out something – anything – about the Freemans, but drew a blank. And then help arrived from an unexpected source.

She sat looking at the email that had just arrived in her inbox. It had 'Ivory Family' in the subject line, and was signed 'Jack Ivory'. He explained that he was researching his family history and was following up all Ivorys that he could find, in the telephone book, on the internet and in her case, in the public library. It was an unusual surname and he thought it most likely that they were related. All Ivorys were related at some point in the past, he said.

He gave details of his parents' and grandparents' names and approximate dates of birth, and wondered whether any of them were familiar to Kate.

I'm sure you know that we're a far-flung clan, descended from Roger de Iueri, who came over with the Conqueror. We spread to Ireland and Scotland and then, much later, across the Atlantic and to Australia. The Ivorys who interest me are those who stayed behind in England, settling in Oxfordshire, Berkshire, Buckinghamshire and Hampshire.

He gave the origin of Ivory as 'yew-army', which made Kate think of stout yeomen (in spite of their Norman antecedents) carrying sharpened staves, or longbows perhaps. They didn't sound artistic or literary, certainly – more like a crowd of soccer hooligans – but who knew what they might have become in the centuries between? In spite of herself, she felt a twinge of curiosity about the family from which her barely known father had sprung.

At first she had been inclined to ignore the appeal, or send a brief reply saying that she had never heard of any of these Ivorys. But Jack Ivory had a very engaging way of writing, and had taken so much trouble. What was more, he hadn't made any errors of spelling, punctuation or syntax. It might be small-minded of her to be swayed by such things, but as a writer she couldn't help believing they were important. On the other hand, she really didn't know much about her father's family, so she had little information to offer Jack Ivory in return. Her father's name, she knew, was John, but who his parents or grandparents had been, and where and when they were all born, she had no idea. Family history and genealogy were interests that had passed her by.

Then it occurred to her that she could ask Roz about it – and that this would be a way of approaching her mother without broaching the tricky subject of her health. And surely even the Freemans wouldn't butt in on a conversation about Roz and Kate's family tree.

So she sent a friendly reply, explaining that she knew little about her family, but would make enquiries. When she had sent off the email two new messages dropped into her inbox. The first was from her agent, Estelle Livingstone:

How's it going, Kate? Any chance of a new MS for me to read soon?

That was Estelle for you. No time to waste on small talk: she got straight to the point, and if she asked for something it was as well not to disappoint her, Kate had found. The second message was from her editor at Foreword Publishing, Neil Orson:

I wonder whether you could give me a date for the completion of the new book, Kate? No pressure on you, of course, but I need to put it into production by the end of November if we're to make the April publication date.

With all the worry about Roz, she'd managed to forget the deadline for the delivery of her new book. She would get on with it this afternoon, or possibly this evening, if she could find the time. Or else it could wait until tomorrow morning. She was sure there were only ten or twenty thousand words left to write, and she knew she could manage those in a couple of weeks if she had to. For the moment she was going to concentrate on getting her mother to see sense.

She sent a couple of cheerful, confident emails to Estelle and Neil, promising delivery of the manuscript in plenty of time for the November deadline, then printed out the message from Jack Ivory to show to Roz. Her mother ought to be working on site with Avril this morning, if she was feeling well enough, but Kate might catch her at home around lunchtime. She'd give her a ring on her mobile to check. It would be good to have a friendly conversation when she saw her, rather than launch into another argument.

Roz had sounded wary when Kate had phoned her, but when she learnt that this had nothing to do with the Freemans or her health she asked Kate to call in for a sandwich and coffee.

'Let me see the copy of the email,' she said, when she and Kate were seated, as in the old days, at the kitchen table. 'Yes, he does seem to have done his homework. This is more than I ever knew about the Ivorys – not that I ever thought there was anything worth knowing about them, I have to say.'

'Do you recognise the names he mentions?'

'No. But then your father didn't have much to do with his family. He was an only child, his parents died when he was in his late twenties, and I don't think he had any cousins of his own age – the few he did have were all much older, I gathered. I do know that John was a common name in his family, but then it must be common in a lot of families, and it occurs to me that your Jack could be a John too.'

'He could be a grandson of one of my father's cousins, I suppose.'

'Or he could be such a distant relative that it really has no relevance for you and me. Would you like some more salad?'

'It sounds as though he's working on a family tree,' said Kate. 'I wouldn't mind taking a look at that. I know you're not interested in the Ivorys, but I'd like to find out something about them – it might tell me more about my father, and about myself. I didn't know him very well, and all I'm left with is a series of mental snapshots. Daddy at the beach – wet grey shingle, not golden sand. Daddy coming home from the office carrying a brown leather briefcase with scuffed corners and straps that were curled with age. I remember the briefcase more clearly that his face! And yes please to salad: this is a very good dressing.'

'The secret's in the balsamic vinegar. Your father wasn't a wildly interesting man, I'm afraid, so I'm not surprised that you have no vivid memories of him. I can't get up much enthusiasm for tracing any other descendants of Roger de Iueri – even if that's what you are – and I'm afraid that you'll be disappointed even if you manage to do so. If Jack Ivory wants to trace his family back to some Norman who came over with William the Conqueror, I think he's indulging in wishful thinking. Have you had enough to eat? Shall I make the coffee?'

'No thanks. I'd better get back to my novel. And I don't suppose that Jack Ivory will get in touch again, since there was nothing I could add to his knowledge of the family.'

Kate sent off an apologetic message when she returned home, telling Jack Ivory that she had learnt nothing from her mother, believing that would be the end of the story.

But that evening there was a new message from him. He thanked her for her efforts, even though they were fruitless, and then told her that it just so happened that he was staying in Oxford at the moment, in one of the guest rooms of his old college. If she was by any chance interested, they could meet so that he could show her the family tree that he was building, although much of it was still rather tentative. If she agreed, she could leave a message at Leicester College – the one that was tucked in behind Blackwell's – and they could meet in one of the town's coffee shops. His day was his own, so he would leave the choice of time to her.

It was an appealing idea. Since he was an old member of Leicester College, where she had known one or two of the

Fellows, Jack Ivory no longer seemed like a complete stranger. She pictured a retired academic or teacher, filling his empty days in the harmless search for his ancestors.

She sent a swift reply – after all, he might well be leaving Oxford in a day or two – suggesting that they meet in Blackwell's coffee shop at four o'clock the next afternoon or, if that wasn't convenient, at the same place and time one day the following week.

The next morning there was an answer: he would meet her at four that very afternoon. And he would recognise her from the photograph on the flap of the Kate Ivory novel he had recently been reading. He described himself as tall and greyish, and wearing a dark jacket. Given the vagueness of this description, Kate hoped that the photograph he had seen of her was one of the more realistic and less air-brushed images used by her publisher, or they would never find one another.

# 8

Kate arrived early at Blackwell's, giving herself time to purchase a paperback novel on the ground floor to take with her to the coffee shop. Having bought an espresso on her way in, she managed to find a seat on a leather sofa near the window, facing into the room, so that she could scrutinise all the customers as they entered.

The coffee-drinkers were students, mainly, she saw, gathering at the start of the new academic year. Some had spread files and books out across the small tables, or were tapping away at laptop computers. She supposed it was warmer working here than back in their digs – or maybe they liked to give a public display of hard work early in the year before relaxing their standards later on. She didn't think she'd be able to concentrate on writing a book amid the chattering groups, but she could see the appeal of being surrounded by other people, enveloped in the aroma of coffee, instead of shutting herself up in a room alone with her thoughts and her computer.

So far she had seen no tall, greyish men in dark jackets, and she was about to fetch herself a second espresso from the counter when she saw someone entering through the History section, moving rapidly and glancing at his watch. Tall man, dark hair sprinkled with grey, dark blue jacket. It could well be Jack Ivory. She watched him as he looked around at the crowded tables. Quite attractive, really, and somewhat younger than the ageing academic she had been expecting. The touches of grey in his hair suited him, and although there were crow's-feet by the blue-grey eyes, his face was tanned and he moved like a younger man.

At that moment he caught her eye, looked hard for a moment, then smiled. A very pleasant smile, she considered. He negotiated a gaggle of chairs and reached her sofa.

'You must be Kate Ivory.' She nodded. 'And I'm Jack Ivory.' He saw her empty cup. 'Let me get you another coffee. Espresso? I'm sorry if I've kept you waiting, but I was delayed by a phone call just as I was leaving – yet another Ivory, if you'd believe it! I've been tracking them down all over the south of England.' He handed across an A3 portfolio bearing a label saying *Ivory Family*. 'Look after this for me, would you mind, while I get our coffees. And would you like anything to eat? They have chocolate cake, I believe.'

Kate assured him that coffee was all she wanted.

While he stood at the counter, ordering coffees for them both, she could carry on her inspection of him with impunity. A pleasant voice, difficult to place as to geographical area. Age, in his early fifties, she would have thought. Clothes, casual but prosperous. Build, wiry. Manner, energetic. OK so far. She looked down at the portfolio and wondered whether she might open it and eyeball the contents. Better wait for him to return.

'Here we go. This one's yours.' His own was a large latte, she saw. 'Do open up the family tree, by the way, though I must apologise for that fact that large areas are quite vague. I have to get confirmation of the names and dates of the people I've found before I can fill them in with any certainty.'

'That's not important as far as I'm concerned: I'm grateful for anything you can tell me. I've never seen any details at all of my father's family. He died when I was a child and my mother has never been very interested in where or what he

66

came from – she prefers to live in the present. I assume his family lived in Oxfordshire since that's where I was brought up, but my birth certificate tells me that I was born in London – I believe that's where my parents met – so I can't even be sure he originally came from this area.'

'Haven't you seen his birth certificate?' He looked concerned to find such a rootless person.

'No, I'm afraid not. I'm not even sure that Roz still has it. She did a lot of travelling when she was younger and wasn't inclined to take much luggage with her. She had half a dozen photographs from the time of her marriage and she gave them to me years ago. I must have them in a box somewhere, but with the recent move I really couldn't say where they are – or whether I still have them.'

'What a pity.' He paused as though waiting for Kate to offer to search her house for errant photographs. 'What about your parents' marriage certificate? Surely she still keeps that. It might give us a little information about them.'

'No, I haven't seen that, either – though I'm sure that one exists somewhere. Don't they keep copies at St Catherine's House?'

'I'll try there eventually, if all else fails. But it's so useful to be able to connect the certificate with the actual person. That's what I was hoping to achieve here.' He sat looking at her so expectantly that Kate felt guilty at letting him down.

'This is hopeless, isn't it? I'm afraid I'm being no help at all to your researches,' she said.

'It's very kind of you to have met me like this, taking time out of what I'm sure is your very busy schedule. Now, why don't we look at the draft family tree.' Jack Ivory pulled off the elastic holding the corners of the portfolio and opened it up. They pushed their coffee cups out of the way so that he could he could spread it flat. The good thing about

Blackwell's coffee shop was that no one thought their behaviour the slightest bit strange.

'Perhaps with a little hard work we'll find an extended family for you. I do think it's important to know where you come from. We who are living now, in the early twenty-first century, are the inheritors of our medieval ancestors' talents, of their virtues and their faults, of their eye colour and their physical build, as well as of any material goods they may have left us. If we discover our forebears, we discover more about ourselves as well, don't you think?'

'I hadn't thought of it like that before,' said Kate, who was wishing that she'd said yes to the chocolate cake. Maybe she'd discover a distant Ivory who had been the village baker.

'Now here, at the bottom on the right, are my sister and I,' said Jack, pointing at the relevant spot. 'And just above us are our parents, Ruth and Donald, and above them, our two sets of grandparents. I can be quite sure of the eight of us because I've seen our birth certificates and marriage lines, too, where appropriate.'

Kate saw that she'd been right about his age: he was fifty-three. He must have taken early retirement. And his name was John, just like her own father. *John Donald Ivory* was written in a neat black hand, *known as Jack*. The sister he mentioned was ten years younger than him and had apparently been both married and divorced. There was no note of a wife for Jack. She wondered why not: at first sight he had all the signs of being excellent husband material. But maybe he was in a long-term relationship and had seen no need for a formal arrangement, especially since there were no children. Up at the top of the tree Jack had written in *Roger de Iueri*, firmly, in ink, but it looked as though he had a long way to go before he could join the top to the bottom of the diagram. She ended her musing and turned her attention back to what he was saying.

'Now, over here,' he pointed to the bottom left quadrant, 'are some more people I've contacted, and their names and dates have all been confirmed, too. Do any of the names seem familiar?'

'No, though I see there's another John over there.'

'A popular name among the Ivorys. I'm trying to establish a connection between this group and my own, probably in my grandparents' or great-grandparents' generation. I've found some names and dates that match, but that isn't good enough without proper corroboration in the form of entries in registers or other written evidence.'

'I'm afraid you're losing me,' said Kate, who had just come to the limit of her interest in family history, even if it did appear that the history was her own. 'Where are you hoping to fit my parents and me into this scheme?'

'Here, in the middle.' He took out a pencil and lightly wrote in Kate's name. 'Your parents are Rosemary and John, aren't they?'

'Yes, that's right. Though everyone calls my mother Roz.'

'Do you happen to have their dates of birth?'

'I'm afraid not. I can give you approximate years, but I couldn't be sure.'

He looked disappointed. 'I hadn't realised you were so unaware of your forebears. I suppose that if your mother wasn't interested there was no one to tell you about them. An elderly unmarried aunt is usually the repository of the family history, they say.'

'We don't go in for such people, unfortunately. I'm the nearest to a spinster aunt you'll find, and as you can see, I'm sadly inadequate.'

'I don't suppose you have any old family letters, or diaries?' He sounded hesitant. 'And of course, even if you had, you might not want to lend them to a stranger.'

'Again, I haven't.'

Jack smiled his charming smile again. 'We really aren't getting very far, are we? Now, does your mother live locally, by any chance?'

'In East Oxford. Why?'

'I was wondering if it was worth applying to her for the information I'm looking for. She probably knows more than she's told you, and she might remember details of her husband's family with a little prompting.'

'You're very persistent,' Kate couldn't help remarking. 'You're not going to give up on my branch of the Ivorys without a fight, are you?'

'Oh, I do apologise. I am being a little too insistent, aren't I? I can only give the excuse that this is a new hobby for me, and since I gave up full-time work it's taken over all my spare time. Blame it on the fact that I'm an old bachelor with nothing better to do with his days.'

Kate looked at her watch. 'I'll try her mobile,' she said, taking her own phone out of her bag.

'Are you sure you can hear above this noise?'

Kate covered her free ear and listened to the dialling sound.

'Roz Ivory.'

'It's Kate. I wondered whether I could bring someone round to see you.'

'What?'

'Can I bring someone. To see you.'

'As long as it's not someone who wishes to lecture me about my health.'

'NOTHING LIKE THAT.' Kate was having to speak up to cover the background noise.

'And where on earth are you? It sounds like a school canteen.'

'Blackwell's. Coffee shop. WITH JACK IVORY.' A few feet away an elderly woman glared disapprovingly at Kate. 'Sorry. I can't make myself heard unless I shout.'

'What was that?'

'Just apologising to someone for SHOUTING.'

'I'm not surprised. This Jack Ivory wants to pump me about our family history, I assume.'

'Yes.' It was hopeless trying to hold a normal conversation, so Kate kept to basics.

'Now?' asked Roz.

'Is that OK?'

'Make it six o'clock.'

'Six o'clock?' queried Kate at normal volume, turning to Jack.

'Fine,' he said.

'FINE,' she repeated, at top volume.

'See you at six,' said Roz, and rang off.

'That was very kind of you both,' said Jack. 'Now, how do I find my way to your mother's house?'

'Why don't I pick you up? Would you like to walk, or shall I bring my car?'

'If I'm going to carry the portfolio, it had better be by car, I think. Are you sure you don't mind? I could take a taxi if you like.'

'It's no trouble. I'll see you outside the college lodge in Parks Road at ten to.'

'I'll be ready and waiting for you. I don't want you to get a parking ticket!'

At home, Kate checked her emails – nothing of interest – and then decided to ring Avril to keep her up to date. There was one avenue, too, she felt they hadn't yet explored.

'Hi, Avril. It's Kate.'

'Any progress to report?'

'Nothing concrete yet, but someone who's researching the Ivory family history has contacted me, and we're both going to visit Roz in about an hour's time. It's an opportunity

71

to see her without the dreadful Freemans, and when we're talking about a neutral subject.'

'Well, good luck. But you know how stubborn your mother can be.'

'Yes, I'd noticed.'

'And who is this researcher?'

'A Jack Ivory. He contacted me by email.'

'Are you sure you can trust him?'

'He seems genuine enough. I'm picking him up at Leicester lodge later on. What makes you so suspicious?'

'You can't trust anyone these days, Kate. When I think of the letters . . . well, I won't go on about it now.'

'Is everything all right, Avril? You sound upset.'

'No, I'm fine.'

'I was wondering, which was the estate agent's where you first met the Freemans?'

'Rafe Brown. Do you know him?'

'Yes. I saw him several times when I was looking for a new place, before I found this house.'

'I don't think he'll be able to tell you any more than I could, I'm afraid.'

'Well, I might give him a try anyway.'

Jack Ivory was as good as his word. As she drew up outside the college he appeared out of the crowd of undergraduates milling around the lodge so that they held the traffic up for only a minute or two as he stowed his portfolio on the back seat and then slid into the front and closed the door.

'So kind of you,' he said to Kate, and again, when they arrived at Roz's and she opened the door, 'So kind of you to assist me in my search for ancestors.'

'Come in,' she said. 'Can I offer you anything to drink?'

But Jack wouldn't impose on her generosity.

'I hear that you want to find out more about my husband's family,' said Roz.

'That's the general idea, but I gather that you don't know much about them. Would you allow me to show you my attempt at a family tree? It might prompt you to remember something,' said Jack, indicating the portfolio.

'Why don't you use the table, over here?' suggested Roz. And there it was again, the big sheet of paper with Roger de Iueri at the head and John (known as Jack) Ivory at the bottom.

'Kate's explained to me that you know very little about your late husband's family, but I was wondering whether there weren't any birth or marriage certificates that might give some clues?'

'I'm afraid that I'm not one for keeping unnecessary things,' said Roz. 'I like to travel light through this world, and I throw away papers when I have no further use for them.'

'That goes for people, too,' put in Kate.

'Now, Kate, that was uncalled for,' said Roz.

'I suppose that you would include diaries or letters in that category, though,' said Jack.

'I'm afraid I would. My husband died nearly thirty years ago and I've kept only a handful of photos of that time. My daughter is the only thing of value that I carried away from my marriage.'

Roz would have made a great actress, thought Kate. Considering that she had taken the hippie trail as soon as her daughter was seventeen, leaving her to fend for herself for the next ten years – with her share of the money from the sale of their house to console her, she had to admit – Roz's comment was a bit rich!

'Oh. I see.' Jack Ivory was obviously cast down by Roz's news, but he wasn't going to give up immediately. 'In that case, could I ask you for a few details.' He produced a notebook and pencil. 'Dates and places,' he explained. 'Could you tell me John Ivory's date of birth?'

'Well,' Roz began, making a visible effort to remember, when there came the now familiar sound of a key being turned in a lock and a trilling voice called, 'It's only me!'

# 9

'Hello, Roz dear. And Kate, too. How lovely to see you again. No, please don't get up. Marcus and I will sit on the sofa and stay as quiet as mice until you've finished your little chinwag.'

Of course, it was the Freemans.

'But I see you have another guest!' exclaimed Marcus.

'A distant relative,' explained Roz. 'This is Jack Ivory, a visitor to Oxford. And Jack, these are my friends, Marcus and Ayesha Freeman.'

Ayesha was saying, 'Lovely to meet you,' but Marcus and Jack were staring at one another.

'Marcus! My goodness!' said Jack.

'It must be . . . well, a great number of years. But you've hardly changed!'

'Do you two know each other?' asked Ayesha, superfluously in Kate's opinion.

'Well, yes. But a very long time ago,' said Jack.

'Jack and I were at Leicester together,' explained Marcus. 'But I never saw you at a Gaudy, Jack.'

'I'm not a great one for reunions, though I do happen to be staying at Leicester at the moment,' said Jack. 'Once I'd graduated I thought it was time to leave Oxford behind and find out something about the real world.'

'That sounds a sensible course of action,' said Roz, who had been listening to their conversation with interest. 'I did much the same thing when my husband died.'

'So you must be related to Roz's husband?' said Marcus. 'And to Kate, too, of course.'

'We're not sure about that,' said Roz. 'I know so little about the Ivorys, and Kate knows even less. Still, Jack seems determined to connect us all to each other and to someone who came over with the Conqueror.'

'How very fascinating. But don't you approve, Roz?' asked Ayesha sympathetically. 'Of course, you have a pessimistic view of families, don't you, dear? I do hope this isn't too upsetting for you.'

'Not upsetting at all. I just have little interest in finding out who was or wasn't related to my late husband.'

'But I'd like to know,' put in Kate. 'They're my family too, you know. In fact they're more mine than they are yours.'

'Of course they are,' said Roz. 'And if you're determined to hunt them down, then I'll do everything I can to help.'

'Oh, good!' said Jack. 'So you might be able to find those dates for me?'

'Yes, yes,' said Roz wearily, worn down by Jack's single-minded resolve. 'I'll see what I can do. But you'll have to give me a day or two to look them out for you.'

Reassured, Jack turned back to the Freemans.

'How extraordinary to meet again after all this time!' he said.

'Not really,' said Marcus. 'If you're staying at Leicester, and we're living in Oxford, it was quite likely that we'd meet. This is a small town, after all.'

Kate took the opportunity to look at the two men. They were of the same age, she could see, but where Jack was wiry and fit-looking, Marcus's face was starting to soften around the chin, and he even had the beginnings of a slight paunch. And then there were their hands. How different Jack's, with their long thin fingers, tanned like his face, were from Marcus's.

Then Kate caught Roz's eye. Her mother was looking exhausted again. If the Freemans and Jack Ivory wanted to go through a grand scene of reunion it would be better if they did it elsewhere. She liked the idea of getting rid of the Freemans, too.

'Why don't we all go off to eat somewhere?' she suggested.

'I'm signed in for dinner in Hall,' said Jack.

'I'm sure you could be signed out again,' said Kate helpfully.

'I suppose so.' He sounded doubtful, but then said, 'If I could borrow your telephone, Mrs Ivory?'

'Call me Roz,' she said, and showed him to the phone.

'Where do you think we should go to eat, Kate?' asked Ayesha. She didn't sound at all pleased at the idea of leaving Roz's house.

'Or perhaps I could throw together a little something in the kitchen here,' suggested Marcus.

'Oh, no. We couldn't possibly expect you to produce a meal – and from nothing! – for so many people,' insisted Kate.

'Well, I'm sure—'

'No, we wouldn't hear of it, would we, Jack?'

'What's that?'

'We all want to go out to eat, don't we?'

'Oh, yes. Of course. I thought that's what we'd decided on,' he said.

'What sort of food do you like?' Kate asked him, afraid that the Freemans would want something impossibly healthy and unobtainable in Oxford.

'I'm quite fond of Italian,' he said. 'Or anything except Indian, really.'

Kate thought for a moment, then asked her mother for the phone book. 'OK if I use your phone?' she asked.

'Of course.'

She booked them in to a pleasant, reasonably priced Italian restaurant in the city centre. Then, without asking anyone's consent, she called for a taxi.

'I know it's a bit early, but the two of you have so much to catch up on,' she said when she told them what she'd arranged. Ayesha was looking even more put out by now, but Kate just smiled at her in a friendly manner and pretended not to notice.

The taxi arrived within ten minutes and somehow, without much effort on their part, the Freemans and Jack Ivory found themselves on the path outside.

'Aren't you joining us?' asked Jack, surprised to see that Roz and Kate remained inside the house.

'I'm awfully sorry. Didn't I mention, Jon's calling in on his way back to London this evening. He's my boyfriend, so I'd better be at home when he arrives. I can't stay very long at all. And anyway, we'd only be in the way. I'm sure you've got loads to catch up on,' said Kate, and she closed the door on the three of them.

'Now,' she said, walking through to the kitchen, 'why don't we open that bottle of wine I brought the other evening?'

Roz had retreated to the sofa and had put her feet up, as though her legs were aching. Her face was alarmingly pale, and she leant her head back on the cushions.

'Jon's on his way back to London, is he? Where from?'

'Oh, Devon I think,' said Kate vaguely.

'A well-known hotbed of serious international crime.'

'Maybe I was stretching the truth a little.'

'I'm quite glad they've all gone. I was finding them a little tiring.'

'Can I get you something to eat? You look as though you've had a busy day.'

78

Roz opened her eyes. 'I quite fancy some of that lovely French cheese. There should be a baguette in the bread bin. You could put it in the oven for a few minutes and it'll be as good as new.'

'And a small salad?'

'Perfect.' And Roz closed her eyes again.

It was tricky, Kate thought. It seemed like a perfect opportunity to talk to her mother about her health, but if she did, then Roz would start arguing again and the pleasant atmosphere would be ruined. She would have to approach the question obliquely.

'I can't imagine that Jack Ivory and Marcus Freeman were ever great mates, can you?'

'It's always difficult to imagine what people were like thirty or forty years ago. We all change.'

'Some more than others. I can't visualise Marcus as a young man, certainly. Can you see him enjoying himself with a crowd of fellow students?'

'I expect he was the sporty type: up at dawn and out on the river, breaking the ice with his oar and training for some frightful race.'

This was the first time Kate had heard anything approaching criticism of Marcus Freeman from Roz, and she found it an encouraging sign.

'You don't mind that I brought Jack Ivory round? He is very insistent.'

'I could see that. But you have every right to find out what you want to know about your father and his family. I'm sorry I can't help. I really don't know very much about them. John only kept in touch with them through Christmas cards, and when he died, I didn't keep up the acquaintance with his family. There seemed no point at the time, but I can see now that I should have kept some kind of link, for your sake.'

79

'I don't suppose I've missed much,' said Kate. 'There was no one else my age, was there?'

'Not as far as I know.'

'I think the bread should have revived by now. I'll go and fetch our supper.'

For the next half-hour Kate was expecting the Freemans to return. She found herself listening out for the sound of the key in the lock and that honey-sweet voice calling out, 'It's only us!' But they must have settled themselves into the Italian restaurant and by now be deep in reminiscences of their time at Oxford. And what of Ayesha? Was she an Oxford graduate too? Or was she sitting there feeling left out? Well, as long as she didn't come running back to Roz's house, Kate could live with that thought. She wondered how she could broach the subject of front doors, and bolts.

To her surprise, it was Roz who raised the subject of her friends.

'I can see that you don't like Marcus and Ayesha,' she said.

'They're not really my type, are they?'

'I suppose not. And in some ways, they're not my type, either. But you must be friendly towards them for my sake, Kate. They've been very kind and helpful to me, you know.'

Kate was about to say that she wished they hadn't been quite so helpful, since their interference was preventing Roz from seeking medical help, but her mother went on, 'I received a letter, you see. Not a very nice one. I know I should have ignored it, Kate – but then, hindsight is a marvellous thing, isn't it? I was curious. So I replied. And then the avalanche began. Hundreds of letters. Including one that I found particularly disturbing.'

She stopped, staring into space.

'What letters are you talking about?'

'They spoke of warnings and prophecies.'

'Prophecies?'

'Yes, that was my own reaction to begin with. But you see, the first prophecy came true.'

'What sort of prophecy was it? Something very general, I suppose?'

'No, I'm not stupid. Not yet at least, Kate. If it had said that Wednesday was a unpropitious day for me, and on Wednesday there'd been a thunderstorm and I'd been caught without an umbrella, I'd have laughed about it. But it was more specific, and nastier than that.'

'Have you still got the letter?'

'Yes, it's upstairs.'

'Can I see it?'

'Perhaps, but not this evening. I'm just not feeling up to it. I think I need to go to bed and get some rest. Give me a ring in the morning, there's a good girl.'

Her mother never called her 'a good girl'. Kate wondered whether to offer to help her upstairs, but Roz would hardly thank her for that, even if she did need help. All she could do was wash up their plates and cutlery while her mother made her way upstairs.

'Good night!' Kate called, as she left. From her mother's bedroom came a faint reply, 'Good night.'

Well, she thought as she drove back to Jericho, at least she and Roz had spent an evening largely free of the Freemans. But she'd talk to Jon about the letters. Surely Criminal Intelligence would know all about the people behind them.

That evening, when she rang Jon, Kate decided to bring up the subject of Roz again.

'Apparently she's received dozens of letters containing what she calls "prophecies" – warnings that something nasty is about to happen. Is this some kind of a scam? Have you heard of anything similar?'

'Yes, I've heard about it, but I haven't been involved in any investigations myself. Is Roz worried by the letters?'

'Oddly enough, she is. You'd have thought she'd just tear them up and throw them away, but she's kept them – or at least some of them – and they're on her mind, I can tell.'

'Has there been a demand for money?'

'Not yet, or at least, not one she's told me about.'

'Usually there's no outright demand, but a polite request for a modest sum to cover expenses. What they're after is the victim's credit card or bank details, then they charge a regular fee for expenses, usually one that increases steeply with time. You see, if they're not asking for money, they're doing nothing illegal.'

'I'm sure that Roz wouldn't have sent money, let alone her credit card details. She's much too canny for that.' She paused. Was Roz, in her present state, quite as streetwise as she used to be? 'She started to tell me about it and then felt so tired that she had to go to bed. It was only about half past eight.'

'That's not like her! She and I have sat up until past midnight with a bottle of wine in the old days.'

'I told you: she's not herself.'

'At least you managed to avoid the Freemans for once.'

'Rather cleverly, I thought. I palmed them off on Jack Ivory – you know, the man who wants to know about his ancestors.'

'I don't think you've mentioned him before.'

Kate quickly filled Jon in on the missing details. 'Anyway,' she finished, 'Roz and I were left on our own for a while.'

'If the letter-writer hasn't asked for money he or she may be a simple nutter. Try to persuade Roz to tear the letters up and forget about them. I have to say, though, that the usual pattern is to target elderly—'

'Roz isn't elderly!'

'On paper it might appear that she could be,' said Jon carefully. 'They target comfortably off women of a certain age—'

'That's marginally better.'

'And the letters contain vague threats couched in other-worldly language. Only the letter-writer can keep the danger at bay.'

'Roz says the threats were specific, and one at least has come true.'

'Otherworldly language makes me think immediately of the Freemans,' said Jon.

'Face it, you don't like the Freemans—'

'You're not that taken with them yourself.'

'True. But I do think they're very kind to Roz, and she certainly likes them.'

'Fond as I am of your mother, I have to say that her judgement of people isn't always the same as mine.'

'That's putting it very diplomatically. Do you remember the dreadful Barry?'

'The one who disappeared just before the police caught up with him?'

'That's the man.'

'Yes. Vividly. But to return to the scams. The people who run them are mostly based in the Iberian peninsula. I don't think they turn up on people's doorsteps to threaten them with violence. It's all done at a distance, and by inference rather than by wielding baseball bats. And they do succeed in extracting large sums of money from vulnerable people.'

'How large?'

'Tens of thousands. All the victim's savings.'

'How can people be so gullible?'

'Perhaps as we get older we become more fearful of the unknown. I don't know. I do know that the victims are often educated, intelligent women who have held down senior jobs during their working lives.'

'Shouldn't she go to the police?'

'If there are no demands for money – and there aren't, usually – then it's difficult to see what crime has been committed. And as I mentioned, the letter-writers aren't based in England. There's not much that the local police can do about them.'

'I can't see Roz having the energy to go to the police, to be honest, even if there were some point in it.'

'Do you think the Freemans are really up to being this callous – and clever?'

'No. And I think they're genuinely fond of Roz. I could find out whether they've spent any time in Spain, though, couldn't I?'

'If it would make you feel happier. Be careful, Kate.'

'You know me, Jon. Cautious and circumspect to a fault.'

When he'd stopped laughing, Jon changed the subject. 'Have I mentioned it before? I'm giving serious thought to changing my job. I've been looking around to get an idea of what's on offer to someone of my experience and I'll be sending out a few copies of my CV in the next week or so.'

'So you don't think you'll be happy in the new set-up?'

'I haven't made a final decision, but I'll see what my options are. If I'm going to make a change, this is the time to do it.'

Kate wanted to ask what effect this would have on the two of them, but it wasn't the right moment. It sounded as if Jon had enough on his mind without adding an aggrieved girlfriend to the list.

# 10

Next morning when she checked her emails she found two new messages. The first was from Estelle:

So glad to hear you're making good progress, Kate. I've made a note in the diary to expect the completed MS in three weeks.

She'd forgotten all about the book she was writing. She might get on with it in the afternoon, but it was a question of priorities. She must contact Jack Ivory again before he left Oxford – and that was something she would ask him: just how long was he planning to stay? And for how long was Leicester prepared to give him a room? With the new term into its second week, they must be needing every inch of space they possessed.

Jack Ivory might be anxious to discover how his grand-parents were related to hers, but Kate was more interested in researching the background of the Freemans – and it seemed to her that Jack might be able to answer some of her questions. She rang Leicester College and asked to speak to him, but was told by the porter that he was out, so she left a message for him to ring her back after lunch.

Meanwhile, she would walk into Oxford and talk to Rafe Brown, estate agent. He must have learnt more about the Freemans than Avril had been able to extract from him.

Before leaving the house she went to switch off her computer, and then remembered to look at the second email.

To Kate Ivory
This is a warning to you to change your ways. If you do
not then bad things are waiting to happen to you. Don't
interfere in other people's business but look after your
own. You are running into a trap and falling into danger.
Watch out, Kate Ivory.

For a moment she felt frozen with shock. This must be the
sort of thing that Roz had been receiving. It was nonsense, of
course it was, and she should delete it immediately.

She clicked on 'File' and 'Properties' to see where the
message originated from.

There was only a jumble of letters and digits and an
unheard-of service provider. But instead of deleting it, she
left it there in her inbox. Next time Jon was in Oxford she
might ask him to take a look at it and see whether he could
discover anything useful about the sender. Yet at the same
time she felt ashamed that she could find such rubbish
disturbing.

She walked slowly across the centre of Oxford, unable to
put the message out of her mind. Of course it was a fake. A
joke, even. Was this what Jon had been talking about? Did
it sound as though it had been translated from the Spanish?
(Though the people operating out of Spain were more likely
to be English, surely.)

And was it possible that someone was targeting both
mother and daughter? But this was an email, and Roz's
messages had come in the form of letters.

Letters. Someone else had mentioned letters recently. Jack
Ivory had wanted to see any letters Roz might have received
from family members, but it wasn't that. No, it was Avril.
When she had been warning Kate against con men, she had
mentioned letters. Did that mean that Avril had been a victim

of the letters scam too? Even if she had, those letters couldn't have been linked to the email she had received.

Jon had said that the victims were elderly, comfortably off women. Kate wasn't old enough, and she certainly wasn't rich. She was seeing connections where none existed.

By the time she reached Rafe Brown's door she was feeling a lot better, and when she entered and found the place deserted except for Rafe himself, she knew she was in luck.

'Hi, Rafe. Remember me?'

'You were selling a three-bedroomed Edwardian mid-terrace in Fridesley, right?'

'Right. And I'm Roz Ivory's daughter, Kate.' This was one place where Roz's name might carry some weight.

'How is your mother? She was looking a bit under the weather last time I saw her.'

'She is a bit peaky still, I'm afraid.'

'I'm sorry to hear that. What is it I can do for you? You're not thinking of moving again just yet, are you?'

'I'm very happy in Jericho, Rafe – but you'll be my first call if I change my mind. Actually, I was wondering whether you could help me over something else. Do you remember a couple called Freeman? Marcus and Ayesha.'

'Yes. Though she told me her name was really Sheila. They were interested in your mother's North Oxford property. I seem to remember taking them up there as soon as it was ready to view. But it turned out the place wasn't big enough for them.'

'They bought a house in East Oxford in the end, didn't they?' asked Kate, thinking about the meeting in Tesco's.

'No, they'd made up their minds it had to be a Victorian house in one of those quiet, leafy roads in North Oxford – Summertown, preferably, they said. I know they found something they liked in the end, but I didn't sell it to them, unfortunately. Why do you ask?'

'They've made great friends with Roz, and now they're influencing her business decisions, too.' Kate thought she was justified in stretching the truth a little, and she went on, 'I was just a little worried that they might not be all they appeared. No one knows anything about them, as far as I can tell, so I thought I'd try to find out what I could about their background. What did you think of them, Rafe?'

'Whatever business decisions Marcus Freeman's taken in the past must have been pretty good ones, don't you think? I don't think you need worry that Roz is being led astray!'

'Do you know where they lived before they came to Oxford?'

'They mentioned Kent, but I couldn't tell you more than that, even if I knew it myself.'

On his desk stood a terracotta pot with a half-dead plant drooping over its rim. It might once have been an anaemic daffodil, or maybe a narcissus. Rafe noticed Kate looking at it. 'You think I should throw it out?'

'You never know with bulbs; often they revive in the spring.'

'OK. I'll give it a second chance if you say so,' he said without enthusiasm.

The phone rang and Rafe turned to answer it.

'Thanks for your time, Rafe,' said Kate, and left him to get on with his work.

Kent. Still, as she had noted before, Kent was a big county and she couldn't imagine herself driving aimlessly around it, hoping to bump into someone who knew the Freemans. She hoped that Jack Ivory would ring after lunch, otherwise she had nowhere else to go and would have to give up the search.

* * *

'Hello, Kate?'

'Jack? Thanks for getting back to me.'

'Not at all. What can I do for you? Have you found out any more details of your father's family?'

'Nothing, I'm afraid. But there was something I'd like to talk to you about.'

'It sounds intriguing. I'm rather busy at the moment, but would you like to meet for a drink this evening? We eat at seven fifteen, so perhaps we could say six o'clock?' And he mentioned the name of a pub near Leicester College. 'I expect we can find a quiet corner to talk.'

'It sounds ideal.'

When she had rung off Kate wondered whether she should have invited him back to her place for a drink, or even a meal. But Avril's distrust of strangers and Jon's account of how victims were carefully targeted were having their effect on her. Jack might be very different from Marcus, but she knew him no better than she did the Freemans, and it would be as well to be cautious. Could this be the onset of middle-aged paranoia? she wondered.

# 11

Although it was another misty evening, Kate walked across town to the pub that Jack had chosen. The temperature was dropping and she was glad that she had worn a warm jacket. The damp air brushed her cheeks and pearled her hair and her breath came in small white clouds.

When she reached the pub she found Jack already seated at a corner table with an open bottle of sparkling mineral water, beaded with condensation, standing next to his glass. The clock on the wall said that it was only two minutes past six, so he must have been early. He rose to his feet as soon as he spotted her.

'Kate, how lovely to see you.'

'It's very kind of you to agree to meet, Jack.'

'It's my pleasure, I assure you. Now, what would you like to drink – and it doesn't have to be mineral water, by the way!'

'In that case, I'd like a glass of white wine,' she said, removing her jacket and sitting down. 'This place is very civilised,' she added, when he returned to the table with her drink.

'Yes. I thought it would be quieter than the King's Arms,' he said. 'But do tell me why you wanted to meet, if it wasn't to talk about the Ivorys. I'm really curious to know.'

'It is about the Ivorys in a way. At least, it's about Roz.'

'Your mother?'

'Yes. I'm sure you noticed that she didn't appear to be at all well.'

'I thought she didn't seem very strong, certainly, though of course I had nothing to compare it with, knowing her for less than an hour, as it were.'

'Usually she's full of energy, and sparkle, and life. But now she seems to be permanently tired, and so pale. Worst of all, she appears to have given up the struggle. Up to now she's always been a fighter.'

'Do you know what's wrong with her?'

'I wish I did. That's the crux of the problem: she won't see a doctor.'

'Some people can be awkward about visiting a doctor. They think up all sorts of reasons, but it boils down to one thing: fear, I believe. You'll have to coax her out of her house and down to the surgery.'

'I've tried that, and failed. No, I hate to say this, Jack, but the real problem lies with your friends, Marcus and Ayesha. They're doing everything they can to prevent her from seeking help.'

'Surely not! Why would they do that?'

'I'm sorry, I didn't mean to offend you. I've no idea why they dislike conventional medicine. But they go round to Roz's place every day with herbal remedies and . . . I don't know what you'd call them – "alternative therapies" perhaps, if you were being kind.'

'And you don't think these remedies are doing her any good?'

'Not that I've seen, anyway. In fact she seems to have got worse in the past week or so.'

'I'm not an expert. I don't know how you think I can help.' He doesn't like my criticism of his friends, she thought. I shouldn't have been so direct about it, but what could I do? Jack sipped at his glass of mineral water.

The pub was filling up. A party of young people sat down at the table next to them, deciding loudly what they

92

would drink and how they would pay, and it was difficult to carry on a conversation against this background. Kate leant towards Jack so that he could hear.

'You've known Marcus a long time, so I was hoping that you could tell me whether he and Ayesha are genuinely concerned about Roz or not. If I really thought that they had Roz's interests at heart I might feel happier about their being in her house every day.'

'I know I'm in your debt for the help you've given me over the history of the Ivorys, and believe me, I really appreciate the way you took me to see your mother. It was hardly your fault that I learnt nothing new, so really, Kate, I would like to help you if I can. But I do feel awkward about discussing my friends behind their backs. I'm sure you understand.'

'I'm not asking you to gossip about them, only to tell me whether you believe they're sincere. I'd like to know that they're seeing so much of my mother because they're good people, to put it simply. Really, that's all.'

'But you're afraid that they might have an ulterior motive? They could be after her money, for example.' Jack had followed her lead and was leaning forward so that their heads were only a few inches apart. This close, she could smell the aftershave he had applied that morning, a faint citrus scent.

'Yes, you're right, I can't help wondering about that,' she said. 'How can I know whether they're acting out of the pure goodness of their hearts?'

'Well, if it helps you to trust them, Kate, I'll tell you all I know. But there's no need to doubt them. Believe me. Marcus and I no longer have as much in common as we did when we were young, I admit that. And seeing him again yesterday after such a long time I can see that he has become perhaps just a little overbearing, just a little too pleased with himself.'

Kate said nothing. She thought it diplomatic not to agree too enthusiastically with what Jack was saying.

'And Ayesha can also be a little overwhelming at first meeting. They seem to have gained a, what shall I call it, a theatricality in the way they present themselves, so I can understand why you are dubious about their good intentions. But I hope, for all your sakes, that I am able to correct this impression.'

'So what can you tell me? I need to know what kind of a man Marcus Freeman is. Is he just what he seems, or is there something in his background I should know about?' She wasn't going to apologise for asking him to give her the lowdown on a friend of his; Roz's health was too important for that.

'As I've said, and I can't emphasise the point too much, I don't really like talking about an old friend – and fellow Leicester man – behind his back, but you have been so helpful to me over my researches into the Ivory family that I feel it is the least I can do to repay your kindness.' He paused to drink some more of his mineral water while Kate waited, hoping that at last she was going to learn something solid about the Freemans.

'It's more than thirty years since we were at Oxford,' he began, then paused as his chair was jostled by a young man pushing through to the bar. 'I knew Marcus quite well in those days – we both rowed for our college, and those training sessions in the misty dawns on the Isis formed bonds that can never be broken. I think I gained an insight into the mettle of the man, and I don't believe that can have changed over time. So perhaps what I have to tell you will be useful for your purpose.' Jack leant to one side to allow someone else to pass. 'I should have chosen a quieter pub,' he apologised.

'I imagine that all the pubs in the town centre are crowded

at this time of year,' said Kate. 'The students seem to be out in force tonight.'

'So many more of them than when I was here. I hardly recognise the place.' Jack looked around, as though searching for his lost youth.

'Go on with what you were saying about Marcus, please.' For a moment the sound level had dropped and she had no difficulty in hearing his voice. Imperceptibly, she moved back so that their faces were no longer only inches apart.

'He was a very open, generous young man, though this sounds very trite in this day and age.' He looked around at the young people with their knowing, experienced faces, their cigarettes, their designer clothes. 'Not at all cool, as they would say.'

'Well, we are talking about a different time. The late sixties? Early seventies?'

'Yes, that's right.'

It was hard to imagine now, in the twenty-first century, that there were once young men like Jack Ivory and Marcus Freeman – decent, clean-living, idealistic. Had anyone ever offered them a joint? They wouldn't have known what to do with it. 'Do tell me more about Marcus.'

'He was not, perhaps, one of the brightest of his year. In fact, if I'm to be honest, everyone thought he would be lucky to achieve anything better than a 2.2.'

'That's bad, is it?' asked Kate, who was always aware in conversations like this that she wasn't a graduate of any university, let alone Oxford, and found it difficult to understand these distinctions.

'By Oxford standards it means that you are irrevocably second-rate.'

'But you don't agree?'

'Not as a human being, certainly. And in fact he

95

confounded everyone's expectations and gained a respectable 2.1. But that's hardly pertinent to the present examination, is it?' He smiled at his own mild joke. 'As I say, his was a straightforward character and I don't believe there were any hidden, dark depths to him.'

'A creature of the light,' said Kate.

Jack nodded, hearing no irony. 'He was an idealist, always ready to believe the best of everyone, and this laid him open to being taken advantage of on occasion. He never lost his belief in his fellow man, however. I expect that with the passage of the years he has become less, what shall I say, naïve, but that is only to be hoped for and expected. No one could go through life with an attitude like that without being destroyed.'

They were both silent for a minute or two, then Kate said, 'Tell me more about Ayesha. Please.'

'I didn't know Ayesha in those days, of course, but I do remember that the object of his affections in his second year was an equally good-natured and open young woman, not particularly pretty, but with a sweet nature and a great love of music.'

'They sound like an ideal couple,' said Kate drily.

'Perhaps they do. But the relationship lasted less than a year. Perhaps the girl – I forget her name, I'm afraid – was just a little too anodyne. Marcus needed someone to oppose him, someone to sharpen himself against, if you want. He needed to question his beliefs. That was what would bring out the best in him.'

'And you think that Ayesha fulfils these needs?'

'Kate, I've spent only one evening in her company. How can I answer that question?'

'I'm sorry. Of course you're right.' She would have to rely on her own judgement of Ayesha. Perhaps it was the woman who was the evil influence in this marriage. Kate looked around her. For a few minutes she had been immersed in a totally different world, one that she could scarcely imagine any of the young people around her inhabiting.

'Do you know anything about his recent past, I wonder? We know nothing about them before they turned up in Oxford.'

There was a short silence while Jack thought about what he was going to say. 'I know that what I am about to tell you isn't generally known, and I'd be grateful if you kept it to yourself. The memory is too recent and too raw for them to talk about.'

'I'll keep it to myself,' Kate assured him.

'Marcus and Ayesha had been living for some years in Kent, in a village on Romney Marsh. They had one child, a son, when they were in their late thirties, but he was born with a defect of the heart. I know that they can do wonders with such children these days, and the boy spent time in a children's hospital, having several operations to repair the damage, but in the end it was in vain and he died last year. As you can imagine, they were devastated, and decided that they must leave the place that reminded them every day of his death. So they sold their house and moved right out of the area.'

'Why Oxford?'

'Why not? That was their attitude, I believe. It's a beautiful city, which Marcus knows well and where he was once happy. It's within easy reach of London and Birmingham, and they believed they would meet plenty of people who would share their cultural interests.'

'Did they mention that they'd been living in Spain?'

'No. That sounds most unlikely. Marcus was laughing at me and accusing me of having itchy feet. He said he preferred to stay in one place and "collect some fat around him", as he put it – and from what I've seen, I'd say he'd succeeded in doing that.'

'And did he tell you what he did for a living?'

'I gather that as a young man he was in business – don't ask me what kind – and made enough to retire on by the time he was forty. He then decided to repay to society some of what he had taken out, and became a teacher. Not a teacher in a prestigious school, you understand, or even a good one, but somewhere where the children came from underprivileged backgrounds and had an unwillingness to learn. A dozen years on, and following the tragic death of his son, he was ready to retire for a second time.'

'He's not old, though. Will he take up some other work?'

'He already has. I should have thought you'd noticed, Kate. Marcus and Ayesha quite simply like to do good – not in any formal way, but in the normal course of life. When they meet someone with a need, they do their best to fulfil it, often at some cost to themselves.'

'And are the recipients always grateful for their help?'

'The Freemans aren't looking for gratitude, believe me.' Which was probably just as well, thought Kate privately. They certainly hadn't received any from Kate and Avril.

'I can see you aren't convinced by my judgement,' said Jack, watching Kate closely. 'So I have a suggestion to make.'

'Yes? I'm open to any suggestion that will convince me of the Freemans' good intentions towards my mother.'

'Although I haven't seen anything of Jack over the past thirty-odd years, and anything I can tell you is consequently out of date, there is someone who has known them more recently. I could put you in touch with her.'

'Really? That would be very kind.'

'She's nearer your age than mine, and you might get on

well with her. Her name is Laura Wilton, she lives in Hythe, and she's my sister.'

'How does she know the Freemans?'

'Oh, it's a long story, but I'll try to condense it as much as possible. She's ten years younger than me, and when she was twenty she married an old Oxford friend of mine, Kevin, and went to live in Kent, on the south coast. Kevin also knew Marcus from our Oxford days, and they met up again by chance, through some common business interest.'

'But you didn't meet Marcus then?'

'I was abroad, teaching English in Hong Kong.' Jack looked at his watch. 'Look, this has been most interesting, and I do want to help, but I have to be going now, I'm afraid. It's nearly time for dinner in Hall.'

'If you could just give me your sister's address or phone number?'

'Of course.' He found a biro and notebook in an inside pocket and wrote a name and address in his neat handwriting. 'The marriage didn't last long, I'm afraid. I think that Laura still wanted to go out to parties and restaurants every evening while Kevin thought it was time to settle down and start a family. He behaved very shamefully, going off with a friend of Laura's, and leaving my sister quite badly off and very unhappy. The other woman was older and less lively than Laura, so I can see they might well get on better together, but it was a great blow, at least to her pride, at the time.'

'And Marcus and Ayesha stepped in and helped her?'

'Yes. You sound sceptical, but that is exactly what happened. Perhaps you're thinking that I should have been the one to offer assistance. I confess that I had little patience with my sister at the time, and anyway, I didn't want to return to England until I'd cured my wanderlust.' He tore the page from his notebook and handed it to her. 'I've written down her phone number as well as her address so you can ring her up this evening if you like.'

'Thank you very much, Jack. And thank you for your patience, too. I really am grateful.'

'Goodbye, Kate. I must run or I'll be late.' And he left the pub a few paces ahead of her and turned in the direction of Leicester College.

Kate walked back towards Beaumont Street mulling over what Jack had told her. There was a touch of frost in the air and she pulled up the collar of her jacket and stuck her hands in the pockets to keep warm. The mist was still lingering as she approached the canal, and the damp air penetrated her clothing, making her hurry towards the warmth of her kitchen.

The Freemans still sounded just a little too good to be true, she thought, as she strode through the streets. But perhaps this sister of Jack's would have a less rosy view of them. She wondered what sort of person she was. She imagined a schoolteacher, a paler version of her brother. Was she the type to take the Freemans at face value? Or maybe, she thought gloomily, they really were the paragons that Jack believed them to be.

When she had eaten, and fed Susanna, Kate decided to phone Avril again.

'Yes, Kate? Is there any news about Roz?'

'None, I'm afraid, Avril. But last time we spoke you were talking about trusting people and you mentioned that you'd received some letters – unpleasant ones, I gathered. I wonder whether you could tell me what they said.'

'I didn't mean to let that slip. I found them most upsetting at the time and I don't like talking about them.'

'I do have a reason to ask you about them, believe me. Did you receive any kind of threat?

'Only in an indirect way. I forget the exact words now, but they warned me that something nasty was about to happen and I needed to contact them to learn more and ward off the danger.'

'Did they ask for money?'

'Again, only indirectly. They asked for a contribution towards their expenses – they were very insistent that they didn't charge for their services, but I'm sure they were expecting payment eventually.'

'What did you do with the letters?'

'I know I should have put them through my shredder and then into my recycling bin.'

'But you didn't?'

'No, and the odd thing is, Kate, that the thing they threatened came true, just a week later.'

'Wasn't it a vague threat that could have applied to any number of things that might happen?'

'No, that's what frightened me and made me feel that these were truly wicked people. It was something specific which meant a lot to me but which wouldn't have occurred to anyone else, I should have thought.'

'Can you tell me what it was?'

There was a pause, and then, sounding as though she was close to tears, Avril said, 'It was my mother's grave. She's buried in Wolvercote Cemetery, you know.' Her words were disjointed and Kate felt guilty at having revived the painful memory. 'I visit it every Sunday afternoon and make sure the plot is free from weeds. I bring fresh flowers, of course. I was devoted to my mother, you see. But someone desecrated it. Tore down the headstone and tried to gouge out the wording, dug up the earth, scattered the spring bulbs I'd planted there. Who would do such a thing? What can be going through their minds? It felt awful, Kate. I can't describe it. It was as though she'd died for a second time.'

'I am so sorry, Avril.'

'Well, now you know what I mean when I say that you should be careful. There are wicked, callous people in this world.'

Kate wanted to ask her if she thought that the people who had sent the letter had also vandalised her mother's grave, but this wasn't the moment.

When she had rung off she thought about it for a while. She couldn't believe that the letter-writers had come all the way from Spain, or wherever they were based, to vandalise one old woman's grave. From what Jon had told her, they sent out thousands of these letters and relied on getting a response from a fraction of them. It wouldn't be worth their while to chase up the sceptics, especially since those who did reply were so lucrative for them.

Where did they get the names and addresses from? There must be mailing lists for sale, she imagined. And once someone responded to one of the letters, she knew that their name and address would be sold on to other criminals who preyed on the vulnerable.

Kate wished that Roz and Avril had done the right thing and ignored their letters.

Kate sat looking at the torn-off page with Laura Wilton's address and phone number. She wanted to ring Jack's sister and find out what she knew about the Freemans, yet she couldn't put what Avril had said out of her mind. But she had to do it, for Roz's sake. She picked up the phone and dialled.

'Laura Wilton.' The voice was low and pleasant, sounding a lot younger than Jack Ivory. It occurred to Kate for the first time that if Jack was right, she and Laura could be cousins, even if several times removed.

'My name is Kate Ivory and—'

'You've been talking to my brother, I believe.' She sounded friendly, not at all resentful that a total stranger was ringing to find out all she could about a couple of friends of hers. And Kate was glad that Jack had given her at least some of the background so that she didn't have to go through a long explanation of who she was and what she wanted.

'So you know who I am?'

'Probably my cousin! I was Laura Ivory before I married. But of course you know that.'

'And do you mind talking about Marcus and Ayesha Freeman? It is important, or I wouldn't ask.'

'Ayesha!' Laura giggled. 'You do know she's really called Sheila, don't you?'

'Someone did mention it.'

'Whatever possessed her to change it!'

'I don't really know, but I suppose she can call herself whatever she likes. Plenty of people don't like their given name, after all,' said Kate, trying to be as reasonable as she could.

'I can hear you're determined to be charitable, so I'll say no more. Look, Kate, the problem is that it isn't possible for me to talk this evening. In fact, this phone isn't very private, I'm afraid.'

'Would it be better if I rang you on your mobile?'

'I must be the only person in the south of England who doesn't own one.'

'Should I email you?

Laura laughed. 'I'm not much of a one for modern technology. Phone calls and the occasional postcard are as high-tech as I get.'

'So what do you suggest?' Kate didn't think she could bear the slowness of an exchange of postcards, even if

103

Laura replied by return of post. How much could you fit on a single card? No, it was better to gauge your correspondent's reactions, either over the phone or face to face.

'I don't suppose you could drive down to visit me?' said Laura. 'No, sorry, that's a ridiculous suggestion. It must be over a hundred miles.'

It wasn't such a bad idea. There could well be other people in Hythe who knew the Freemans. She could find out from Laura where they had lived and visit the place. This could be the opportunity she had been searching for.

'As a matter of fact, I believe I could come down in a day or two, if that would be OK. It's time I visited a few bookshops in your part of the country. My agent's always suggesting that I should spend more time promoting my work.'

'You're an author?'

'Jack didn't mention it?'

'No. He only seemed interested in the fact that you were an Ivory and therefore had to be related to us. Are you turned on by all that genealogy stuff too?'

'Not really. He is rather intense about his family history, isn't he?'

'And that's putting it mildly! You'll have gathered that he and I aren't really alike, and there's rather a large age difference. Though I am very fond of the old boy, don't get me wrong.'

'May I ring you again tomorrow? I'll contact some local bookshops and see if they'd like me to sign stock for them. If I get a positive response, I'll drive down in a couple of days. When's a good time for you?'

'Oh, afternoons are best. I'm not at my brightest in the mornings, and evenings I'm often out. And I'm free in the afternoon all next week, as it happens. OK?'

'Sure. I'll be in touch.'

When she'd hung up, Kate wished she'd found out a little more about Laura Wilton. What did she do for a living? Did she live on her own? A more worldly person than Jack Ivory might have filled her in on these facts. Never mind, she'd find out for herself soon enough.

# 12

It was still dark when Kate left the house the next morning. In a couple of weeks' time, when the clocks went back, it would be easier to lace up her running shoes and get out through the front door by six in the morning. It was only that initial effort of will that was so hard – leaving a warm bed and climbing into T-shirt and tracksuit while the sky outside the window was black and her body-clock was telling her that she should still be sleeping. But five minutes into a run her spirits started to rise and she was glad that she'd overcome the initial resistance.

This morning it wasn't just the darkness that made her think twice about going out. There was a thin layer of ice over the cars in the street, and a mist that would probably rise by the time most people left for work, but which was cold, damp and unwelcoming at this hour.

She set off in the direction of the canal, since this was her favourite run, but the mist thickened as she approached the towpath and she wished now that she had crossed the Woodstock and Banbury roads and run through the University Parks. Still, visibility wasn't so bad that she was in any danger of missing her step and falling into the canal.

As she ran on the soft surface, sounds were muffled, reflected back by the murk, and she heard the echo of her own footsteps giving the impression of a second runner, perfectly in time, sometimes close, sometimes receding, always behind her.

A plinking on her left could have been a fish surfacing,

or a small mammal slipping into the water. A sudden quacking and splashing ahead signalled the presence of ducks. Smaller birds occasionally cheeped disconsolately from the twigs above her head. Condensation dripped from the trees on to her forehead and beaded her hair. On her right she could still hear the sound of cars on the Woodstock Road and from the bypass. Then she saw a welcome glow of windows ahead as canal-dwellers switched on lights and cooked breakfast, and heard the slapping of small waves against the hulls of narrow boats as they moved around inside.

The smell of coffee reminded her that she would soon be sitting down to breakfast at her own kitchen table. The gloom was lightening as she turned for home, but for the moment the mist was as thick and damp as ever, and she increased her pace to keep warm.

Soon she was off the towpath, back in Cranham Street, the mud soft under her trainers, and with the deadening of her own footfalls she became aware that there were footsteps behind her. This time it was not an effect of the mist; this was a real person. In fact, there was more than one, for she could hear them talking, and they were gaining on her. Not that there was anything to be nervous about: there were plenty of people who went out for a run before breakfast, and this was hardly a likely time of day to get mugged. But still it was disconcerting to hear people near her without being able to see them, and there was something menacing in the tone of their voices.

And then another person approached from her right, as though he had been waiting for her arrival, catching her in a pincer movement. She looked around to see if there was someone, anyone, who could help her, or simply by their presence act as a deterrent. A car door slammed and an engine reluctantly turned over, but the car and driver were some distance away, and invisible, as she must be to them. She heard the car move off in the opposite direction and felt more vulnerable than before.

There were at least two people behind her, at her shoulder now, and another one, wearing a sweatshirt with the hood pulled down over his forehead, just two feet in front of her.

'Give us your mobile,' he rasped, but even so she could tell he was young, maybe only fourteen or fifteen. His accent was broad, his voice muffled by the hood and his lowered face. Could she push past him and escape?

'We got a knife,' said the one at her shoulder, and his voice sounded a little older, but still that of a youth. 'Your mobile. Give it over.'

'And your wonga,' said the third.

'What?' For a moment she couldn't think what he wanted. Something sharp pricked her left shoulder blade and she felt real fear for the first time – the fear that roots you to the spot and drains the blood from your skin, leaving you as cold and helpless as a rabbit caught in headlights.

'Money,' shouted the first, growing impatient. 'All you got.'

One of them was holding her left elbow in a painful grip. She could smell them now, the sweaty scent of their nervousness, the cigarette smoke in their clothing mixed with the sweeter smell of cannabis.

'I don't have any money on me.' Her voice wavered. She made an effort to sound less afraid of them. 'I don't carry money when I'm running.'

Then someone's hand was in her tracksuit pocket. 'Got her mobile,' he said. 'No money.'

'Bitch,' said the first. 'Let's see your watch.' But it was only a cheap digital one and they didn't bother to take it. No rings, no jewellery either.

Then her elbow was released and she was pushed roughly

to the ground, but she was free. Ahead of her the three indistinct running forms were swallowed up by the mist, their feet thudding on the pavement for a moment until that sound, too, was gone.

She got to her feet, rubbing her arm where it had hit the edge of the pavement. She was so angry that she wanted to run after them and demand that they return her phone, but her legs were shaking and she couldn't move. She felt in her other pocket: her doorkey was still there. At least they hadn't taken that. She could still feel the point on her shoulder blade where the knife – if it was a knife – had rested, and the painful spots on her elbow where the other lad had taken hold.

Minutes later she was still shaking, but the blood was returning to her face and hands and, cautiously, she started to walk home. As she approached her house she saw that the mist was rising. She could see the shapes of the cars the length of the street, and the first workers appearing from their doorways and walking towards Walton Street. The muggers had timed their attack well: another ten minutes and they would have been in full view.

As she filled the kettle for coffee she wondered whether she should report the incident to the police. The three youths must have been waiting for one of the many joggers who frequented the towpath and the streets of Jericho in the early morning, using the mist and the darkness to hide both their appearance and their escape. Could she describe them, except in very general terms? No, they could have been any three teenagers. Would the police be interested? Probably not. And even if they were, they were unlikely to find the muggers. Would she get her phone back? Even less likely.

Just one of those things, she told herself. And it could have been worse. She wasn't hurt, just shaken. And furious. She'd had no money on her, and she realised that she was lucky they hadn't been angry about that and hit her, or worse. She regretted the loss of her phone, which was new and could do all sorts of clever things. And there was at least twenty-five pounds of credit on her account.

She rang the phone company to let them know about the theft, Susanna complaining all the while that she wanted her breakfast too.

'Not an auspicious start to the day,' Kate told her, as she shook a pouch of beef-flavoured pellets into the cat's dish.

She didn't feel much like writing when she went into her workroom, but she turned the computer on and then checked to see if she had any new messages. As she waited for the system to connect, her eyes fell on the message she had received the previous day. There was one phrase in particular that caught her attention: *running into a trap and falling into danger*.

Of course, it was a coincidence. It was absurd to think that it could be anything else. And in any case, who knew she was going to run along the towpath that morning? She hadn't known herself until she turned left out of her gate rather than right.

She shouldn't even be thinking this way. Someone had sent her a daft email; three youths had stolen her mobile. The two facts were unconnected. She concentrated on reading the perfectly sane messages that had just arrived in her inbox and tried to put the rest out of her head. She would make another pot of coffee and relax for half an hour with a book (other than her own), and then she would start to contact bookshops along the route from Oxford to Hythe.

# 13

There were three booksellers who seemed happy for Kate to call in and sign the copies of her books that they had in stock – though they had to warn her that these weren't very numerous. Never mind, it was a case of making her face known, Estelle had told her, and Estelle was one of the few people that Kate was inclined to obey.

She sent emails to Estelle and Neil telling them rather smugly what she was doing. Neil sent a reply thanking her for her efforts. Estelle's answer said:

> A good idea in principle but I hope you're not wasting precious writing time, Kate.

Next Kate rang Laura Wilton to tell her that she'd be visiting her on Thursday afternoon.

'Do you want to stay overnight?' asked Laura. 'It's a long way to come for such a short visit.'

'I have to return to Oxford. I need to get on with some writing on Friday.'

'OK. But the offer's there if you want it.'

'Thanks.'

It made Kate think, though. If she stayed overnight – or even until Saturday, since she and Jon weren't meeting this weekend – she could have a good look around and see what more she could find out about the Freemans.

If she was going to stay in Hythe for a couple of days she wanted to be independent, though. And it sounded as though Laura's social life was riotous enough for Kate to be in the way if she stayed there. She went on the internet and found what looked like a suitable B and B, far enough away from Laura Wilton for them not to bump into one another in an embarrassing way on Friday. She phoned up and booked for one night, with the possibility of staying for two since it was the low season.

By then it was too late in the morning to settle down to serious work, so she pottered about in the garden until it was time for lunch. In the afternoon she would walk into town and buy herself a new phone. Then she'd have to let everyone know that she'd changed the number of her mobile.

Before making herself a sandwich at one o'clock, Kate called in to see her neighbour, Brad. Like her, he worked from home, so she could be sure of finding him there. Brad's exotic looks came from his Sri Lankan mother and Malaysian father, and his name was really Rohan, he had told her. 'Brad' was a relic from his not-too-distant student days.

'Would you mind feeding Susanna for me for a couple of days?'

'You know I love that cat as much as you do: of course I will.'

'Thanks. You've still got the key, haven't you?'

'And I know where the cat food is, and when she's fed. Yes, don't fuss, Susanna will be fine. Are you going somewhere nice with that exciting man of yours?'

'No. I'll be on my own, down on the south coast, doing research.'

'For the new book?'

'Could be,' said Kate, not wanting to explain.

'Well don't leave the lovely Jon on his own for too long, sweetie, or someone else will snap him up.'

Kate had long been aware that Brad admired the lovely

Jon, but they both knew that the attraction was strictly one-sided.

'Don't worry. He's busy himself this weekend and won't have time to miss me.'

'Are you all right, by the way, Kate? You're looking a bit pale.'

'Oh, I got stopped by three youths when I was out running this morning. They stole my mobile.'

'Are you hurt?' Brad looked horrified.

'No. Just a bit shaken.'

'I hope you've reported it to the police.'

'It's not too serious. I didn't think I'd bother.'

Brad looked as though he was about to lecture her on her duties as a resident of Jericho, so she said quickly: 'Thanks so much for agreeing to look after Susanna. I know she'll be happy with you. I'll see you when I get back at the weekend, but now I have to go into town to buy a new phone.'

Before she did so, Kate nipped back home to ring Avril. There was another question that she had been afraid to ask.

'Kate? Nice to hear from you, but do you mind if I ask whether this call is urgent? I have just ten minutes left before I have to leave the house, I'm afraid.'

'I'll be brief. Avril, what do you think is wrong with Roz? Is it serious, do you think, or are we making a fuss, as she keeps telling us?'

'I'm not a doctor. I wouldn't like to speculate since I would probably be wrong and would only worry you needlessly.'

'So you do suspect it could be something serious?'

'Yes.'

'What?' Kate asked, hoping that Avril's guess wasn't the same as hers.

'I had a friend once, Kate, and her husband had that

same tiredness, the yellowish tinge to his skin. And he was losing weight. He'd been quite a plump man, but after a while his skin looked too big for him. Oh, I've described that badly!'

'I know what you mean.' It was something Kate was noticing about Roz these days too. 'Do you know what was wrong with him?'

'He was suffering from leukaemia.'

And that was the word that Kate had been dreading to hear.

'But it's not certain, is it? We're not experts, Kate. We couldn't be certain until she saw the doctor and had the tests done.'

'And that's the problem, isn't it? I'm sure that she needs to see someone soon, Avril. Surely the sooner she's diagnosed the better her chances are?'

'I'd have thought so. But we mustn't lose hope. You know how impulsive she is: she might suddenly decide to go to the surgery tomorrow morning.'

'Yes, of course.' But Kate didn't think Roz did much on impulse these days; she just didn't have the energy for it. She had one more question. 'I mustn't keep you Avril, I know, but can you tell me what happened to your friend's husband?'

There was a short silence, then Avril said, 'He died, eventually.'

Jon Kenrick read the letter once more. They wanted him to come for an interview in ten days' time. The company was one he respected and the salary they were offering was an improvement on what he was receiving at the moment. And then there was the fact that the job would be based just ten miles outside Oxford.

How would Kate feel about that?

On the one hand, they had such good times when they

were away on holiday, but he felt with Kate that she needed to keep a certain distance between them. She was always pleased to see him when he came down for the weekend, and she always accepted his invitations to spend a weekend on the boat, or in his London flat. But there was a part of her mind that belonged somewhere else – maybe that was because she was a novelist. He felt that from time to time she liked to leave everyone behind and live in that imaginary world of hers quite happily, for weeks on end.

When they had been apart for a few days, he missed her, especially when it was a weekend like this one coming up when they wouldn't see one another at all. But did she miss him in the same way? He doubted it.

If he took a job near Oxford she might feel trapped, unable to escape from him, pushed into a corner. Or was he underestimating her? And anyway, he hadn't been offered the job yet. There was no guarantee that he'd get it, but he should let her know he'd be in her area for the interview. They could meet up afterwards and discuss the future.

He lifted the phone and dialled her number, but Kate wasn't answering. He left a message on her machine, asking her to call back. He knew it was no use trying her mobile: she always switched it off during the day, and then she forgot to pick up her voicemail. He wondered if she really was out, or whether she was sitting at her computer, too engrossed in her work to want to answer the phone and let in the outside world.

It was a cool, blustery day when Kate arrived in Hythe. She found a place to park and then took a walk through the town centre to stretch her legs after the journey. On the way down she had visited the three bookshops and smiled relentlessly at their owners as she signed the four or five copies of her works that they had in stock.

A pleasant town, she thought, as she peered into shop windows. An attractive place to retire to, obviously, so why was it that Laura Wilton – who had sounded very far from retirement and not at all sedate – had decided to come here to live? Perhaps there was a bright and noisy set of forty-somethings hidden away somewhere. Above her, the seagulls wheeled across the sky, screaming like lost souls, the fitful sun catching their white breasts and changing them to silver. She looked at her watch: a quarter to three. It was time to find Laura Wilton and the answers to her questions.

She easily found Charlotte Road, where Laura lived, which was wide and tree-lined, leading down towards the sea. The houses here were mostly detached, and as white and pretty as wedding cakes. Number thirty-two had a dark red front door set in the pristine white stucco. Kate lifted the small brass knocker and let it fall, twice.

The door was flung wide almost immediately, as though Laura had been standing in the hallway waiting for her. She was, like her brother, tall and spare, and her hair, too, was dark, but without the grey that was showing in Jack's. The first impression Kate received was that she resembled her brother, but when she looked again, she saw that they were entirely different, and the difference lay in the personalities stamped on their features.

'Hi! You must be Kate! Come inside! Are you exhausted? What can I get you? You can put your jacket on one of the hooks here,' and she paused long enough for Kate to hang up her jacket, noticing as she did so that there was a man's parka on the next hook. Then she was leading Kate through the narrow hall into a long, pleasant room with high ceilings and a fireplace with a real log fire burning in it, although it was hardly cold enough yet.

Before Kate could get a word in, she went on, 'I expect

you'd like me to show you where the bathroom is, wouldn't you, after your long journey? You can use this downstairs cloakroom, if you like. Shall I make tea, or would you prefer coffee? It's a bit early for gin, isn't it?'

Kate managed to say, 'Tea would be fine,' before opening the cloakroom door while Laura went through into the kitchen, a sunny room overlooking the garden.

Although in general appearance she did resemble her brother, Laura had an extraordinary face, where Jack's was conventionally good-looking. Perhaps the rest of us have all those bones, thought Kate – knobbled, fine-planed, complex – but ours are hidden under subtle layers of muscle and fat, and thick pink skin. Laura's skin was the colour of pearls, and drawn so tightly over ivory bones that it was translucent. Her face was angled and moulded into shapes that distracted your eye so that you didn't notice that her hair was too thick, too curly and too wild. Kate wouldn't have been surprised if she had spoken with an Irish brogue, but in fact her accent was the one that you heard all over this south-eastern corner of England.

'Come and sit down,' cried Laura when Kate returned to the sitting room. Tea was served in blue mugs on a low table before the fire. The sofas, set at right angles, were deep and comfortable, with a collection of embroidered and beaded cushions strewn along their backs, reminding Kate of Roz's place.

'How was your journey? Did you find the bookshops you wanted? Did you sign lots of copies? Are you sure you wouldn't like to stay overnight?'

The questions came so fast that there was no time to answer, as though Laura was bored by these conventional enquiries and couldn't be bothered to hear the replies. She wore a skimpy green and pink top which revealed a taut midriff and a pierced navel, and artistically faded blue jeans.

Her feet were bare, in sandals decorated with large pink and green flowers.

Just as Kate was about to launch into the subject that had brought her here, Laura jumped up again and said, 'I've forgotten the biscuits. Or would you like something more substantial to eat?'

'No, I'm fine,' Kate managed to insert into the stream of words. She wanted to say that she didn't need a biscuit either, but Laura had already left the room, so Kate amused herself by studying her surroundings. As she did so, she realised that there was a perfectly conventional, rather staid room underneath Laura's additions. The sofas were covered in a dark blue material, as were a couple of chairs. The curtains were of a matching blue, with a small gold pattern. But everywhere, on top of this traditional decor, there were objects, brightly coloured or sparkling, home-made or bought from craft shops, threaded through with strings of small white lights. It was as though Laura had come to stay with a great-aunt and scattered her belongings all over her house. She looked around for signs of the great-aunt herself, but could see none. And, come to think of it, if there had been a great-aunt, she would have removed the dust from the polished surfaces, or instructed Laura to do so.

Kate had noticed a pair of size ten walking boots in the cloakroom, though, which could well have belonged to the owner of the parka, so maybe there was a boyfriend somewhere in the background.

But as Laura breezed back into the room, carrying a dish of flapjacks in one hand and a plate of chocolate biscuits in the other, Kate reminded herself that she wasn't here to take stock of Laura Wilton's taste in decoration, or wonder about her love life. She hadn't forgotten what Avril had said about Roz's illness. If she could find out what the Freemans were really about underneath that wholesome exterior, she might be able to get them out of her mother's house and set Roz on the way to diagnosis and recovery.

'Do try the flapjacks – take a couple. They'll keep you going till suppertime. Personally I can't resist anything with chocolate in so I'm sticking with the biscuits. You don't need a plate, do you? You needn't worry about the crumbs.'

At last the torrent of words stopped, as Laura took a chocolate biscuit for herself and bit into it, so that Kate, parking her flapjack on the table, managed to ask, 'I was wondering what you could tell me about Ayesha and Marcus. Did you know them well when they lived in this part of the world?'

'I can't get used to calling Sheila that! I suppose I shall have to, though, shan't I? I wouldn't like to offend her by getting it wrong when we next meet. They were more Kevin's friends than mine, you know – they're both quite a bit older than me, you may have noticed – but they were very kind to us when we first came to live down here. It's hard, isn't it, moving into a place where you know nobody, except Kevin's colleagues from work, of course. And it took a bit of getting used to, after London.'

'You didn't think of moving back to London after your divorce?'

'Oh, I thought about it. But it's such a bore, isn't it, moving house? I expect I'll get round to it one of these days. I wouldn't mind moving down the coast to Brighton – it's got more life to it than this place, certainly. But I have some good friends here,' she ran her hand through her hair and smiled as though remembering good times, 'and I don't want to say goodbye to them just yet.'

'I suppose that Marcus and Ayesha had lots of friends down here too?'

'Oh, yes. They were very sociable, and they had

barbecues in the summer and a drinks party at Christmas, and introduced us to loads of new people.'

'You don't sound wildly thrilled by them.'

Laura laughed. 'I sound horribly ungrateful, don't I? Of course it was kind of them, making an effort to ease us into the local social life like that, but as I said, they were at least ten years older than me, and I'm not really the golf club and bridge type, if you know what I mean.' She wriggled her toes in their summery sandals, and Kate did see what she meant. Laura's toenails were each painted a different shimmering colour, and she couldn't see her fitting in easily with the bridge set.

'Marcus and Ayesha were a bit on the staid side, were they?'

'Very much so. And church-going.' Laura pulled a face at this. 'And heavily into healthy eating and moderate drinking. I like my gin in immoderate quantities, personally!' She looked up at the clock on the mantelpiece. 'I suppose it is still a bit early for our first G and T of the evening.' She sounded as though she hoped that Kate would contradict her. 'Oh, and they were very keen on keeping fit. Yoga and cycling, that sort of thing.'

'How awful!' said Kate hypocritically. 'I'd be surprised if Ayesha had kept it up, though.'

'She's put on weight, has she? She did have that tendency.'

'Did they live very near here?'

'About ten miles away. We weren't always popping into each other's houses, if that's what you're thinking.'

'I expect you were all too busy to do that anyway.'

'I found a part-time job as a buyer in one of the craft shops – it's quiet here at this time of year, but we get our fair share of visitors in the summer. But Ayesha had plenty of time on her hands to carry out all her good works.' She laughed again. 'Honestly! We used to say that she collected lame dogs! If she saw a deserving case, or even an undeserving one, she couldn't pass it by. I don't know how she did it. She had infinite patience, that woman. And she was keen on pills and potions. She believed that she had gifts as a healer. Did you know that?'

'I did wonder.'

'I'm not a great believer in that kind of thing myself. I prefer to go down to my GP and pick up a prescription for some proper medicine when I'm ill. You know what you're getting then, don't you? But I must say that she does have a gift.'

She paused, and Kate prompted, 'A gift?'

'It was when Kevin walked out on me. I was in a bad way, as you can imagine. I really would have overdone the G and T if it hadn't been for Ayesha. I couldn't even get into work in the morning.' There was a platter of grey and white pebbles on the floor by Laura's feet. She had picked out a couple of them and was turning them over in her hands, inspecting them as though she had never seen such things before. 'I just lay there under the duvet all day, crying much of the time. I looked a mess! If you'd seen me then you wouldn't have blamed Kevin for walking out. But Ayesha used to come round and make me a cup of fruit tea and feed me some herbal pills or other – though I don't think any of that did me any good.'

'So what did?'

'This is going to sound weird, but she used to hold my left wrist and put her other hand on my forehead, and I felt this warmth, like energy, passing from her to me, and I started to feel better. Oh, don't get me wrong: it wasn't a miracle cure or anything. I didn't get over Kevin leaving in just a week. But that was the other thing. She persisted. She came in every day for a couple of months or more, and each time she calmed me down and I started to feel that a day would come when I would get over it and life would begin to mean something once more.' She paused again and threw the pebbles back to join their companions. 'Sounds daft put like that, doesn't it? And I don't know how she did it, but it was her hands that pulled me through, nothing else. God knows what I'd be by now if it wasn't for Ayesha.'

'And she drove ten miles each way, so it wasn't as though she was on your doorstep. That was real devotion.'

'Yes, they had a place out on Romney Marsh. It's too rural and isolated for me, but it was very grand – a tastefully converted farmhouse – and you wouldn't get anything that size in the town.'

It didn't sound as though the Freemans had many close neighbours that Kate could just happen to call in on, so she didn't press Laura for the address.

'Do you think she practised healing on her lame dogs?'

'Her other lame dogs, you mean? I don't really know, but I should think so. If she had a gift like that she was the sort to share it around.'

'Where did she find them?'

'I think they found her. Haven't you noticed that she has the ability to focus on you, and really listen, so that you feel immediately that she's your friend, and then you'll tell her anything.'

'You're right. She did have that effect on me.'

'I think the vicar at her church was a bit wary of her gift, but then she was treading on his toes, wasn't she? It must have been annoying for him to think that his flock would rather go to her with their problems than to him.'

'Perhaps he was grateful,' suggested Kate. 'These rural vicars have to cover four or five parishes these days.'

'No, I don't think she was C of E. This was a church in the town – it looks more like an old Scout hut than a church, just a red-brick shed, really, at the other end of the high street. I don't know what it's called. But I don't think you'd be very interested in it.'

'No. You're right, it doesn't sound my kind of place.'

Laura looked up at the clock again. Kate might have expected something in plastic with a Mickey Mouse face and big white gloves on the hands, but the case was square and made of mahogany, with pilasters and Roman numerals.

'I'm sure it must be time for a drink by now.'

'I have to be moving on, I'm afraid. But it's really kind of you to see me and to set my mind at rest about the Freemans.'

'No trouble at all. Do give my love to Jack when you get back to Oxford, and tell him he must come and visit in the very near future.'

In the car Kate consulted her map again, working out how to get to the house where she had booked a room. She would have to drive down through the town centre to get there, she reckoned.

As she reached the end of the high street she looked for the red-brick Scout hut that might be a church and – by a coincidence that Ayesha might have put down to Providence – just as she saw a likely building on her right, she spotted a convenient parking space to her left. It seemed ungrateful not to pull in and stop.

# 14

'Hi, Roz. It's Jon here.'

'Jon, how nice to hear from you. And what I can I do for you?' It wasn't late – not yet nine o'clock – but Roz sounded tired, almost as though he'd woken her from sleep.

'I was just wondering if you knew where Kate was.'

'Why? Have you lost her?'

He was never quite sure whether Roz was laughing at him. 'I've tried ringing her a couple of times but I only get her bloody machine. I have to stay in town this coming weekend, but I was hoping to talk to her on the phone occasionally.'

'She doesn't take me into her confidence, I'm afraid, Jon, but as far as I know she hasn't gone off with another man, if that's what you're worried about.'

It wasn't, but Jon said, 'Thanks, Roz. That's very reassuring.'

'What I do know, however, is that she's walking round with that eager look on her face – you know the one? She's up to something, I'm sure, and it probably means that she's poking her nose into other people's business in the firm belief that she's doing good. Probably to me. Or to you, of course.'

Jon tried not to sigh into the phone. 'You could be right. She hasn't told me what she's up to either, but she's got that evasive look in her eye again.'

'You'll probably manage to talk to her before I do, but if she does contact me I'll let you know.'

127

'Thanks, Roz. How are you, by the way? I thought you were looking—'

'Oh, no! Not again! I'm fine. Just a little tired.'

'Yes, of course. I'm sorry.'

There was an awkward pause, then Roz said: 'I don't usually offer advice, especially if it's unasked for, but I would suggest that you back off a little. Remember that her father died when she was a child and I was never a suffocating mother, just as she wasn't a clinging child. She's used to having space around her.'

'You think she might dump me if I try to find out where she is and what she's doing?'

'I think she's very fond of you, and I think it would be a pity if the two of you split up over a misunderstanding.'

'I'll keep it in mind.'

'Goodbye, Jon.'

He'd wanted to talk to Kate about the possibility of the job in Oxford, and he felt disappointed at not reaching her. Why couldn't she have told him if she was going to be away? She'd probably say that it was because she was doing research on the new book and she couldn't plan far in advance where she would be, but he didn't quite believe that. There had been very little evidence of work-in-progress recently, and he had a nasty feeling that Roz was right, and that she was spending her time interfering in her mother's business.

And why had Roz given him that warning? He wasn't over-possessive – if anything, in the past he'd been accused of being too remote and unemotional. He'd take her advice, though, and ring again tomorrow evening, and not mention that he'd been hurt that she'd gone away without telling him beforehand.

It had been too much to hope that on a Thursday afternoon there would be a service going on at the church and that the congregation would pour out on to the pavement and shower Kate with information about Ayesha Freeman. She had rattled the door handle, but the door was firmly locked and no one heard her or came to find out what she wanted. She learnt from the noticeboard inside the porch, however, that this was the Chapel of Enlightenment, that there were two services on a Sunday, and that the Leader was Mr L.E. Brutton, who very helpfully had added his address. Kate's map informed her that the street where he lived was on her route to the B and B.

Why shouldn't she call in, since she was virtually passing his door, and ask for news of her old friend Ayesha Freeman? On second thoughts, she'd better refer to her as Sheila, since she wasn't sure when the name-change had come about.

She crossed the road to where she had parked the car, then looked back at the squat red-brick chapel. She couldn't place the extravagant figures of Ayesha and Marcus in the doorway, somehow. The entrance was too low, the style of the building too restrained. Not enough bling, she thought. And she was sure that that was a term that Ayesha under-stood perfectly, while she couldn't imagine the devotees of the Chapel of Enlightenment having any use for it. But maybe she was underestimating the Freemans' devotion to all forms of enlightenment. Maybe they really were very good people, she thought as she started the car and aimed for 27 Jubilee Street, the residence of Mr L.E. Brutton.

The street was narrower than the one where Laura lived, and there were fewer trees. The houses were lower and more closely packed together, like unsightly teeth. There were cars parked all along the kerb and Kate had to drive nearly to the end before she found a space large enough to accommodate her reversing skills.

She walked back to number twenty-seven, peering into gardens and front rooms as she went. Most of the gardens had been paved to make space to park one or two cars, and she could see the stumps of trees that had been felled to make room for them. Hardly any shrubs or perennials, only a little rank grass. And the front rooms were universally screened by impenetrable net curtains.

The house she was looking for stood in the centre of a red-brick Victorian terrace. Unlike its neighbours, its paint-work was fresh, there was a clipped bay tree in a wooden container by the front door, and the car on the paved-over garden was old but lovingly polished. There was still no view of the front room through the net curtains, but Kate rang the doorbell and waited.

She heard slow footsteps approaching, and the door opened to reveal a diminutive woman with white hair drawn into a knot on the back of her neck, a face as wrinkled as an ancient oak, and an expression as innocent as a young child's.

'Yes?'

'I was wondering whether I could speak to Mr Brutton.'

'My son's not home from work yet. Is there anything I can help you with?' Of course, it should have occurred to Kate that the chapel in the Scout hut would hardly bring in enough to support a man and his elderly mother, and a wife and children too, for all she knew.

'I was trying to trace an old friend of mine. We've lost touch recently, I'm afraid, but I know that she was one of your son's parishioners and I was hoping he could help me.'

'We call them the members of our congregation rather than parishioners,' Mrs Brutton corrected gently. 'And I'm sure that Leonard will help you if he can, but I doubt that he'll feel comfortable at passing on a member's address to a stranger.'

Kate felt it was time to fish in her bag and produce one of her business cards, which gave her name and address, but no indication of what she did for a living. 'Novelist', rather like 'journalist', sounded unreliable and bohemian, and was inclined to increase your car insurance and reduce your credit rating, and that wasn't the image she was hoping to create.

'Here's my card,' she said, handing it to Mrs Brutton, who held it close to her face while she inspected it minutely.

'What is the name of this old friend that you're trying to trace, may I ask?'

'Her name is Sheila Freeman and her husband's name is Marcus, though I'm not sure whether he was a member of your congregation or not.'

'Oh yes. Not as regular an attender at Sunday Enlightenment as his wife, but then men aren't as spiritual as their womenfolk, are they?'

'And I know what a friendly and good-hearted person Sheila is, so I'm sure there are many fellow members who will remember her. I don't suppose you know anyone who was close to her?'

'She spent a lot of time with old Mrs Leverett, of course. Such bad arthritis that she could hardly get out of her chair, but a lovely person, right to the end.'

'The end?'

'She died, I'm afraid, earlier this year. Sometime in the spring, it must have been. A terrible tragedy.'

'So I'm too late to contact her. Did she live alone? Were there any relatives I might get in touch with, perhaps?'

'She was quite alone. That was why it was so kind of dear Sheila and Marcus to befriend her like that. Sheila used to visit every day, I believe, and she had to drive all the way into town to do so.'

'I suppose it was a fall,' said Kate, imagining the elderly

woman, her joints stiff with arthritis, moving painfully across the room, her foot catching the edge of a rug, and then losing her balance.

'Oh, no. She died in a fire, in her sleep. Though even if she had awoken I don't suppose she would have been well enough to escape, poor thing. It was the smoke that killed her, they say, so I like to think that she slipped away in her sleep and knew nothing about it.'

'Let's hope so. Sheila Freeman must have been dreadfully upset when it happened.'

'I expect she was, if she heard about it. But the Freemans had moved away from Kent some weeks before it happened.'

They were still standing on the doorstep, and the wind was growing colder as the day advanced. Mrs Brutton looked light enough to blow away if there was a strong gust, and Kate reckoned it was time to bring the conversation to a close. But on an impulse she said, 'Whereabouts did Mrs Leverett live?'

'It was in one of those streets leading down to the sea, but I'm afraid I can't remember the name of it, or the number.'

'Thank you so much, Mrs Brutton. You've been very helpful.'

As Kate drove away it occurred to her that Laura Wilton also lived in one of the roads leading towards the sea. But then so did several hundred other people. And if Sheila – sorry, Ayesha – was visiting Laura daily to keep her away from the gin bottle, she could conveniently visit Mrs Leverett as well. That made good sense.

So far she had found out nothing about the Freemans that wasn't to their credit. If she was going to persuade Roz that they were charlatans, she was going to have to try harder.

Later that evening she asked her landlady whether she had ever met the Freemans.

'No, I can't say I know anyone of that name, though it's a common enough one.'

'Marcus and Sheila.'

'Oh, definitely not. I'd have remembered names like those.'

'And do you know anything about the Chapel of Enlightenment?'

'That funny little place down at the end of the high street?'

'That's the one. Looks like a Scout hut.'

'I wouldn't go in there! Chapel of spirits and lights and mumbo-jumbo! They've got some very funny practices, they say.'

But when Kate tried to find out from her what funny practices these might be, her landlady was unable to be more specific and Kate could only put her comments down to gossip and prejudice.

'I was trying to find Mrs Leverett, too. But I gather she died in a fire earlier this year.'

'You do ask a lot of questions!'

'It's to do with my family history,' improvised Kate. 'While I'm here I thought I'd find out all I could about the local branch of my family.'

'Ivory? I've never heard of anyone of that name round here.'

'Another blank then,' said Kate cheerfully. 'But I've still got tomorrow to search. I might get lucky yet.'

Kate was down to breakfast as early as possible the next morning, declining the fried eggs and sausages, helping herself to muesli and an apple, and accepting a large cup of strong coffee.

She was looking forward to a long walk along the seashore before driving back to the town centre to continue with her researches. The wind had dropped and the sun was

133

shining, though rain, she was told, was forecast for later in the day.

'I don't think I'll be staying for two nights after all,' she told the landlady when she returned from her walk.

The sea air and the brisk exercise had helped her to think more clearly: she had explored two culs-de-sac already, and although she had one last idea to follow up, she wasn't confident of finding anything of real use. She was coming to the conclusion, however reluctantly, that the Freemans might be exactly what they declared themselves to be. It was only her prejudice against Marcus's hands and unctuous manner that was persuading her otherwise. But since she was getting nowhere, she might as well get back to Oxford this afternoon. Instead of pursuing her fruitless research, she could sit down at her computer this evening and draft out another chapter of her book.

So she packed her bag and stowed it in the boot, then paid her bill and thanked her landlady for a pleasant stay, before driving back into the town. It wouldn't take her more than an hour or so to follow up the story that Mrs Brutton had told her, then she could be on her way.

The library wasn't hard to find, and she was soon in the hands of a helpful librarian.

'We don't keep back copies of the *Herald* for more than a few months, I'm afraid. It's a question of space, you see. Let me know which dates you're interested in and I'll see what I can find.'

'The spring. I suppose that would be March or April.' Wasn't that when the Freemans had first been seen in Oxford?

'You might just be lucky. If we can't help you, you could try the main library in Folkestone, or the *Herald* offices. They'll have all the back issues.'

To Kate's relief she could leaf through the newspapers

134

themselves rather than strain her eyes on a microfiche. She started with the earliest available issue and found what she was looking for in the following week's paper: a report of the terrible fire that had claimed the life of Mrs Hilda Leverett, 90. It had happened at about three in the morning, when no one was around in the street or awake in their bedroom to notice what was happening. By the time the alarm was raised, the fire had taken a strong hold. By that point, although most of the ground floor was relatively unscathed, there was no hope whatsoever of saving Mrs Leverett from her upstairs bedroom.

The police didn't believe there was anything suspicious about the fire, but the Fire Investigation Officer would be looking into the circumstances, gathering evidence and sifting it, as he always did, and he would not give up until he had found the cause. Of course, Mrs Leverett suffered from severe arthritis, added to which it was known that she enjoyed a cigarette, and was even known to smoke in bed. She was too old to give up now, she told her friends. 'If I was going to catch cancer, I'd have done so by now. And anyway, in my young day cigarettes were considered to be good for you! These modern doctors don't know everything, do they?'

It looked as though the smoking had killed her after all, even if it wasn't through cancer. When smokers' houses burnt down, the cause was usually a cigarette left smouldering in an ashtray at bedtime. (A box on the left of the page gave brief advice to smokers who didn't wish to share Mrs Leverett's fate: make sure your cigarette is completely extinguished; empty ashtrays before going to bed; don't smoke in bed.)

Following the story through the next two issues, Kate learnt that Mrs Leverett was a faithful member of the congregation at the Chapel of Enlightenment and that she was a sober and respected inhabitant of Charlotte Road.

Just a moment! Kate stopped and turned back to the first account of the fire. There was a photo taking up half the front page of the paper showing the fire at the point where the Fire Service succeeded in bringing it under control. The house was partially concealed by the smoke that still billowed out from the upper windows, and there were ladders and hosepipes and very large firemen obscuring much of the building. What a pity they didn't give the house number in the paper. Most of the houses in Charlotte Road had been built in a similar style, so it was impossible to tell which of them it might be. Below the dramatic picture of the fire they had inserted a photograph of Mrs Leverett ('Hythe Widow Perishes in House Inferno'). Her face was thin, dominated by a bony nose, but her eyes were still bright and challenging, and her chin was pushed forward at a determined angle. She looked, thought Kate, as though someone had just advised her to stub out her cigarette, and she had given a very definite negative.

Kate continued to look through the papers, just in case there was more news about the cause of the fire. There was: when the Fire Investigation Officer reported his findings, he found that there had been no accelerant used (so arson was not suspected), and he was convinced that the cause of the fire was not after all a cigarette which had been insufficiently extinguished before Mrs Leverett fell asleep, but old and faulty wiring and an overloaded socket. Her death was due to smoke inhalation. This time there was advice to the elderly about getting their electrical wiring checked, especially if it hadn't been renovated for a number of years.

Kate was in need of coffee, but she might as well be as thorough in her researches as she would have been if it had

been for one of her books. She returned the pile of newspapers and asked to see the more recent ones. She was
rewarded by finding that in September there was a tiny
paragraph reporting that Mrs Hilda Leverett, the widow who
had met her death in a house fire, had left an estate of only
£2,316.

So neither the Chapel of Enlightenment nor the Freemans
would have benefited by more than a few hundred pounds,
once the funeral expenses were paid, Kate concluded. It
looked as though she could forget about suspecting the
Freemans of doing away with her for her money. (And what
other reason could they have had?)

But what about her house? Charlotte Road was full of
desirable residences, she would have thought, and Mrs
Leverett's could hardly have been an exception. Even before
repairing the fire damage, it must have been worth at least a
hundred and fifty thousand.

Kate looked through the notes she had made. Really,
there were no grounds for believing that Mrs Leverett's
death had been anything other than a tragic accident from
which no one appeared to have benefited. She couldn't
blame the Freemans. They had moved away from Kent by
the time Hilda Leverett met her death. Sheila Freeman must
be the kind-hearted woman that Roz believed her to be: she
had visited Mrs Leverett; she had called in on Laura Wilton
and kept her away from the gin bottle. What was there to
complain of?

Interesting as it had been to read through old newspapers,
Kate knew that she had reached another dead end. And she
didn't know where to look next.

It was time to return to Oxford.

Still, the rain that had been forecast to fall that afternoon
had so far held off, there were several hours of daylight left,
and it seemed a pity to hurry back when there was no real

need. Somehow, she found herself driving towards Charlotte Road. Just one more look, she promised herself, before she headed home.

# 15

Her route took her back past the chapel, and while waiting for the traffic to move she saw the door open and two people emerge. One of them she recognised at once as Mrs Brutton; the other, from his appearance, had to be her son. He too was diminutive, and rather stooped, and his grey clothing matched his hair and did nothing for his pale complexion. Someone behind her hooted and she realised that the stream of cars at the lights had moved on, so she pulled forward to catch them up, losing sight of the two Bruttons as she drove on to Charlotte Road.

She parked as far away from Laura's house as she could get, though she had a feeling that by this time Laura would be well into the G and T and quite uninterested in anything Kate might be doing. She walked slowly down one side of the road and back up the other: it was only a quarter of a mile or so and didn't take her long. She saw no indications on any of the houses that there had been a serious fire, though she did see quite a few net curtains twitching as she made her leisurely way along each pavement.

She looked for fresh paint and evidence of rebuilding, but many of the houses looked as though they had been painted within the past year, just as the cars in the driveways and against the kerb were clean and polished – it was that kind of neighbourhood, she concluded. She took out the small digital camera that she always carried with her. It might be useful to have a record of the street to take back to Oxford with her. And it was at that moment, just as she raised the viewfinder to her eye, that she felt a hard finger prodding her left shoulder blade. She whirled round, startled, half expecting to see three hooded youths brandishing a knife and demanding that she hand over her wonga. But no. This wasn't Jericho.

'Well, young woman, do you mind telling me what you're doing here? You've walked up and down Charlotte Road, staring into our gardens, peering at our motor cars, and now you are taking photographs. Who are you and by what right do you invade our privacy? You will find no so-called celebrities here, you know.'

Kate stared down into the intensely blue eyes of a woman not unlike Mrs Hilda Leverett. She thought rapidly about what version of the truth her interrogator would be likely to accept, and found it a tricky question to answer. She gained a little time by dipping into her bag and coming up with another of her business cards, grateful yet again that she had gone in for such a respectable font and classic design.

'My card,' she said as firmly as she could.

The card was inspected as carefully as it had been by Mrs Brutton.

'Yes. This tells me your name, and that you live in Oxford – and a raffish place I've always considered it – but it tells me nothing of your intentions and why you are here in Charlotte Road.' Now that she looked at her properly, Kate could see that this woman had smaller features than Hilda Leverett, and there was certainly no whiff of cigarette smoke coming from her clothes, just the slight scent of flowery toilet water.

'I'm a writer,' began Kate in her most conciliatory tone, and without being too specific about what she wrote. 'And I've been looking into the circumstances of the fire in Charlotte Road in March.'

'And why would you be doing that?' She evidently still thought Kate was up to no good, in spite of the business card.

'I'm writing about it,' said Kate simply.

'Are you seriously telling me that someone is going to pay you for an article about a fire that happened some seven months ago and in which one elderly woman, of no interest to anyone except her small circle of friends, lost her life?'

'It hasn't actually been commissioned,' conceded Kate. 'I'm writing it on spec.'

'Then you're more stupid than you look.'

They glared at one another for a long moment. 'I don't believe a word of it,' said her tormentor. 'Why don't you tell me what you're really up to?'

'I haven't the time to talk now, I'm afraid. I have to be going.'

'I don't advise it. I shall ring the police and give them your car registration number and a description of you. In this area their time is not wasted in hunting down gunmen and breaking up drug gangs, so they are able to protect law-abiding citizens who live in a respectable neighbourhood. They will doubtless stop and question you.'

'I'd like to stay and tell you all about it, but it's a long story,' said Kate.

'I have plenty of time.' There was nothing conciliatory about her reply.

'Very well then, if you insist. It starts with my mother, who is ill and who should see a doctor, but is being encouraged not to do so by a couple whom she's met only recently. It sounds melodramatic, but I want to find out if they're all they seem or whether they have an ulterior motive in, well, in keeping her ill.'

'What's wrong with her?'

'Since she won't see a doctor, I don't know for sure. But her symptoms could indicate something serious. Like leukaemia. She needs a diagnosis, soon.'

'And she won't listen to her daughter's advice, I assume.'

'Right.'

'And what brings you to Charlotte Road?' There was more genuine interest and less aggression in her face now.

'I was trying to trace what my mother's friends were doing before they came to Oxford earlier this year, and apparently they lived ten miles from here. They attended some odd chapel in Hythe, and they also had friends here.'

'Not that preposterous Chapel of Enlightenment establishment!'

'That's the one.'

'Then they're either loonies or thieves.'

'Why are you so sure?'

'Hmph. I still have the use of my eyes and ears. That place is full of the old and vulnerable, and thus attracts the kind of people who prey upon them.'

'Perhaps there are also some who genuinely want to help.'

'I suppose their minister is a good enough man, although stupid. Tell me more about these friends of your mother's.'

'Mrs Freeman was a great friend of Hilda Leverett's, I've been told,' Kate continued. 'Did you know her, by the way?'

'I knew who she was, but she wasn't my sort of person,' and it was clear from her face that the difference was one of class. She would write Laura Wilton off for the same reason, Kate guessed, so she didn't ask about her, either.

'When I checked in the local newspaper, I found that Mrs Leverett had died in a fire in Charlotte Road, and so I came back here to have another look. I don't know what I expected to find. I suppose I was just desperate to find something.'

'What do you mean, you came back?'

Kate had given away more than she intended. 'Yesterday afternoon I came to see Laura Wilton, across the road at number thirty-two, to ask her about what the Freemans were doing when they lived in this area.'

'And that's someone else I don't care to know,' said the other woman, confirming Kate's guess. 'Who's paying for her to live in Hilda Leverett's house, I wonder?'

Kate thought it might be the owner of the parka and walking boots, but she said, 'So she hasn't lived in Charlotte Road for long, then?'

'She's been here all summer. This road isn't what it once was, I regret to say.'

Kate dropped the subject of Laura Wilton. 'I've learnt nothing new about the Freemans here in Hythe. They seem to be just what they say they are. I'm not going to be able to persuade my mother to throw them out of her house when I get back to Oxford on the basis of the skimpy facts I've managed to uncover.'

'It sounds as though they're running her life for her.' The woman sounded disapproving. Kate could imagine that no one had ever run her life for her, or at least not since she passed the age of six.

'It wouldn't normally happen,' said Kate. 'It's because she's ill and she just has no energy to spare to fight them. And they are very helpful. Too helpful.'

'I'm being very ill-mannered, aren't I?' said her companion suddenly, sounding much friendlier. 'My name is Anne Morson and I'm a widow.'

The house behind them – presumably Mrs Morson's own – was separated from the pavement by a low brick wall with a rounded top, just the right height for a seat.

'Let's sit down,' said Mrs Morson. 'They say it's going to rain later, but I think we're safe for the next fifteen minutes.' When they had seated themselves she continued,

143

'The odd thing is that your story seems familiar to me. I can't quite pin the memory down – that's the trouble with growing older: the other mental faculties may be unimpaired but the memory becomes increasingly unreliable. Describe these Freemans. Let's see whether it triggers off a response.'

'Well, Marcus is tall and good-looking in a conventional way. Silver hair. Suntan. Inclined to put on weight, I would have thought, but fights against it. Smooth, persuasive voice. Large, well-formed hands, and you feel he's about to ask you to kneel down to receive his blessing.'

Mrs Morson, in her neat blue tweed jacket and skirt, a strand of pearls visible at the neck, sat on the wall, swinging her legs and ruining the heels of her expensive shoes by banging them against the brickwork. She looked as though she hadn't had this much fun in years.

'Now tell me about the woman, whatever her name is.'

'Sheila originally, but she renamed herself Ayesha – though of course she has every right to do so,' she added.

'Rubbish. It's a silly name for an Englishwoman. At least, I suppose she is English?'

'She certainly looks and sounds it. Round-faced and fair-haired,' said Kate, guessing that Mrs Morson would not easily accept modern ideas about Englishness and ethnic diversity. 'She's just over five foot, and somewhat overweight. Flowing, vaguely Eastern garments purchased from an expensive shop.'

'She sounds like Madame Arcati.'

'As played by Margaret Rutherford, but perhaps just a few years younger,' agreed Kate.

'Yes,' said Mrs Morson slowly. 'I'm getting the picture. I'm seeing them quite clearly.'

'And have you ever come across them?'

'I'm sure I once met a couple who match their descrip-

144

tion, but their name wasn't Freeman,' she said. 'It was . . . oh, damn this memory!'

'A time? A place?' asked Kate, trying not to sound too excited. This was the best piece of news she'd had since she'd started her search. If they both stayed very calm, Mrs Morson might be able to put a name and place to the fugitive impression.

'It must be at least five years ago. The place . . . Hove!'

'Seaside town in Sussex,' Kate affirmed. 'Home to retired, well-off people.'

'My sister lived there,' continued Mrs Morson, just as excited as Kate to be tracking down these distant electrical impulses in her brain. 'And the Freemans – no, that definitely wasn't their name – had something to do with a friend of hers.'

Keep going, prayed Kate. Don't stop now, Anne Morson.

'We could have spoken to my sister,' said Mrs Morson, 'but unfortunately she is no longer with us; that is to say, to put it plainly, she died.'

'I'm sorry,' said Kate, not certain whether she was sorry about Mrs Morson losing a sister or about herself losing information on the Freemans.

'She was several years older than I, and not in good health. But my brother-in-law is still there, and in possession of most of his faculties.'

'Could you manage to recall just a few more facts?' asked Kate. 'I wouldn't like to approach your brother-in-law without something a little more concrete, as it were.'

'You're right, of course,' said Mrs Morson, who had lost some of her sparkle at this failure on her part, and was starting to look her age. Laura would suggest gin, thought Kate, but even if she had some handily about her person, she didn't think it would work. It hadn't been doing much for Laura, that was obvious.

They sat side by side on the wall, silent, each engrossed with her own thoughts.

'Harding,' said Anne Morson suddenly. 'That was their name.'

'Are you sure?'

'Yes, of course I am!' she snapped.

'I meant, are you sure that the Hardings and the Freemans are the same people?'

'There can't be two such odious couples in the south of England, can there?'

'I'm afraid that there may well be dozens of them,' said Kate, trying to suppress the thought that her Freemans and Mrs Morson's Hardings were almost certainly different people.

'It was your description of his hands that I recognised. And his oily way of speaking. And did she gaze into your eyes with her little piggy blue ones and make you think that you were the only person in the world who mattered to her?'

'Oh, yes!'

'I do hope you didn't confide all the secrets of your heart to the loathsome woman.'

'I managed to resist the temptation, but she does have that effect on one, doesn't she?' said Kate.

'I believe so. But, like you, I too managed to resist her.'

'So what have we got? The Freemans were once known as the Hardings, and they lived in Hove—'

'They could have lived in Brighton, or St Leonards, or perhaps Rottingdean, or even Lewes.'

Or even Romney Marsh, thought Kate. The distance wasn't very great. 'I get the idea. And—'

'And they prey on gullible old women!'

'I wouldn't describe my mother as gullible, or old, if it comes to that.'

'If she's your mother, she can't be very young,' said Mrs

Morson shrewdly. 'And if she's as ill and as frightened as you say she is, she might easily be taken in by people like the Freemans. Or Hardings. Whatever their real names are.'

'We don't really know that they are preying on anyone,' said Kate, trying to be fair. 'Don't you think you might be jumping to conclusions?'

'You think they're up to no good, or you wouldn't have driven all the way down here and asked so many questions,' said Mrs Morson.

'I was trying to keep an open mind. As a matter of fact, I don't even dislike them all that much. I know they irritate me when they interrupt my visits to my mother, but they can also be very charming when they want. But tell me, were they known as Marcus and Ayesha five years ago? Or Sheila, perhaps.'

'I think not. Not Ayesha, certainly. And I do believe I would remember a Marcus, since I once knew someone of that name, many years ago, and in a different place.' She smiled reminiscently.

'So where do we go from here?'

'Where do *you* go, you mean. I think you travel to Hove to visit my brother-in-law. I will write to him to warn him of your arrival, and explain the bones of the problem to him, so leave it a few days before undertaking the journey.'

'Why are you helping me like this?' asked Kate.

'I could say that I was acting out of pure goodness of heart, but I have to say that I find your search quite exciting, and nothing exciting has happened to me for a long time. Are you staying here in Hythe for much longer?'

'I have to get back to Oxford tonight. I have a cat dependent on me and I can't let her down.'

'It sounds as though you should marry soon and start having children. You're too young yet for this sentimentality over fluffy animals.'

147

'I know a very kind and dependable man who would agree with you.'

'Kind? Dependable? He sounds dull! Can't you do any better for yourself?'

'Probably not,' said Kate, not sure that she wanted to do any better than Jon, in any case.

'I'll go inside now and write down my brother-in-law's name and address for you.'

'Does he have a telephone number? I could telephone to alert him to my arrival.'

'I believe I told you that he has retained most of his faculties. His hearing, alas, is not one of them.'

Oh well. Shouting into an ear trumpet would make a change from sparring with lively elderly women, thought Kate philosophically.

Mrs Morson climbed down from the wall and disappeared inside her house, returning a few minutes later with a piece of paper on which she had written a name and address.

'Thank you,' said Kate, taking it from her.

Mrs Morson looked up to the sky. Above them a seagull screamed. 'I do believe the rain is arriving at last,' she said.

'And it's time I returned to Oxford,' said Kate. 'Mrs Morson, it has been a great pleasure to meet you.'

'And to meet you, Kate Ivory. I doubt whether we will meet again, though. At least not in this life.'

'Don't be so morbid! I'll drop you a line to let you know how my investigation goes, and next year I'll send you an invitation to my book launch, and I shall be greatly offended if you're not there.'

The sound of a telephone ringing, the volume magnified, came from the house behind them.

'There is just one thing I meant to ask you,' began Kate.

'I'm sorry. I have to answer the phone. It's probably my friend Enid, and she does worry about me if I don't answer.'

Kate sat for a moment or two more, looking at the name and address on the paper Anne Morson had given her. Now it was raining in earnest, but she turned and stared back at the house. Was Anne Morson perhaps mistaken in thinking that the Freemans and Hardings were the same people, or had she really told Kate something useful?

Even the gulls had muted their screams as the relentless downpour continued. It was time to go. Kate climbed into her car and turned the key in the ignition.

# 16

Ayesha had placed herself close to Roz on the sofa and had even accepted a small glass of red wine.

Her voice was confidentially low as she said, 'Now, don't take this the wrong way, Roz, but have you thought about your will at all recently?'

'It never occurred to me that what I had to leave was enough to worry about.' As a matter of fact she had made a perfectly good will, leaving everything to her daughter, but she felt reluctance at discussing it with Ayesha and Marcus, however kindly meant their interest in her affairs.

'In our work,' said Marcus earnestly, leaning forward with his hands clasped, 'we have seen too many instances of people whose wishes weren't carried out after their demise.'

'I was hoping that my own demise wouldn't be for a year or two yet,' said Roz as cheerfully as she could.

'But we don't know, do we,' said Ayesha. 'None of us can be sure of the day or the place.'

'And on that happy thought, what was it that you wished to suggest?'

'A trust,' said Marcus, ignoring the irony.

'Why would I need to put my money into a trust? I know nothing about them.'

'But Marcus does,' said Ayesha. 'Do listen to him, Roz dear. He has so much experience in this area and he will make sure that everything is done just right.'

'The purpose of the trust is twofold,' said Marcus, as though she had asked a question. 'Firstly it is to minimise the payment of inheritance tax, and secondly – and most importantly – it is to ensure that your money is spent in ways that you would approve of after your death.'

Roz wanted to say that she was quite content for Kate to spend her deceased mother's money in any way she pleased – the more frivolous the better, in her view – but she didn't feel up to having the argument with Marcus. If the Freemans had a fault, it was perhaps their lack of humour.

'You see, the trustees are obliged to deal with the property according to your instructions,' continued Marcus. 'You set them out in a letter of wishes.'

Roz thought vaguely that this sounded like the letter she had written as a child to Father Christmas, but this couldn't be what Marcus was talking about.

'Of course, it might be necessary to set up a non-resident trust,' said Ayesha.

'That's where the property is held outside the United Kingdom's jurisdiction,' explained Marcus patiently.

'Really, this is very kind and thoughtful of you both, but I don't think I want to be bothered with such things at present.'

'Don't worry about a thing, Roz dear,' said Ayesha soothingly. 'We know just the man to help, don't we, Marcus?'

'A solicitor,' said Marcus. 'One who specialises in setting up your trust with the minimum of fuss and as swiftly as possible.'

'Not just now,' repeated Roz.

'Of course not,' said Ayesha. 'We'll wait a few days, until you're feeling a little better. And you know that Marcus is willing to answer any questions you might have. We wouldn't want you to worry about a thing.'

* * *

Once she was back in Oxford, Kate made herself a mug of tea and sat down to make a fuss of Susanna, who was sulking at being left on her own for a couple of days. Then she picked a bottle of wine out of the rack in the kitchen and went to knock on Brad's door.

'Thanks so much for what you did,' she said, handing him the wine.

'I hardly deserve this for looking after Susanna for such a short time. And I do love your cat, you know. If only Patrick wasn't allergic to their fur I'd have one of my own. Would you like to come in, by the way? It's wet out there on the doorstep.'

'I have some catching-up to do, so I'd better not. There was just one little thing more.'

'You know you only have to ask!' As a matter of fact, Kate did know that Brad, who was an architect, enjoyed wandering round her house to see what she'd achieved since she'd moved in less than a year ago.

'I'll be going down to the south coast again, probably next week, and it's more convenient if I can stay the night. It gives me more time for visiting libraries and so on.'

'Your new book sounds most exciting. What's it about this time?'

'Oh, I can't discuss work-in-progress, I'm afraid. It breaks the spell.'

'Well, just let me know when you're going to be away, and don't worry about Susanna. She and I have a lovely time together. I do hope you don't mind that I come in and watch your television. Susanna prefers being in her own home rather than mine while you're away. She sits on my knee and purrs, you see.'

'Of course I don't mind. Thanks, Brad.'

'You can stop sulking now, Susanna,' she called, back in

her own house. 'I've heard how you've been spoilt while I was away. You didn't miss me at all.' Susanna must have left through her cat flap, however.

Kate went into her workroom and switched on the computer. Time to look at her emails. There were several messages from friends, and something from her agent with the subject line *Your New Novel*, which she ignored since she didn't want to be nagged at so soon after arriving home. And then there was one from an address she didn't recognise. She opened it.

To Kate Ivory
Did you think it was all over? You took no notice of our first warning and so you fell into danger. Next time the blow will fall not on you but on one you love. Do you want to risk such misfortune? You cannot afford to ignore our second warning.

What was wrong with her? Usually she would have laughed off such an absurd message. She would have deleted and forgotten it in an instant. It reminded her of those round-robin emails where you had to send some ludicrous message on to ten of your friends within the hour or be visited by unspecified bad luck. That's all this was, surely? But it referred to falling into danger, which was what had indeed happened to her. What if next time they turned their attention to Roz – whoever 'they' were. Her mother was in no state to be mugged for her mobile phone.

And it struck her that if Roz were to be the target of an attack, then it was the Freemans who were in the best position to carry it out. She just had to hope that Anne Morson would get back to her in the next few days and say she could visit her brother-in-law. She checked the paper

Mrs Morson had given her. His name was Eric Brayne and the address, as she had mentioned, was in Hove.

One thing was clear, however: she was in no mood to write another chapter of her novel. It would have to wait until the morning – though Monday morning would be even better. She would work more efficiently after a little break. This evening she would pour herself a glass of wine, cook herself a meal and relax with whatever was showing on television.

Of course, she thought later, she couldn't really relax without checking on Roz, especially after the email she had received. She would have to hide her anxiety, though, or Roz would start getting stroppy and uncooperative again.

'Hi, Roz.'

'Kate. How very diligent you're being at checking on your aged parent.'

'I went down to the coast for a couple of days, doing some research.'

'I hope it was for your new novel,' said Roz drily.

'Mostly,' prevaricated her daughter.

'How are you getting on with it? You must need to deliver the completed manuscript soon, surely?'

'Fairly soon. But don't worry, it's nearly finished.'

'Good. Because I had the impression that you were so busy scurrying around after all sorts of irrelevant matters regarding friends of mine that you were neglecting your real work.'

'What an idea! Of course not.' Kate was beginning to feel uncomfortable, and wished she'd poured that glass of wine before dialling her mother's number.

'I just wanted to be sure everything was OK while I was away,' she said. 'How's the new project?'

'Avril and I have just completed a renovation, if you remember.'

'But I thought you were searching for a new property. How are you getting on with it?' She might as well use her mother's own weapons against her.

'We haven't found anything suitable yet, but we're working on it.'

And that's about as honest as my own report on the progress of my novel, Kate guessed.

'Maybe you'd like to come over for a meal this weekend?' If Roz accepted, it would get her out of the clutches of the Freemans for a couple of hours.

'Sorry, Kate, but I'm not free. Maybe another time.'

Kate was still glowering at the phone when it interrupted her silent diatribe against the Freemans by ringing.

'Hi. It's me. Did you get my message?'

'Oh, yes, of course,' said Kate, who had forgotten all about it. 'How are you? I can't tell you how glad I am it's you, Jon.'

'That's very flattering. What's been happening?'

'I've just had a frustrating conversation with Roz. She won't come over for a meal this weekend.'

'That doesn't sound too serious.'

'And I've been talking to Jack Ivory's sister, because she used to know the Freemans, and after going all that way I learnt not a thing.'

'It's possible that there's nothing to learn, of course,' he said mildly. 'Whereabouts does she live?'

'Hythe.' Too late she remembered that she had failed to tell Jon about her trip. 'Didn't I tell you about it?'

'You must have forgotten in the excitement of the chase.' He didn't sound pleased.

'There was one fact that didn't fit. They belonged, apparently, to an odd church in Hythe, some ten miles from where they were living. It's called the Chapel of Enlightenment, the minister is a man called Brutton who enjoys polishing his car and wears a baggy grey suit, and the chapel itself looks like an old Scout hut. That's not like the Freemans, is it? If I'm right about them, they'd go to some Norman church in a picturesque village and drink sherry after the service with the posh rector and the rest of the well-heeled congregation.'

'But that's the whole point, isn't it? You don't know them. You're trying to find out, and you'll have to adjust your opinion as you're presented with facts that contradict your preconceptions. But you're trying to deny anything that disagrees with your prejudices.'

Kate managed to ignore this unpalatable truth and continued, 'And then the next day I met someone who did appear to know about them, but really I'm not at all sure that we were talking about the same people.'

'Very trying for you.' Was he trying not to laugh? Surely not.

'And now I'm banging on about the Freemans and Roz again and I haven't even asked you how you've been getting on. Tell me what you've been doing while I've been away.'

While Jon was speaking, Kate took the phone into the kitchen and poured herself the promised glass of wine. Jon broke off in the middle of a sentence to ask, 'Is that a glass of something or other you're pouring?'

'I need it.'

'I wasn't criticising, I was just thinking that I wish I'd poured myself one before ringing you.'

'I'll hold on if you like.'

'It's OK. I'll wait till later.'

'Go on with what you were saying.'

'I told you I was looking at alternatives to moving to SOCA – you know, the Serious Crimes unit.'

'Yes, you mentioned it the other day.'

'Well, I've been offered an interview, the week after next, with a company I really like the sound of.'

'That sounds promising, only you're about to add a "but". I can hear it in your voice.'

'It isn't really a "but". Personally, I think it's a definite plus. I just hope you do too.'

'What? Don't keep me in suspense.' Kate swallowed another mouthful of wine to prepare for his news.

'They're based just outside Oxford. Of course, I could commute from West London for a while, but eventually I'd want to relocate. How do you feel about that?'

Kate knew that she should respond positively and immediately, but for the moment she just didn't know how to react. And her silence was saying far too much.

'Kate?'

'Sorry, Jon. That came as a bit of a surprise.' They both knew she had nearly said 'shock' rather than 'surprise'.

'I was hoping you'd be pleased. It means we can see more of each other, without having to get up and drive off into the dawn.'

'Of course I'm pleased.' She infused her voice with as much delight as she could manage. And anyway, she *was* pleased about it, wasn't she?

'I wasn't going to suggest we moved in together immediately,' Jon said. 'We could take it gradually. Let's see how we go.'

'Yes. Though I have to warn you that writers don't make very good partners. I disappear off into my own world for months at a time. I sit and stare out of the window with a blank expression on my face for days.'

'I know. I've noticed. And you're perfectly happy with your own company – well, I suppose you share it with so many characters of your own creation, and none of the rest of us can compete with those sparkling personalities.'

'I do need other people. I'm not a complete loner.'

'But you also need time to yourself. I accept that. Really, I do understand, Kate. I'm perfectly prepared to adapt. I love you the way you are, after all, and I do know you quite well by now.'

She wondered about that word 'love'. It was not one that often entered their conversations. She said, 'You're wonderful. And I'm very lucky.'

But later she wondered if he was prepared for the reality of life with her. Wouldn't he get annoyed with her when she failed to answer a question for the fifth time of asking, or sat up until three o'clock in the morning because she just had to complete a chapter? Or disappeared off for several days because she needed to visit the setting for a scene, or look up a minor fact in a distant library? Sometimes she was so absorbed in her work that she forgot to comb her hair for days on end. And it wasn't even as if she made shedloads of wonga to make up for it! (Where on earth had she picked up that expression? Oh yes. From the youth who mugged her.)

She was nervous about the future, she realised, because it was so important to her. This was one relationship she didn't want to screw up, but she wasn't sure that she had learnt how to make it succeed.

When Jon rang she had been worrying about Roz. She had sounded more exhausted than ever on the phone, however hard she had been resisting her daughter's efforts to help: and that resistance was just a front. She had probably retired to bed as soon as Kate had rung off.

Would it have helped if she had had Jon here? Of course he would have been supportive – he was that sort of man. He would have been a help, a solid presence Kate could bounce her fears off.

Yes, he would definitely be an asset around the house. Could she ask for any more from a man?

When she checked her emails again later that evening, she found a message from Jack Ivory. Now there was a man who didn't intrude. He might have phoned her to ask about her talk with Laura, but he sent her an email instead so that she could read it and reply at her leisure. She thought about it and then wrote:

I met your lovely sister yesterday, Jack, and she sends you her love. She was so hospitable and friendly, and I could see her resemblance to you. She answered all my questions in such an open way and, although she had certain reservations about the Freemans, she confirmed that they were exactly what they seemed: honest, good people (even if sometimes misguided!). Thank you so much for putting us in touch with one another.

I hope that your own investigations into the Ivorys are going as well. I'm sorry that I could contribute so little to your knowledge of our family, but I do hope you will let me know if you find out anything that affects Roz and me. I would like to think that you could fill in the blank space in the middle of your family tree with a line that connected you to my father.

When she had sent it, Kate wondered why she had been so effusive about her meeting with Laura. In truth, she had been left with questions about the Freemans and their sincerity, and she wasn't at all sure that after her daily ration of gin Laura was capable of judging anyone, let alone a couple as manipulative as the Freemans. Yet she had expressed none of these reservations to Jack. What would have been the point? It wouldn't do any good, and he had done his best to help her. It wasn't his fault if she came away dissatisfied.

The phone rang once more that evening, and it was not a call she was expecting.

'Kate dear?'

'Yes.'

'It's Ayesha Freeman.' Of course, she should have recognised that warm and friendly voice.

'Ayesha. How are you? What can I do for you?' She infused warmth into her own voice: she wasn't going to have Ayesha telling Roz what an ill-natured daughter she had.

'I was just ringing to find out how you were after your trip down to the south coast. You're not too tired after all that driving, are you?'

'Not at all. It was most invigorating, and I managed to call in on several bookshops as well.'

'I do hope you don't mind my quizzing you like this, Kate, but dear Jack mentioned that you were going to visit his sister.'

Kate hoped that Jack hadn't told Ayesha why she was going all that way to pay a social call, but certainly Ayesha hadn't asked about her reasons. Maybe Jack had made some bland excuse.

'And how did you get on with Laura?' asked Ayesha.

'Very well. She seems a lovely person.' If she hadn't seen fit to share her reservations with Jack, she certainly wasn't going to share them with Ayesha.

'Oh, good. I do so worry about the dear girl. I expect you heard about her difficulties. She was well on the way to disaster at one time, I fear.'

'She did tell me something about them. And I gather that you were instrumental in bringing her back to normality, visiting every day and supporting her while she went

161

through the pain of the separation from her husband, pulling her back from the very brink of the abyss.'

'You give me too much credit. I did very little except hold her hand and listen to her. She was very distressed about her husband leaving her, and all too apt, I'm afraid, to attempt to lose her sorrows in the bottom of a glass.'

'Well, we drank nothing more sinful than tea while I was there,' said Kate.

'I expect you drove straight back to Oxford,' suggested Ayesha. Now, why should she care about that?

'No, it's such a lovely place that I stayed overnight and drove back today. I had a lovely bracing walk along the seashore and then meandered home along the back roads, instead of using those boring motorways.' She didn't feel like telling Ayesha about Anne Morson.

'I expect you needed a little break. You do toil so diligently and for such long hours, you creative people.'

'Relatively speaking, I suppose we do,' said Kate, only glad that she didn't teach in an inner-city school, or try to rehabilitate drug addicts, or chip out coal half a mile beneath the surface of the earth.

'You're being very modest, I can tell. I'm sure you work under enormous pressure to produce your wonderful books.'

'I didn't realise you'd read any of them.'

'Oh yes, of course I have. It provides such an insight into a person's mind, doesn't it, to read the story they have created from nothing – just from the pool of inspiration deep inside themselves.'

'I hadn't thought of it like that,' said Kate, who found herself warming just a little to someone who had taken the trouble to buy one of her books and read it.

'In my own small way I feel that I too am part of the creative process, though in a much less direct way than writers like yourself, of course.'

'It's very kind of you to phone like this,' said Kate.

'I wanted to find out how you got on with Laura – she can be a trifle touchy and emotional sometimes, I fear, but it appears that you caught her on a good day. And I wanted to let you know that you have nothing to worry about over Roz. Marcus and I called in to assure ourselves that she was well while you were away, so you need have no anxiety on that score.'

'Is she eating properly, do you think?'

'Marcus cooked her something light and nutritious while we were there today. And Kate, I do admire the way you and your mother have decided to take the independence route. It's so sad when you see a mother and daughter still clinging together, even when they're both getting on a bit. But you and Roz have your own lives. It's quite splendid, really it is.'

'I don't think we look at it quite in those terms.'

'Really? Well, I do tell Roz what a lucky woman she is to have such a successful daughter.'

When she had rung off, Kate looked around for Susanna. She needed the undemanding presence of the cat to get her back into a calm frame of mind. Even when she was attempting to be warm and friendly, Ayesha managed to get on her nerves. But Susanna was out on her own travels, apparently.

When she checked her emails later that evening, Kate found a short message from Jack Ivory.

Dear Kate,

This is just to let you know that I have completed my researches in Oxford and will be returning home tomorrow.

My sister has told me of your enjoyable visit and I do

163

hope that she managed to put your mind to rest over my good friends Marcus and Ayesha.

It was such a privilege to meet you and your mother and I hope that I will one day manage to establish a close connection between our two branches of the Ivory family. I'll be in touch when I do find out anything, and I hope you'll contact me if any of our family history comes into your own hands.

It was only nine thirty, but Roz was on her way to bed. In spite of all the infusions and supplements that Marcus and Ayesha pressed on her, the massage and the scented oils, she still wasn't feeling herself. Sometimes she wished she could ask the two of them to leave her alone. She really didn't like people fussing over her like that.

But if she asked them to go, the letters might start arriving again.

If Avril or Kate received one of them, she was sure they would ignore it, and even if something unpleasant happened to them, they'd write it off as a coincidence. She should do the same thing, but she just wasn't feeling up to it. All she wanted to do was go to bed and sleep the whole night through and then stay in bed all the following morning.

Was Ayesha right in suggesting that she'd feel so much easier in her mind if she sorted out her finances and her will? In the past she'd had nothing much to leave, and Kate appeared to be doing well enough on her own, so there was no need for her to worry about her daughter's future. And now there was Jon Kenrick solidly in the picture. A nice enough man, but lacking the dangerous edge that she personally had always found attractive. But Kate was different, she could probably settle down with someone quite ordinary, and she might make a go of it. She could see them getting married before another year had passed, as long as Jon didn't push Kate too hard. Maybe it was time her daughter settled down and had a child or two before it was too late.

And if that happened, then she would think seriously about Ayesha's proposition.

# 17

It was less than a week later that Kate heard from Anne Morson.

'I'm using the telephone rather than writing you a letter because Eric is going to visit his son in the Lake District on Friday, and he'll be staying there for at least a week, if not more. He could well embark on one of his royal progresses, visiting every relative north of the Wash and postponing his return for a month or more. But he will be able to see you if you pop down to Hove tomorrow.'

'Tomorrow? I think I can manage that.'

'He suggested you might care to arrive in the early afternoon. Two thirty was the time he mentioned.'

'Two thirty,' Kate repeated obediently.

'That's correct. I believe he is partial to a number of television programmes in the afternoon, and although he is willing to forgo *Countdown* this once, he would be quite upset if you and he hadn't completed your conversation by the time *Richard and Judy* appeared on the screen.'

'I'll be there at two thirty, and I'll be sure to leave in plenty of time for *Richard and Judy*,' said Kate, though to tell the truth she had lost some of her enthusiasm for the trip. She was despairing of ever finding any concrete evidence against the Freemans, though she hadn't quite given up her conviction that it existed, somewhere.

'That's good. I told him to expect you unless he heard from me to the contrary. Do you need directions to his flat?'

'I'm sure I can find my way there if I print out a map.'

'Would that be from the internet? How clever you are. All that kind of thing is quite beyond me. My brother-in-law said that you have permission to leave your car in one of the visitors' spaces, and there's just one other matter that's relevant.'

'Yes?'

'Make sure he's wearing his hearing aid and that he's switched it on when you talk to him. It must be his vanity, but he doesn't like to wear it when he's meeting someone new.'

'I'll remember to check.' Kate made a note to work out in advance a mime for 'Have you remembered your hearing aid?'

'And if he offers you tea, refuse. He buys the cheapest he can find and lets it stew before pouring it. Very nasty.'

'I'm glad you've warned me.'

'I do hope that your journey will be worthwhile.'

'I'll let you know either way. And thank you for arranging this meeting with your brother-in-law. It's very kind of you. Goodbye, Mrs Morson.'

At lunchtime she called round to see Brad.

'I have to drive down to Hove tomorrow and I'll probably come back straight away, but just in case I'm delayed, could you feed Susanna for me? I'll give you a call to let you know what I'm doing, of course.'

'What an exciting life you're leading! All these lively seaside resorts!'

'Perhaps you think I should search out more exotic locations for my next project?'

'It might make your life a little more invigorating.'

In the distance she heard the ringing of her telephone. 'Must dash, Brad. And thanks again.' She ran the short distance between the two back doors and made it to the telephone before it stopped.

'Kate? It's me.'

'Hi. What's up?' Jon didn't usually contact her during the day.

'You remember I'm coming over to Oxford for the job interview tomorrow, don't you?'

'Yes, of course.' Damn. It had entirely slipped her mind.

'I should be out by one o'clock, so why don't we meet for lunch somewhere – you could take an hour or so out of your working day just for once, couldn't you? A country pub with a log fire and good food would be nice.'

'I can't make it, I'm afraid,' said Kate, her heart sinking. This was one of those times when she had promised herself she would put her own problems to one side and be supportive of Jon for a change. And now she was going to have to say no. 'I've arranged to interview someone. It's research, and tomorrow at two thirty is the only time this person is available.'

'Two thirty? We can have a quick lunch in town and you can still make it.'

'I have to drive down to Hove.'

There was a pause. 'Is this actually to do with your work?'

'It's to do with Roz.' She could hear the note of obstinacy creeping into her voice as soon as she got on to the subject of her mother, and she was sure that he could too.

'You're not tracking the Freemans again, are you?'

'Yes, but I promise it's the last time. I can't miss this opportunity, Jon. It just fell into my lap and I feel that's got to be a good omen.'

'Now you're sounding like Ayesha!'

'It's to see someone who may have known the Freemans before they lived in Kent. And if it is the same couple, they weren't calling themselves Freeman, but Harding.' She didn't like explaining herself, but she made the effort as she knew she was in the wrong for forgetting about his interview.

'That's a very big "if". In fact, it sounds like an outside chance. Look, I'm only asking you to give it a miss for tomorrow, Kate. You can see this person another day, surely? If I get this job it's going to affect our future quite radically and I'd like to talk to you about it. You haven't been forthcoming about your feelings and I don't know where I stand.'

'Could we meet at the weekend to discuss it? We wouldn't be so rushed. Why don't you come down to Oxford?'

'I'm going to be tied up again. We'd better leave it for the moment.' She could hear the disappointment in his voice.

'Shall I come up to London on Saturday?'

'No. I'd rather you didn't. I have things to do, and to think about.'

'Good luck for tomorrow.'

'Thanks.'

She made herself a mug of coffee and sat at the kitchen table staring morosely into it. She had played the conversation all wrong and now she was left with a wild-goose chase to Sussex tomorrow instead of a celebratory lunch with the man she loved. He might forgive her, since he wasn't the kind to bear a grudge, but it would always be there: the day she couldn't give up her own selfish concerns to be with him, just for once.

On the other hand, if their relationship couldn't survive a little glitch like this, what hope of survival did it have in the long term? She would ring him in London as soon as she got back from Hove. Her meeting with Eric Brayne couldn't take more than an hour, probably only half that, so she could be home soon after five, traffic permitting. It was a pity that Jon always switched his mobile off when he was in the car or she could have called him as soon as his interview was over. Even if she got a frosty reply, it would show him that she'd made an effort, that she cared.

*　*　*

Kate decided that she'd use the motorways on the return
from Hove, but as she didn't feel like facing the M25 twice
in one day, on the journey there she would amble down the
A34 before turning east when she reached the Winchester
bypass.

It was a pleasant enough day for the time of year, cool
and cloudy, but with nothing worse than the occasional
shower forecast for the rest of the day. In her bag she had a
notebook as well as her voice recorder and camera. She
only hoped that the inhabitants of Hove were less suspicious
about her activities than Anne Morson had been.

She thought of Jon, coming out of his interview at about
this time. What would he do? Have a pint – no, a half, being
Jon – on his own? Or maybe there'd be an attractive young
female executive who would smile at him and offer to show
him a pleasant local place to eat, and tell him how well he
had done, and how everyone was really enthusiastic about
his joining the company.

But no, this was just the first interview. The final four
candidates would be called in again next week, he'd said.
Well, she would make quite sure that she was available at that
point – for lunch, or dinner, or whatever else he had in mind.

The Channel was grey and choppy when she reached the
coast, the breakers foaming against the shingle, and a brisk
wind was moving the pedestrians along the front at a good
pace. Kate needed some exercise, but she declined to join
them as they scurried past, hats pulled down, jackets zipped
up to the chin.

She pulled off the road and consulted her map, then took
a turning away from the sea. It was easy enough to find Eric
Brayne's block of flats, a dun-coloured 1920s building with
rounded corners like an ocean liner, with a paved area to
one side, neatly laid out for visitors' cars.

She checked her watch: two twenty. She had time to try Jon on his mobile. It was just possible that he'd switched it on. But she only reached his voicemail, so she left a brief message hoping that everything had gone OK at the interview.

As she locked her car it occurred to her that this was one of the safest places she could have left it. There was not a trace of vandalism in this road: no graffiti, no children kicking footballs around, no youths in hooded sweatshirts. Actually, there were no people at all in view, and apart from the distant drone of traffic and the occasional cry of a gull, the place was quite silent. Like the waiting room at the crematorium, she thought, though even there one could probably listen to piped music.

Eric Brayne's flat was on the third floor. He buzzed her in on the entryphone, and as she entered the hallway she heard a door open on an upper floor. There was a lift, which she was confident would be in working order, but she took the stairs anyway, proving to herself that she was not quite ready yet for the easy life.

'Come in, Miss Ivory. Let me take your jacket and bag.'

'It's very kind of you to see me at such short notice, Mr Brayne. And I'll keep my bag with me, thank you.' She didn't like to stare at his ears to see if he was wearing his hearing aid, but since he took her jacket to hang on a hook by the door, and left her with the bag containing her notebook and voice recorder, she came to the conclusion that he must have remembered to wear it.

'May I offer you a cup of tea or coffee after your long journey?'

'Thank you, I'm fine,' she answered, mindful of what Anne Morson had said about his dreadful stewed tea as well as his devotion to afternoon television. She had, in any case, stopped for a coffee in Petersfield on her way down.

172

As they settled themselves into armchairs, placed on either side of an electric wall fire, Kate took a good look at Anne Morson's brother-in-law. He was of medium height and spare build, with sparse white hair and a fresh pink complexion marred only by the brown marks of increasing age. He wore a tweed suit and Viyella shirt, all in shades of beige and brown. His eyes were a very bright blue, and the general effect would have been of a jolly uncle out of a children's book if the corners of his mouth weren't pulled down and if there hadn't been a vague look of discontent about his eyes. If Mrs Morson's sister had been miserable, it might have had something to do with her husband, Kate thought, as much as her own nature.

'Now, tell me what it is you want to know,' he said, with a touch of impatience. He glanced to his left, and she saw that a large, old-fashioned television set stood on the sideboard, reminding her that she was encroaching on his watching time. Her chair was covered in stiff dark green velvet and the cushion was so hard it was doubtless doing her back a power of good, but Kate was uncomfortable enough to agree with Mr Brayne that they should get down to business as soon as possible.

'My mother has made two new friends called Freeman: Marcus and Ayesha – or Sheila as she's also known – and I am worried that they are not all they seem and that they are planning to take advantage of her in some way. Your sister-in-law thought they might be the same people you knew as Harding when they were living here in Hove.'

'I don't think they actually lived in Hove. It could have been Rottingdean, or even Brighton, I believe.'

'I don't suppose you have a photograph of them?' she asked.

'I'm afraid not.'

'No, I didn't really expect it. And I haven't one of the

Freemans, either.' She wondered whether to ask him if she could take one of him, now, but decided to leave it until the atmosphere thawed a little.

'Why don't you describe them to me,' he said. 'I have a description from Anne, but it consists mostly of words like "evil" and "scurrilous" and so isn't very useful from a practical point of view. If they appear to be the same couple as my Hardings, I'll tell you what I know about them.'

The room they were sitting in was very clean and neat, with none of the clutter that most people manage to collect around them. There was a single row of books, of uniform height and in perfect alignment. On top of the small desk in the corner there were two or three silver-framed photographs, presumably of his family. That was as far as it went in terms of decoration. The room might have benefited from a visit by Laura Wilton: a few peacock feathers or strings of beads would have cheered it up a bit.

She made the description of the Freemans as detailed as she could without being confusing. 'Marcus is over six foot, say six foot two, with silver hair and regular features. He's not overweight, but he looks as though he will be one day – a kind of softening round the edges. He's expensively dressed. But the two things you remember about him are his voice, which is low-pitched – consciously so, I would say – and persuasive, as though he wanted to sell you something. And then there are his hands, which are large and well shaped and which he uses all the time, as though he wanted to control you.'

'And Sheila, his wife?' The door had swung open as he spoke and a cat walked in. This was not a beautiful, elegant creature like Kate's long-legged Susanna, but a low-slung tabby with one eye missing. It sat next to Eric Brayne's chair, just within reach of his hand, and glared at Kate through its one remaining yellow eye. Eric's hand reached out and stroked the top of its head, fondling the torn ear, until it stretched its neck in silent ecstasy. Then it bit his finger, but he seemed to be expecting this and only smiled fondly at his pet.

'What a lovely cat,' said Kate politely as the animal settled itself on the carpet, turned its third eye towards her in a pointed manner and then proceeded to groom itself.

'You're a cat person too, are you?'

'I have a ginger and white cat and we're devoted to one another.'

'I've always preferred tabbies myself. They have such loving natures. Haven't you, Nelson?' He crooned to the cat as though to a baby.

Kate wondered whether the cat had been named before he lost the eye, but felt it was impolite to enquire. 'I don't know how you can bear to go away and leave him for so long,' she said.

'Oh, but I don't. Nelson will come with me, in his basket.' Nelson moved from Eric's chair to Kate's, leaving a mat of moulted fur behind on the carpet. The chair leg, she noticed, had been used as a scratching post. How odd that such a meticulously tidy person as Eric should allow his pet to be so badly behaved. 'Are you sure you wouldn't like that cup of tea? I can easily make it, you know.'

'Really, it's a bit early in the afternoon for me,' said Kate.

'Now, where were we? Oh, I know. You were about to tell me about Sheila Freeman.' He sounded a lot friendlier and Kate cautiously laid a hand on Nelson's head and attempted to stroke it. The cat bit her. Eric laughed, a rusty sound, as though he was unaccustomed to expressing his amusement this way. 'He's a one-man cat, aren't you, Nelson?' he said proudly.

Kate gave him Sheila's description – she had it off pat by now – and he sat nodding.

'Oh, yes. That certainly sounds like Monica Harding. And we knew her husband as Edward, though he liked to be called Ned. It does sound remarkably like the same couple. How very interesting.' He was sounding quite cheerful now, and Kate was glad that she'd made the effort to admire his cat. There were cat hairs coating her black trousers which would be hell to remove, and Susanna would probably be jealous when she saw them, but if Eric Brayne told her facts about the Freemans – if they really were the Hardings – which would clinch her case against them when she next saw Roz, it would all have been worthwhile.

'How did you meet Ned and Monica Harding?'

'At church. We're a friendly crowd and the vicar makes a point of welcoming newcomers and introducing them to the rest of us. Of course, my wife was better at that sort of thing than I was.'

'Out of interest, would that be the local Anglican church?' asked Kate.

'Of course. You didn't think I looked like a Papist, did you?'

'No, no, of course not,' said Kate hurriedly, though she hadn't thought it was possible to tell a person's denomination just by looking at them.

'I suppose there are a lot of retired people in the congregation,' she suggested.

'A thoroughly nice crowd. And no nonsense with rubbishy modern tunes, or incense, or any tomfoolery like that.' Kate took this as a yes. 'And at first I thought they were the usual decent sort: she wore a hat to church, you know, and he didn't dress in a flashy way, or anything like that. But then he started taking over. I can't put it any other way. The man was everywhere. I've always thought that if one did so-called good works, one should keep quiet about it, be a bit discreet, you know?' Kate nodded. She couldn't see Marcus Freeman being at all modest about his good deeds.

Nelson jumped down off Eric's knee, no doubt disturbed by his master's vehemence.

'Marcus Freeman is like that too,' said Kate. 'It's as though you're taking part in a meeting and he's the one running it. If they are the same people, they were calling themselves Freeman in Hythe and Harding in Hove so that no one would make a connection between them. Why would they do that?'

'But they are Freeman again now they're in Oxford, you say.'

'It's hardly the way honest people behave.'

'I'm not saying that the things the Hardings did weren't good in themselves,' continued Eric, watching Nelson as he left the room on his bandy legs, stomach nearly touching the floor, tail raised high. 'I'm sure he and Monica would have called it "visiting the sick", but they overdid it, don't you know.'

'Calling in every day with nutritious food and jars full of pills?'

'Exactly that. I couldn't look in to see one old friend without finding the pair of them there, hinting that I was in the way, as though I hadn't called in every week for the past couple of years to chat to her.'

'What was she called?'

'Her name was Dora Prescott. She was a colonel's widow and a very decent sort. Lived in all kinds of far-flung places and never a word of complaint. I don't know how she stood having those two fussing over her all the time.'

'Why didn't she tell them to go away? She doesn't sound the shy type.'

'I can't imagine that they could have had any hold over her, but it was as though she was frightened to tell them to leave. She became quite dependent on them, though if I called in, she would send a look of desperation at me across the room when the Hardings weren't looking. Mary – that was my wife, you know – said it was the same when she visited.'

'What happened in the end?'

'In the end she died, but not peacefully in her sleep, the way it should have been. She was ninety-three, and I suppose that she hadn't many years left to her in the natural course of things, but even so it was a dreadful way to go.'

'How did it happen?'

'In a fire. They said she died of smoke inhalation, but you can't be sure that the flames didn't get to her first, can you?'

'I have heard that the smoke renders you unconscious long before the flames reach you,' said Kate, hoping it was true. 'Was there an enquiry?'

'Oh, yes. There always is an investigation into the cause of a fire, apparently.'

'And were the police involved?'

'No. There were no suspicious circumstances, the investigating officer reported. He found that the cause was faulty wiring – all too common in property belonging to elderly people like Dora, they said. Insulation decayed, bare wires touching and short-circuiting – something of the sort.'

'So the Hardings weren't culpable?'

'I suppose they weren't. No one was blamed, certainly. It was an unfortunate accident. But why should she change her will like that?'

'Did she leave all her money to the Hardings?'

'Questions would have been asked, wouldn't they, if she'd done that. No, there was nothing left when she died – just enough to pay for a decent funeral and a headstone. Apparently she had transferred all her assets into a trust fund, cutting out her grandchildren entirely.'

'So they can't have been acting out of greed. They would

178

surely have found out that she had nothing to leave before investing all that time and effort into looking after her.'

'But who gave her the idea about the trust?'

'You think it was the Hardings? Do you know who the beneficiaries were?'

'Some do-gooding organisation or other. Some shambling crowd of drug addicts and drunks are spending her money at this very moment, I don't doubt.'

'Didn't her family object?'

'Her son was killed at Suez. His young widow was left with a baby to bring up. She remarried a few years later and I don't know anything more about her – it's all such a long time ago, isn't it? Suez was in '56, so the granddaughter must be nearly fifty by now and I suppose she didn't think it worth making a fuss.'

Kate sat back in her chair, thinking. 'There's something all too familiar about this story: I heard something very similar while I was in Hythe. In fact, I was looking for the house that had burnt down in that previous case when I met your sister-in-law. I'd looked up the details in the local paper. They didn't mention that the victim had transferred her property to a trust, only that her estate was worth virtually nothing by the time the funeral expenses were paid. And yet, if she lived in the same street as Mrs Morson, her house alone must have been worth a tidy sum.'

'It can all disappear if you have to move into a nursing home. They cost a fortune, those places.'

'But Mrs Leverett wasn't in a nursing home, and neither was Dora, from what you've said.'

'Mrs Prescott,' said Eric, correcting her informality.

'I don't know anything about trusts and how they work,' said Kate. 'Do you?'

'I'm afraid not.'

'What happened to Mrs Prescott's house?'

'It was sold, I assume by the trustees. And if they had any sense they'd have moved the money they made to some offshore fund where it can't be traced.'

'They can't be planning anything like this in my mother's case,' said Kate.

'Why not?'

'She's not rich enough.'

'I hear that property in Oxford is even more expensive than it is here. Does she own her house?'

'Yes,' said Kate, remembering what Avril had told her: Roz owned a half-share in several properties. And then there was the profit she'd made on the ones that had already been sold. It looked as though the Freemans weren't greedy – or stupid – enough to go for millionaires. They targeted well-off elderly women who were alone in the world. But Roz wasn't alone! She had a daughter to look out for her, though Kate had to admit that earlier in the year this might not have been apparent to an observer. Just for a moment she wondered whether her negligence was the cause of the Freemans' interest in Roz. In which case she would be to blame for what happened.

'We have to report this to someone,' she said. 'They have to be stopped.' It was Roz's life at stake now.

'What are you going to report? You don't even have any proof that the Hardings and the Freemans are the same people. I don't know whether it's possible to find out whether they were Dora's trustees – and they could well have used two associates so that there's no apparent connection with them. And certainly in Dora's case it was agreed that the fire was accidental – and given the state of her wiring, it was all too likely to happen, sooner rather than later.'

'It was accidental in Mrs Leverett's case, too. She smoked in bed, apparently, so no one was surprised when the house

180

caught fire. But the cause was found to be faulty wiring and an overloaded socket. Was Mrs Prescott's house badly damaged in the fire, by the way?'

'Luckily someone alerted the Fire Service in time and only one corner of the upper floor was destroyed.'

'I'm sure the Freemans had a hand in starting these fires but they're so slick about their operation that they must have been doing this for longer than four or five years. I wonder where they came from before they lived near Hove.'

'I can't help you there. Perhaps the vicar knows, but I shouldn't bank on it.'

Kate considered searching out the vicar, but she felt an urgent need to get back to Oxford and make sure Roz was still all right. She would have to question her about her will and whether she had been persuaded to transfer her property into a trust. Roz would have mentioned something if she was doing that, surely? She and Roz had never discussed such things, but she realised that she assumed that Roz had left her estate, such as it was, to her only daughter.

Eric Brayne was looking tired out with the effort of recalling the past. Kate remembered that he had to be over eighty.

'Would you mind very much if I took your photograph?' she asked, reaching into her bag. 'And Nelson's, of course,' she added quickly, seeing the frown reappearing on his face. 'I wish now that I had photos of the Freemans themselves, as well as the other people I've spoken to.'

'What are you going to do with it?' he asked suspiciously.

'Nothing at the moment. And when all this is over, I'll destroy it,' she said.

'Very well.' He picked the cat up and placed it gently on his knee. Nelson showed his appreciation by kneading Eric's thigh in what looked like a painful manner. 'If it's a good picture of Nelson, you might send me a copy.'

'Of course.' Kate took three shots, just in case Nelson was blinking his good eye at the vital moment.

'Yes, it would have been useful to have a photograph of your Marcus and Sheila,' he said, when she had put the camera back in her bag. 'But from your description they could well be the couple that I knew as Ned and Monica, though nothing we've said makes it certain, does it? It's a pity there was nothing really distinctive about their looks, just so that we could be quite sure.'

'A scar or a mole? Something like that?'

'Ned and Monica were quite unblemished, I fear.'

'And the Freemans too, as far as I can see. But now it's really time I got back to Oxford,' she said. 'I hadn't realised how late it was. Thank you very much for all your help.'

'I wish you luck, Miss Ivory, but I believe that, whoever they are, these are clever as well as wicked people.'

'If you think of anything at all that might be useful, would you let me know?' She handed him one of her cards. 'There's an answering machine on my phone, so you can leave me a message at any time.'

'With you they seem to have met their match in persistence, Miss Ivory, even if you're not yet their equal in cunning.'

# 18

Kate was tired when she arrived home: by the time she reached the M25 the traffic had slowed to a crawl, the rain had settled to a steady downpour, and Jon still wasn't answering his mobile. When at last the M40 had travelled past High Wycombe and emerged from the cutting through the Chilterns down into the broad green valley of the Thame, there were glimpses of clear sky once more, and with the rain easing off she felt more cheerful as she approached Jericho.

Even before getting out of the car she dialled Roz's number.

'Roz Ivory speaking.'

'Oh, good. Are you all right?'

'Yes, of course I am. What on earth is the matter with you, Kate?'

'Nothing. Sorry, Roz. I just had one of those funny feelings and I had to make sure.'

'Goodbye, Kate.'

Indoors she made herself a mug of tea and drank it curled up on the sofa, her head still buzzing from the pounding of the car wheels on the motorway. She called for Susanna but the cat didn't appear, doubtless lured away by Brad with sardines and a saucer of cream. She couldn't help smiling when she thought of the old, scabby tom belonging to Eric Brayne, and how he was loved in spite of his many infirmities. Eric still saw Nelson as the young, lithe, handsome cat he had been some fifteen years ago.

And let's face it, she thought, we all hope that one day, when we are old, there will be someone who will overlook our own infirmities and bring us a tin of sardines and a saucer of cream.

On that thought, she found the telephone and dialled Jon once more. Still no reply, and there was no point in leaving yet another message.

When she was feeling a bit livelier she picked up a notepad from her workroom and sat at the kitchen table, attempting to work out what she had heard that afternoon. It would make more sense, she thought as she looked at the jumble of notes, if she tried to fit the events into some kind of chronological order. So she drew a horizontal line a quarter of the way from the top and another a quarter of the way from the bottom. She wrote 1950 at the far left-hand point of each, and the current year on the right. The top line she labelled *Marcus Freeman*, the bottom one *Ayesha Freeman*. She guessed that Marcus was born in 1950 or 1951, since he was a contemporary of Jack Ivory's, and she knew from Jack's family tree that he was fifty-three. She wrote *Born* below the date, and *Marcus Freeman*. If Jack had known him under that name at Oxford, the chances were that it was in fact his real name.

For Ayesha she wrote *Born* just a year or so later, and *Name: Sheila?* She had no idea what her maiden name might have been.

The next known date for Marcus was, within a year or so, 1968, so she filled that in: *Leicester College, Oxford*, and under it she wrote Jack Ivory's name since he corroborated the fact. On the far right of the time line she wrote *Oxford* again, and the name *Marcus Freeman*. Who corroborated this? Jack Ivory again, of course. And Roz, and herself and Avril and, presumably, Rafe Brown, and probably a dozen other people.

She was left with a long empty space in the middle of the page.

She pencilled in *Hove*, added a dotted line between Hove and Hythe and wrote the name *Anne Morson* along it, then sighed. The connection between Marcus Freeman and Ned Harding, and Ayesha and Monica, was tenuous at best.

If she met someone else who had known them in the past under a different name, it would be helpful to have a recognisable picture of them to show him or her. She might even drive down to Hove again and show Eric Brayne such a photo if she could obtain it. It was tricky, though, suggesting that the Freemans should stand by the window, where the light was good, and allow her to take a couple of photographs. 'Why would you want that, Kate?' 'Oh, just for my portrait collection.' No, I don't think so. If they were all they seemed, they would think her as batty as Anne Morson. If they were as evil as she and Avril thought they were, it could be positively dangerous.

Without realising why she was doing it, Kate walked across to the smoke alarm and pressed the red button to check that it was working. It responded with a suitably piercing howl which she then had difficulty in stopping.

She turned back to her diagram and notes, but they told her no more than she already knew, and she could see no way at present of finding out any more about where the Freemans might have come from, or how they had made their money. Jack said he had been 'in business', but no one seemed able to be more specific about what he did for a living. And what about Ayesha? As far as Kate knew, they had no children other than the son who had died, and even if they didn't need the money, she would have thought that Ayesha would have a career of her own, but what?

She glanced at the kitchen clock. It wasn't late. Roz wouldn't be in bed yet. She would at least try to tell her something of what she had found out on her travels. It might just cast a small cloud of doubt over the Freemans.

'Hi, Roz.'

'Kate? Is everything all right?'

'Of course. Everything's fine.'

'I wondered why you felt you had to telephone me twice in the same evening. Why do you need to check up on me?'

'No, no, I don't at all.'

'Good. I'm glad we've got that straight.'

'Would you like to hear where I've been today?'

'I'm sure you're eager to tell me.'

This was worse than she expected. She tried to sound as warm and caring as Ayesha but had a nasty feeling that she fell far short of the Freemans' standard, probably because she'd had less practice.

'Today I went to Hove to meet an elderly widower. He's been living alone with his cat since his wife died a couple of years ago.' She was aiming for the sympathy vote here, but again felt that she might be failing to win Roz over. 'He was convinced that he and his wife had met the Freemans a few years ago, but that they were calling themselves Harding: Ned and Monica Harding.'

'It's terrible, isn't it, the way dementia destroys the ageing brain cells.'

'You're telling me that he's imagining it?'

'No, Kate. You tell me: does this sound a likely story, or the fantasy of a sad old man?'

'They met them through their church. It wasn't a brief meeting – the Hardings were regular church-goers.'

'And where is this story leading? It sounds to me as though it's going to have an unhappy ending.'

'An old woman, a friend of the Hardings' – just as you are of the Freemans' – died in a house fire.'

'And you think they set light to her house and burnt her to a cinder.'

'There was an investigation,' conceded Kate. 'And it was judged to be an accident. But there's more,' she added quickly. 'I visited Jack Ivory's sister in Hove last week, and there I learnt that the Freemans – and they were still called Freeman then – had befriended another elderly woman, a Mrs Leverett, and she died when her house burnt too. I checked the facts in the local paper.'

'And have you any idea why Marcus and Ayesha should be travelling round the country setting fire to the houses of the elderly?'

'For their money, perhaps,' said Kate baldly.

'And did they inherit large sums?'

'Not in so many words—'

'That's a no, I take it.'

'I knew you wouldn't believe me. I should have waited until I had more evidence.'

'It doesn't sound to me as though you have any evidence at all against my friends, merely speculation and the gossip of one old man.'

'Obviously you know the Freemans better than I do,' she said. 'But I'm asking you to be careful. And do you know anything at all about their background, and where they've come from?'

'Kent. I know they used to live in Kent.'

'Yes. That's confirmed by Jack's sister.' No need to add that she was a woman with a drink problem.

'I don't think Marcus could have been born there, though, do you? Have you noticed his accent?' Roz was getting interested in her researches at last. Really she was just as curious about people as Kate was.

'No. I suppose you can hear that he comes from the south of England rather than the north, but that's about all.'

187

'Doesn't he remind you of those persuasive news readers and interviewers?'

'Which ones? Jeremy Paxman? Hardly.'

'I was thinking Huw someone or other. Welsh,' said Roz. 'Not all the time, but when he gets excited or enthusiastic.'

'You think there's a touch of the male voice choir about him?'

'Perhaps we should ask him to give us a chorus of "Bread of Heaven" to make sure.'

'Could you find out whereabouts in Wales he comes from, do you think?' Kate wasn't sure how it would help, but she was getting desperate, and at least Roz seemed to be listening to her again.

But Roz didn't reply, and in the background she could hear that her mother was no longer alone. She didn't actually hear someone calling, 'It's only us!' but she could imagine it.

'I'll talk to you again in a few days,' said Roz quietly into the receiver, and then she hung up.

It was a pity about the interruption, but that phone call had been more encouraging than some of their other exchanges recently, thought Kate. By the end of today's conversation Roz was sounding much more like herself, and although she had been so rude about Kate's recent travels, she had taken in what she was saying, she was sure of that.

Wales? She thought about it. It didn't really help. And what about Ayesha? It seemed as though she knew even less about Ayesha than she did about her husband. She thought about going straight round to Roz's place, while the Freemans were still there, and making an excuse to take their photograph. What excuse? The one about 'I just wanted a snapshot of you all for the family album'? That would have made Roz laugh out loud, as the Ivorys had never gone in for snapshots, let alone family albums. And now Kate came to think of it, that was a pity too, since she could have looked for family resemblances and compared notes with Jack.

Perhaps he had a collection of family photographs. She would ask him next time they spoke. It wasn't just that she wanted to find out more about the Freemans from him, she found that she was also getting curious about the shadowy people who stood behind her father and provided half her genes. There might even have been a successful author perching on a branch a few generations ago, though she did think it was more likely that her creative side came from her mother rather than her father. And what, if it came to that, did she know about her mother's family? She must ask Roz about them one day. It was ironic that she was spending so much time looking into Marcus and Ayesha's background while she knew so little about her own.

Thinking of literary ancestors reminded her that she really ought to take a look at the book she was supposed to be working on. It was now several weeks since she had written a word and she had rather lost the thread of what she had been writing. She went into her workroom and turned on her computer, but Susanna came demanding her supper before she had re-read more than a page or two.

'So you've decided to come home after all,' she said, as she logged off. 'I was starting to get worried about you.'

'It's all a question of priorities,' she told the cat as she filled her bowl with rabbit-flavoured pellets. Susanna, of course, had no doubts as to where her own priorities lay.

It was chilly but fine the next morning when Kate set off for her run, but she wasn't going to risk taking the canal towpath just yet. Instead, she turned in the opposite direction, down Little Clarendon Street and across St Giles' churchyard, aiming for the University Parks and the river. Here there were a reassuring number of fellow joggers and dog-walkers, all looking reliable enough to hasten to her rescue if she were attacked.

Lightning never strikes twice, she told herself, as she found herself glancing around to check that there were no young muggers hiding in the bushes or lurking by the water's edge. It would be a long time yet before she would be comfortable running on her own, though. She would always feel a nervous bound of the heart every time she heard footsteps on the path behind her. Would she ever be able to go out, as she used to, and simply enjoy her surroundings and the freedom of moving in the open air?

Nevertheless, she felt proud to have made the effort to go out on her own, and she was looking forward to a congratulatory pot of coffee when she arrived home. The warning email message obviously relied on coincidence for its effect. Nothing terrible had happened since she received the second one. The people who had sent it were nasty-minded jokers, and she would put them out of her mind: if she ignored them they would lose interest and give up plaguing her.

She made a determined effort to enjoy the rest of her run, and for the full timespan she had decided on, before turning for home.

When she had showered and changed, she pushed two slices of bread into the toaster and put the marmalade out on the table: she'd earned a small reward, she felt. Susanna was off on her own affairs again, and she could sit in peace and enjoy the coffee and toast. And afterwards she really would settle down to Chapter Twenty of her novel. Neil Orson had left her alone for the past couple of weeks, sure that Kate would produce a manuscript when she said she would, but

Estelle was less confident of her ability to work to a deadline without being nagged, and consequently Kate hardly looked at her emails these days.

By ten o'clock she had read through the previous couple of chapters to get into the swing of the story, and had jotted down a couple of ideas on her notepad. She needed another caffeine break, so she went to the kitchen, poured a mug of coffee and heated it in the microwave. Susanna still hadn't appeared for her breakfast. Doubtless she was round at Brad's, licking up the gourmet food on offer there, but still Kate put her head outside the back door and called her. She didn't want her cat sticking her nose in the air at the pouches of nutritious processed pellets that Kate served her.

Brad was dropping a bag of rubbish into the bin next to his back door.

'Has she gone walkabout again?' he asked.

'I thought she might be round at your place, feeding on oysters.'

'I do try not to entice her away from her own home when you're there.'

'I wonder where she's got to.'

'It's no use worrying about cats. They're such independent creatures, aren't they?' Brad wiped the lid of the bin with the cloth he had brought out for the purpose.

'She does keep wandering off these days, but it's not like her to miss her breakfast.'

'She's probably telling fibs to some old lady about how you starve her, and being fed tinned salmon even as we speak.'

'You're probably right, but I wish they wouldn't feed other people's cats.'

'You'll have to blame Susanna's charm and good looks, I'm afraid.'

Kate returned to the computer and tried to forget about

191

her cat. She needed to push ahead with the novel if she was going to get the first draft finished before the deadline. She would try to get five hundred words completed before stopping for lunch.

But it was only about eleven thirty when someone rang her front doorbell. Reluctantly she saved her work and went downstairs to see who was there. She didn't recognise the woman who stood on the doorstep, looking uncomfortable.

# 19

The woman on the doorstep was clutching her hands together and shuffling her feet. 'Sorry to disturb you, but Mrs Butler at number fifteen said she thought you owned a ginger cat.'

'Ginger with a white chest and paws, yes,' answered Kate, starting to feel afraid.

'Oh dear. I didn't want to be the one to tell you, but there's been an accident.'

'Susanna? Is she all right? Has she been hurt?'

'I'm afraid it's worse than that. I am so awfully sorry.'

'Oh my God! What happened? Where is she?'

'She's in the garden at the back of fifteen.'

'I'll come to look. Maybe it isn't her.' Kate's heart was thumping in her chest and she hardly dared to hope that Susanna was still alive. But there were dozens of ginger cats, after all. There was no reason to believe that this one was Susanna.

She grabbed her key and Susanna's wire carrying-basket from the cupboard under the stairs. If it was Susanna she wasn't going to leave her lying alone in someone else's garden.

As she flew out through the front gate, following the woman who had brought the bad news, she was joined by Brad, who must have been watching from his front window.

'You look distraught. What's happened?'

'I don't know. But it's Susanna, she says.' She was incapable of being more coherent than that.

He fell into step beside her, and even if she couldn't say

193

anything, she was glad of his company. After all, he had shown that he was nearly as fond of the cat as she was.

The three of them walked in single file down the path through the side gate and into the back garden of number fifteen. A middle-aged woman stood by the back door and watched them without saying anything.

'Here it is. I'm awfully sorry about it. Is this your cat, do you think?'

For a moment she could almost believe that it wasn't Susanna. The soft, loving cat who draped herself over Kate's knee in the evening and crept on to her bed when the nights were cold had almost nothing in common with the stark, lifeless corpse stretched out on the grass.

Susanna was lying on her side, her head at an unnatural angle, her tongue protruding from her mouth. There was a thin rope tied tightly around her neck. Her fur was damp, and it was obvious that her limbs had stiffened with rigor.

Kate turned away abruptly and clutched at Brad. He was standing with the tears falling silently down his face, and for a while they stood with their arms around each other while the two women looked awkwardly on.

'We have to take her home,' said Brad eventually.

Kate bent down and took the cat in her arms.

'Who would do such a thing?' It burst from her in a wail of useless anger.

'Perhaps it was an accident.' Brad didn't sound as though he believed what he was saying. He leant to stroke Susanna's flank, where the fur was unmarked.

It couldn't have been an accident. Someone had fixed the rope around her neck and then pulled, or had hung her from a tree until her own struggles broke her neck and ended her pain. Then they had cut her down and dumped her in this garden.

'I'm going to find out who did this,' said Kate.

'It was probably kids,' said Brad. 'I doubt you'll be able to find them now.'

Kate thought of the youths who had mugged her as she left the towpath the other morning. Could it have been the same ones? Or was it the result of some random cruelty, the sort of thing one was always hearing about?

'Come on,' said Brad. 'There's nothing more we can do here. Let's take her home now.'

He made as if to take Susanna from Kate, but she said, 'No. You hold the basket a minute. I'll put her in.'

There seemed to be no other marks on her, Kate was relieved to see, and she laid her carefully in the basket, her rigid legs pressed against the side. 'Let me carry her,' she said, taking the basket from Brad.

'Thank you for letting me know about it,' she said to the woman who had rung at her door.

'Poor little thing,' said the one who must be Mrs Butler. 'I bet it was those nasty boys who've been hanging around, looking for trouble. Someone ought to lock them up.'

It didn't seem important any more to Kate as she and Brad walked back to her house. He paused by the back door.

'Would you like to help me bury her?' Kate asked.

Brad nodded. He followed her down the side of the house and into the garden.

'Under the apple tree, do you think?' she asked him. It was only a young tree, barely five feet tall, but there was grass underneath it still dotted with daisies and a few windfall apples left for the blackbirds, so it looked a peaceful place. She could bring her chair down here in the summer and sit and read, or chat to Susanna the way she had done when she was alive. As she approached, a blackbird gave its repeated alarm call, then flew off.

Kate laid the wire basket on the ground and gently took Susanna's body out and laid it on the grass.

'Let me set her free,' said Brad, and he took out a penknife and cut the rope from her neck. 'There, that's better, isn't it?' and Kate knew he was talking to Susanna rather than to her.

'Someone thought about it, didn't they?' said Kate. 'This wasn't done on impulse. I mean, most of us don't walk around with that kind of thin rope in our pockets.'

'Thin but strong,' said Brad, rolling it up and putting it in his pocket. Kate was sure he did this because he wanted to remove it from her sight. 'Picture cord, I'd have said.'

'And that was a proper noose someone had tied, as far as I could see. Don't you think?'

'Yes, I do.'

Kate shuddered, remembering the threatening email she had received. Hadn't it warned her about misfortune happening to someone she loved? But that was laughable. No one could believe the piece of purple prose that the emailer had sent. 'It was just a prank by a warped mind, or some horrible kids.'

Brad didn't argue with her, but she could see he didn't believe her. 'You need to be careful,' he said.

'It's a bit late now. What else could they do to me?'

'Shall we bury her?' he asked, not answering her last question.

'I think so. Do you mind doing this?'

'It might help. I know she wasn't my cat, but I was really attached to her, you know.'

'I do know,' she said, grateful that she wasn't on her own and that there was someone there who wouldn't get impatient with her for being over-sentimental about an animal.

Together they walked to the shed and fetched a spade.

'At least the earth is quite soft over there under the tree,'

196

said Kate. 'And don't think of offering to help with the digging, Brad. You'd ruin your shoes.'

Brad, as usual, was beautifully dressed, but not for doing anything practical, and his shoes were made of soft cream leather.

'Would you like me to find something to wrap her in?' he asked. 'I think I might have a scarf that would suit her.'

Kate nodded. She could trust Brad to find something appropriate. She started to dig. Brad was right: there was something about the simple, repetitive task that filled the mind and stopped it from wandering back and forth over the same sad facts.

'What do you think of this?' he said, returning and showing her a fringed shawl.

'It's beautiful.' It was. It was made from a very fine woollen fabric printed with a pattern in shades of green and a soft turquoise. 'But surely that's a Liberty fabric?'

'Well, I wasn't going to use any old scarf, was I?' he said lightly. 'Now, you lift her up and I'll put this underneath her.'

The cat weighed nothing, it seemed to Kate. She let Brad arrange the square around her, folding it neatly and then finally tucking in the fourth corner to hide her poor face.

'I'll just dig down a little deeper,' she said. 'I don't want anything to disturb her.'

She worked in silence for a while. 'There. I think that will do.' She laid the body in the bottom of the grave, then slowly filled it in again. When she had finished, she and Brad looked at the small mound.

'I'll find stones or pebbles to mark the place,' she said. 'And plant something on top. Some spring bulbs, perhaps.'

Brad nodded.

'Come on,' she said. 'I know it's much too early, but I think we both need a drink.'

She would have offered him lunch, but neither of them felt like eating.

Kate rang Jon again that evening, not wanting to wait for him to ring her – she needed to start building bridges – and finally he answered.

'How did you get on?' she asked.

'Quite well, I think. I should hear in a couple of days whether they're calling me in for the second interview.'

'I'm sorry I wasn't around while you were in the area, but I'm sure you'll get the job.'

'You don't sound very happy about it. Is there something wrong?'

'Of course I'm happy for you. It's just that something really dreadful has happened here.'

'Are you all right? Tell me what's happened.'

'Someone has killed Susanna.'

'Oh, Kate. I'm so sorry to hear that. I know you were very fond of her.' She could hear that he was making an effort to say the right things. 'Are you sure she was killed on purpose? Couldn't it have been an accident?' He was relieved that she was all right, and then annoyed because she had turned an insignificant event into a drama.

'There was a noose round her neck. I don't see how that could very well have been accidental.' She tried to stop herself from getting angry with him.

'It was probably done by kids. They can be unpleasant little sods.'

'And isn't that how psychopaths start out?' she said sharply. 'They begin by torturing animals and then they move on to babies and children, or so I've heard.'

'It must have been very upsetting for you,' he said placatingly. 'I know you've had her a long time, and she was one of the family. It's only natural that you should be upset.' Jon, she knew, barely tolerated cats, but he was doing his best to be sympathetic. She couldn't imagine that he'd ever sacrifice a favourite Liberty wool square for a cat's shroud, though, the way Brad had – not that he'd have such a thing in his possession anyway.

'She was given to me as a kitten ten years ago,' she told him, remembering the dependable young policeman who'd brought Susanna round to the house in Fridesley where she was living at the time because he had considered that she needed something to look after, something other than herself to worry about – though that was before Roz reappeared in her life.

The memory brought back the tears, running down her cheeks, and she rubbed them away furiously with her sleeve. She wasn't going to give in to her grief: that way, whoever had killed Susanna would have won.

Changing the subject, she said brightly, 'Let me know as soon as you hear about the second interview. I'll be sure to be here this time so that we can celebrate your success.'

'Or bury my sorrows,' he said. Then they were both silent as they remembered who Kate and Brad had buried that day.


Roz had a different reaction to the news when Kate told her about Susanna.

'Did you say that someone had killed her on purpose?'

'Yes. There's no doubt about that. She had a noose around her neck.'

'How very unpleasant, you must have been so upset. Were you on your own, or did that nice cat-loving neighbour of yours come round to commiserate?'

'He helped me to bury her.' At least here was someone who understood what she felt – and who appreciated what Brad had done.

'I was wondering, Kate, whether you had received any letters, any messages of any kind, that had warned you that something like this was likely to happen?'

Kate wondered for a moment whether to deny it. 'As a matter of fact, yes, I did. But it must have been a coincidence. I don't believe there's someone out there with second sight, do you?'

'I'm not sure. Perhaps I'm not as adamant as you on the subject of psychic powers. But I do know that you should be careful. And if you get another warning, don't ignore it. I know you: you'll pretend it isn't happening, but it is, Kate. It really is.'

'What do you think I should do about it? What *can* I do?'

'I know that you don't like Marcus and Ayesha, but they are very kind, understanding people who have helped many others who were in trouble, from what I've heard. Why don't you drop your scepticism for an evening and speak to them with an open mind?'

There was a short silence while Kate thought about this. 'I appreciate that you're trying to help,' she said slowly. 'But you're right in thinking that I don't trust them. Can we strike a bargain?'

'That depends on the bargain you have in mind.'

'I'd like to take their photograph. If I talk to them with an open mind, can you help me to get pictures of them?'

'I assume you want to show their mug shots to the old man in Hove.'

'Eventually, yes. He's travelling around the country visiting his many relations at the moment and not due back for weeks, or even months.'

'Can you come round here tomorrow at about six thirty?'

'That's when the Freemans turn up?'

'Usually, yes. I don't know if I can keep my half of the bargain, though. You can bring that small digital camera with you, but I'm not sure I can think of a plausible reason for using it. Perhaps one of us will have come up with a scheme by then.'

'As a matter of fact, an idea is starting to come to me. Tell me, do they know when your birthday is?'

'I don't think so. I've never mentioned it.'

'Well in that case, many happy returns of tomorrow, Mother.'

'I trust you'll bring me round a cake and an original, hand-crafted card with a fulsome message hand-written on it.'

'I'll do my best.' It was good to hear Roz back on form, Kate thought. 'And oddly enough, I have an idea for just the right prezzie for you.'

'You know, Kate, if you would listen to Marcus with an open mind, you might not want to carry on with this plan of yours to unmask them as frauds. You might be convinced of their essential goodness.'

'Then that would be a marvellous result, wouldn't it?' She only wished she was as sure as Roz that she would be won over.


Later, Kate decided to phone Avril.

'I'm sorry to bring this subject up again, Avril, but I'd like to talk to you about the letters you received.'

'Yes?' Avril sounded wary.

'You told me about the first letter and what happened afterwards.'

'Yes. What do you want to know?'

'What did you do when the second letter arrived?'

'I ignored it.'

'That was brave, given the result of the first. Was there any . . .'

'Nothing happened, if that's what you're asking. Why?'

'They've killed my cat.'

'They?'

'Didn't I mention that I'd received a couple of messages too? Emails in my case.'

'I am sorry, Kate. One does get so fond of a pet, you must have been very upset. But do you really think it was connected to your email?'

'I have no proof, of course.'

'It might have been a coincidence.'

'I'd like to compare my messages to the ones you received, if that's possible. Have you still got the letters?'

'Yes, as a matter of fact I have.'

'Could I see one of them? Would you mind posting it to me?'

'I don't believe I have your address in my book. Wait a moment while I find a pencil and paper, Kate.'

Kate gave her the Jericho address and Avril promised to put the letter in the post to her immediately. 'To be honest, I'll be glad to get rid of it. I can't think why I didn't throw it away.'

'It may not tell me anything, but you never know.'

'I hope you can stop these people, whoever they are. And I'm sorry to hear about your cat. Really I am.'

'Thank you, Avril.'

It was obvious that Avril had no wish to carry on with the conversation, so Kate said goodbye and hung up.

There was something about the letters that Avril and Roz had received that made them unwilling to share them with anyone else. It was perhaps that they were ashamed of having been affected so badly by the contents, and afraid that an outsider would find them merely foolish.

# 20

The next morning, Kate was up at her usual time, but she didn't put on her running shoes. Instead, she gathered up all the belongings that Susanna had accumulated over the ten years of her life, and put them into a black bin liner. She added the unopened packets of cat food and Susanna's bowls. It was difficult, but she had to make the effort now, this very morning, or she would be forever tripping over poignant reminders of her cat, and she knew that she couldn't stand that. If she saw Susanna's bowl, with the few remaining beef pellets in the bottom, she would expect her to put her head through the cat flap and come running to rub against her legs. The thought was unbearable.

After she had resolutely put everything out of sight, she ate her breakfast and made a list of things to buy in Oxford.

Before walking into town, she visited the apple tree and had a brief conversation with Susanna. She must tell Brad that he was welcome to come in any time if he felt he wanted to do the same thing.

She found just the right birthday card for Roz in a shop in the covered market – flamboyant and yet artistic, she considered. She bought wrapping paper and ribbon too, and spent the rest of the morning producing a perfectly beautiful present – not at all the sort of thing that she and Roz normally gave one another.

Time for work now, she told herself when it was completed, and she took herself off to her computer. If she was good she could polish off the current chapter and start on the next. Estelle would be proud of her.

At six o'clock in the evening she broke off from work, feeling pleased with herself. When she'd showered and changed out of the disreputable clothes she wore for writing, she set off for Roz's house in East Oxford. She decided to drive rather than walk, almost as though she thought she might need to make a quick escape from the clutches of the Freemans.

'Happy birthday!' she said as Roz opened the door, handing over the decorated envelope.

'What a delightful card,' said Roz politely, putting it on the mantelpiece. Certainly when the Freemans arrived they wouldn't be able to miss it. Maybe she should have brought more than one, though. It did look lonely by itself.

'Oh, no one knows when my birthday is,' said Roz cheerfully when Kate mentioned it. As a matter of fact, Kate herself did, but she could quite believe that her mother didn't want the passing of the years marked in any way that might define her precise age.

'And can I open my present?' Roz asked, eyeing the small, bright parcel that Kate had placed on the low table.

'Not yet. I think we should have a celebratory drink, don't you?'

'As long as you don't mind inviting Marcus's disapproval.'

'I think I can stand it. And surely even Marcus would allow you a glass of wine on your birthday.'

Roz poured the drinks and they sat for a few minutes in companionable silence before the sound of key in lock heralded the arrival of the Freemans.

'Why, Kate! What a lovely surprise!' said Marcus.

'Goodness, Roz, is there something we should have known about today?' asked Ayesha, her eye immediately caught by the striking card on the mantelpiece.

'It's not something I make a fuss about usually,' said Roz easily, 'but Kate likes to mark the occasion in some little way.'

'Can I pour you a glass of wine?' Kate asked Marcus and Ayesha. 'And do come in and sit down, both of you.' She rather enjoyed playing the hostess, as she was sure the Freemans would prefer to be treated as family rather than guests.

'Well, perhaps just a small one, since it is a special occasion,' said Marcus indulgently. He was dressed this evening in shades of dark blue and grey that brought out the colour of his eyes and the silver in his hair. Ayesha's gown was striped in flaming golds and scarlet with touches of emerald green. Not easy colours to wear, thought Kate, especially with that nondescript colouring.

'Why don't you put out some of those nuts and the cheese biscuits, Kate?'

'Not for us,' said Ayesha, doubtless thinking about saturated fats and high salt content.

'But you like them, don't you, Kate?'

And so did Roz, as Kate well knew.

When they were all settled again, Ayesha sipping in a very ladylike way at her wine, their eyes fell naturally on the decorated parcel on the table.

'Aren't you going to open your present?' asked Kate.

'Very well. I'm dying to know what it is, but you're very naughty to spoil me like this.'

They were playing the mother–daughter parts rather well, Kate thought, even if the script had strayed rather a long way from their own actual relationship.

Roz started to untie the bows and knots in the gold and silver ribbons. 'And you've even managed without sticky tape,' she said.

'I was rather proud of that,' said Kate. 'It's something I learnt from *Blue Peter*.'

205

Roz pulled the paper back and revealed the small box within. Kate was glad that she hadn't yet thrown out the packaging and instruction manual that had come with her recent purchase of a new digital camera. You'd never guess it had been used, she thought.

'A camera!' Roz exclaimed. 'How clever of you to have noticed that I wanted one.'

'You did admire mine so much that I thought you would like one for yourself. Now you'll be able to record your renovation projects from start to finish. And you don't have to bother with processing. It's very practical, you'll find.'

'You think I'll get the hang of this technology?'

'It's dead easy. Just switch it on, point it at whatever you want to shoot – look, you can see the subject on the screen at the back here – and then push the button. Couldn't be simpler!'

'Like this?' asked Roz, pointing the lens at Kate.

'I think you need to put a memory card in first,' said Kate, taking one from the box and inserting it into the slot for her, wondering whether Roz wasn't overdoing it. Surely they'd suspect that she was quite used to a digital camera.

'Is this the "on" switch?'

'That's right.'

'And I just point the camera at you – oh yes, here you are on the screen – and then push this button.'

There was a click, a flash, and a soft whirring noise.

'And it even has in-built flash,' said Roz. 'All that in such a tiny package.'

'There are lots more things that it can do. You'll learn about them if you read the manual, but really it's all very simple,' Kate was saying, but Roz was taking no notice of her. Instead, she was pointing the camera and clicking, at the card on the mantelpiece, at the vase of scarlet poppies in the fireplace, at Kate again, and then at the Freemans. She

206

kept coming back to her friends, Kate noticed, and since she knew full well that her mother had borrowed this same camera to record the progress of her work just a few weeks ago, she was pretty sure that they would be in focus.

'Well, isn't this fun!' Roz said, sitting down again as though suddenly realising that she felt tired. 'What a very clever present, Kate. I shall enjoy using this.' There was a smile on her face that the Freemans were doubtless interpreting as pure pleasure, but which Kate knew meant that her mother was going to take the opportunity to purloin her daughter's camera and not return it. What with needing to buy a new mobile, and now a camera, it was getting to be an expensive month.

'Why don't I pop into the kitchen and get us all a little something to eat?' said Ayesha, looking bewildered at all this activity.

'You can't possibly risk that beautiful dress,' said Roz. 'No, I'll make us all something simple while you and Marcus talk to Kate.'

'What a good idea,' said Kate, knowing that after Roz's pointing and clicking with the camera to obtain photographs of the Freemans, she now had to fulfil her own half of the bargain.

'Are you sure she's all right?' said Ayesha anxiously, as Roz disappeared into the kitchen.

'Oh, I think so, just as long as she sticks with something simple.'

'And the simple things are so often the most nutritious,' said Marcus. Kate, listening carefully, wondered whether she could detect faint overtones of Neil Kinnock, or whether it was only her imagination.

'Have you always worked in the field of nutrition?' she asked Ayesha, seeing an opening into the Freemans' past life.

'I have always been interested in the whole person,' said Ayesha. 'And of course this includes both the body and the spirit. The body depends so completely on what we give it to eat, how we exercise it.'

'I think I'm following you so far,' said Kate.

'Here in the West,' began Ayesha, hitting her stride, 'the body and the spirit have too frequently been seen as separate, even as in opposition. But what we try to achieve is a fusion of the two, a harmonious way of living so that they are supportive of each other, as it were.'

'How interesting,' she said. 'Have you spent much time in the East, studying these ideas?'

'Not as much as I would have liked,' admitted Ayesha. 'The demands of Marcus's profession have meant that we have stayed in Europe – in fact in the south-eastern corner of England – rather than journeying to India, Nepal or Japan and China in search of enlightenment. There is a far greater acceptance of these ancient ideas nowadays than there ever was before, but still we are fighting against the medical establishment at every turn.'

'I've never really fancied ancient forms of medicine,' said Kate. 'The idea of having a tooth extracted without anaesthetic, rather than filled, for example.'

'But that's not the whole picture—' began Ayesha.

'No,' agreed Kate. 'How about leeches? And purges? Wouldn't you agree that they really do insert poisons into the system?'

'You have to listen to your body, Kate, and then it will heal itself. Using leeches is the old, the natural way of doing things.'

'Not down at my GP's surgery,' said Kate firmly. Then she remembered what she was supposed to be doing: listening for Roz's sake to Ayesha and Marcus's wonderful ideas; and trying for her own sake to find out something about their past. She wasn't supposed to be winning them over to conventional Western medical practices.

Marcus had been sitting listening to them until now, a mildly patronising smile on his face.

'I don't think you're managing to convince Kate of the truth of your ideas,' he said to Ayesha. 'Kate, like so many others who have never had the revelation that we have enjoyed, believes only what she sees in the here and now.'

'I'm a rational human being, yes.'

'Yet you must, at some time, have wondered whether the evidence of your five senses is all that exists in this world. You must, from time to time, fleetingly perhaps, have had a glimpse of what lies beyond. No? Not even once or twice in your life? Standing on top of a hill in the early morning, seeing the landscape veiled in mist, the trees, the church tower, barely discernible and unfamiliar. And then, from near your feet, a skylark rises into the air and breaks into his heavenly song. No? I can't believe you have never experienced miracles such as these. There is something mysterious beyond the world we live in, surely? Suddenly the veil lifts from our eyes and we become aware of something other – a revelation of the future, perhaps, or a new insight about the past?'

Kate was almost convinced by the winning, mellifluous voice. Almost. But then he lifted his right hand, the fingers pointing towards heaven, as though he were about to bestow a blessing upon her, and all her old resistance to the man resurfaced. She picked up her glass and drank more of her wine.

'And don't you think you should consider the place that alcohol has in your life?' asked Marcus.

'It gives me pleasure and provides a convivial atmosphere to share with my friends,' she replied.

'Good fellowship can thrive without the presence of

alcohol in your bloodstream,' said Ayesha. 'You should try it, Kate, and see what an improvement it makes to your wellbeing.'

Marcus inclined his head in what could well be a silent prayer for Kate's salvation. And at that moment Roz re-entered, carrying a tray of food, and Kate rose swiftly to her feet to give her mother a hand.

'How are you all getting on?' Roz asked her, out of earshot of the Freemans.

Kate pulled a face as she followed her into the kitchen. 'I'm doing my best,' she said. 'Really, Roz, I am making a huge effort.'

'Keep going,' said her mother, removing warm bread from the oven. 'Take these into the other room and just remember your side of the bargain.'

It seemed to Kate that she definitely had the wrong side of this transaction: not only was she having to listen to the Freemans – and attempt to take them seriously – but she had lost her camera too. And she hadn't managed to steer the conversation towards the Freemans' past life, either. She knew no more about them now than she had at the beginning of the evening.

Once they had all helped themselves to food, she turned to Marcus again. 'It sounded as though you enjoy the view from a hilltop in the early morning. Have you done much backpacking?'

'I like to integrate my walks into my daily life,' he replied. 'I've always been an early riser, and even when I was working in an office I would spend an hour in the open air – in the hills, if possible – before being trapped in the polluted air of the city. That hour spent communing with Nature would give me the serenity I needed to cope with earning a living.'

'You were lucky to live so near to open country,' said Kate. 'Was this when you were down in Kent?'

'I did go for walks when we were there, certainly, but I must have been thinking of Wales just now. My goodness, but you bring out the child in me, Kate!'

'And you, Ayesha, are you Welsh too?'

'I didn't say I was Welsh,' said Marcus quickly. 'It's just that I spent time there as a child.'

But Kate had heard the Welsh in his voice quite clearly now, though he had quickly returned to standard southern English again. Ayesha, she noticed, hadn't answered her question, but had turned to Roz and was asking why she was eating smoked salmon pâté, because of course it was full of poisonous chemicals and Roz really shouldn't buy it.

'This is delicious, Roz – and packed with wonderful omega threes,' said Kate, helping herself to more of the pâté right under Ayesha's nose. Surely she had done enough to fulfil her part of the bargain by now. When they had finished eating she would leave as soon as she could.

In fact Roz was looking exhausted again, and Kate hoped that the Freemans would take the hint and leave too. She urged her mother to stay seated while she cleared the table, and was pleased to see that Ayesha came into the kitchen to help with the washing-up, in spite of Roz's protests.

'There's a chef's apron here, Ayesha. You really mustn't splash dirty water on your dress.'

'I'm getting rather tired of these colours, as a matter of fact,' said Ayesha carelessly, though she did wrap the apron around herself and push her sleeves up before setting to work.

When they returned to the sitting room, Kate was concerned to see just how pale her mother was. Yet if she urged her to go straight to bed, Roz would only argue with her on principle, she was sure. To her surprise, it was Roz herself who said, 'If you don't mind, I think I'll have an early night. Avril and I have plenty to do in the morning and I need my rest – it must be a result of my increasing age.'

'That's right, Roz. You must listen to what your body is telling you,' said Ayesha. Kate's own body was sending her forceful instructions to push Ayesha and Marcus out into the street and bolt the door against them, but she managed to resist the temptation.

Marcus went to fetch Ayesha's coat and then helped her into it. While he was busy with this, Kate extracted the memory card from Roz's new camera and slipped it into her bag.

'I've taken the memory card so that I can print out the photos,' she said quietly to Roz when she managed to catch her on her own in the kitchen for a moment.

'Well let me have it back as soon as possible. I'd like to play with my new toy again before too long.'

'I'll deliver it back when I go out for my run tomorrow morning,' said Kate, resigned to the sacrifice of one of her favourite possessions. 'But now I wondered whether I could take a look at one of the threatening letters you received.'

'Whatever for? I don't want to go looking for it now, Kate. And anyway, it didn't make any threats, you know.'

'I just wanted to see what it looked like.'

'No, Kate.'

They went back into the hallway, where Kate said good-bye to the three of them and left the house.

She had parked her car some way down the street, unable to find a space nearer to Roz's house. As she prepared to start the engine she saw the Freemans come out on to the pavement and let themselves into a large car almost outside the door. Marcus was driving, and he drew away in the direction of the Cowley Road – the direction in which Kate was facing. She switched on her lights and drove slowly towards the same road junction, keeping a good distance behind them.

Marcus was indicating left, and on an impulse, Kate did the same. She might never again have such a good opportunity to find out where they lived. She dawdled along to the end of the road and then pulled in a couple of cars behind them. For a few seconds she had been close enough to read their registration number, and she committed it to memory in case she should lose them in the traffic in the Cowley Road.

# 21

By the time they had reached the bottom of the Cowley Road and crossed the Plain into the High Street, the traffic had thinned out so much that Kate was once more behind the BMW driven by Marcus Freeman. He drew into the right-hand lane at the traffic lights and Kate didn't dare to hang back any further. If she missed the lights she would lose him, and it wasn't obvious at this point which way he would be travelling. There was no reason for them to have noticed her: the metallic grey Peugeot 206 was a common enough model, and in any case, this was a perfectly reasonable route from East Oxford back to Jericho.

The lights changed to green and they both turned right into Longwall, bumping slowly over the road humps in the university's science area. By now there were two or three other cars behind Kate so that she didn't feel so exposed.

At the next set of lights the Freemans turned north, following the road round until it came out into the Woodstock Road. Marcus was breaking the speed limit, she noticed; for a moment she thought he would be caught by one of the speed cameras, and she felt uncharitably pleased about it. If he used this road frequently, he would know where they were located and slow down, but as he continued to accelerate northwards, drawing away from her all the time, either he must be unfamiliar with the area, or else he had no concern for fines or points on his licence.

Before he disappeared from view, she saw his brake lights come on and a distant yellow flicker indicated that he was turning right into one of the broad, tree-lined streets that in the nineteenth century housed the large families of the senior members of Oxford University.

Kate continued at a law-abiding thirty miles per hour and then turned right, following Marcus. But in this side street she could see no moving car ahead of her, just the wide, empty pavements with street lamps casting pools of light between the heavy, uniform trees. She slowed down at the next road junction and looked to left and right. In the distance, to her left, she saw a vehicle swinging into a gateway, then heard the slamming of car doors and the bleeping of a locking device. She turned off her own lights and pulled into the kerb to wait until the street was quiet again.

When she was sure that the Freemans must be indoors (if indeed it was the Freemans she had heard), she drove on a little way until she was past what she assumed to be their house. Parking halfway between two street lights, in deep shadow, ignoring the 'Residents Only' sign, she closed her own door with only the lightest of clicks.

As it happened, she was wearing dark clothes, so even if the Freemans had been looking out of their windows they would have had difficulty in picking her out against the darker background.

When she arrived at the gate where she thought the car had turned in, she stood back behind the low wall and yew hedge to peer up the drive. Sure enough there was a BMW, but it was too dark to read the number plate, and she couldn't even be certain of its colour. She looked down at her feet: tarmac, not gravel.

Moving back behind the yew hedge again, she wished that she'd brought her bag with her: she always kept a small, powerful torch in one of its sections. Too bad. She'd just have to manage without it. She crouched down so that she was hidden from view by the bulk of the car, then crept forward until she could read the number. Yes, this was the Freemans' Beamer. She rose to her feet and slid into the shadow of a large shrub, silently thanking the Victorian owner of the house who had so thoughtfully planted it there. Now that she was here in the Freemans' garden, she might as well take a good look, even if it was only at the exterior.

It was a solid, double-fronted, brick-built house, with no frivolous decoration and plenty of room for a family, however numerous. There was another car parked on the far side of the BMW, also large and shiny, if not quite as large as Marcus's, and a lighter colour. She guessed that this belonged to Ayesha.

There was a light behind the curtain of the right-hand window, and now another clicked on in the matching left-hand room. Upstairs, a third light went on, and a few seconds later Kate thought she could see the faint blue glow from a computer monitor through the thin curtain.

In the dark she could learn little more from the exterior of the house, except that if the Freemans had bought it the previous spring they must have had serious money to spend. The garden told her only that previous owners had been fond of large, dense shrubbery. She felt something tickling her cheek and gently removed a spider.

She was about to leave when she heard the sound of an approaching motorbike and decided to wait in her laurel bush until it had gone past.

Except that it didn't. It slowed down only slightly, and then the headlight swept in an arc across the garden and the front of the house, missing her by only a foot or two as she shrank back into the concealing shrubbery. The bike's engine roared a couple more times and then was silent. A moment later the front door was flung wide and she saw

Marcus Freeman standing there, silhouetted against the lighted hall within.

'Jefferson!' he bellowed. 'Is that you?'

'You'd be in trouble if it wasn't, wouldn't you?'

'I've told you before not to ride that machine like that in this neighbourhood. Do you want people to come knocking on our door with complaints?'

'Keep your wig on, Marc. It's hardly late, even for this dead-and-alive place.'

'Get in here, you little toerag,' and this Marcus was no longer the urbane, priestly character she had met at Roz's place, his accent more Tiger Bay than Palace of Westminster.

The biker sauntered forward into the light. He was, predictably, dressed in black leathers and holding a black helmet. Where his hair caught the light from the front door Kate saw that it was reddish and curly, his body reminding her of a black pudding in its tight leathers, and as she glimpsed him in profile, she thought he bore a certain resemblance to Ayesha, with his soft, rounded face. Were they related? Or was the likeness to Ayesha just a coincidence?

The young man paused and glanced around the garden. Kate dropped to her knees and, keeping to the shadows, crawled towards the gate. As soon as she reached it, she abandoned caution, rose to her feet and sprinted for the car. Thirty seconds later she was driving towards Jericho. She didn't want to be caught hiding in his front garden by the Marcus she had glimpsed that evening.

On the way home she thought how good it would be if Jefferson turned out to be one of the youths who had stolen her mobile phone, but it wouldn't wash. Although she hadn't seen the two who came up behind her at all clearly, she was sure that neither of them was as substantially built as Jefferson, and all three of them were taller.

* * *

Inside the house, Jefferson Freeman was drinking from a can of lager, one booted foot on the fender, the other planted firmly on the pale carpet.

'Can't you change before you come in here?' said Marcus belligerently.

'Why, are you afraid I'll frighten away your posh friends?'

Ayesha entered from the kitchen, wooden spatula in hand, looking nervously from one to the other.

'Now then, you two, you're not arguing again, are you?'

'I don't want him leaving greasemarks on the new paintwork,' said Marcus.

'I was hoping someone would pour me a large glass of the Australian red to make up for all that herbal tea I've had to drink,' said Ayesha brightly, changing the subject.

Marcus crossed to the counter, where bottles and glasses were set out. Red wine glugged into a goblet.

'I wouldn't mind one of those myself,' said Jefferson, tossing his empty lager can into a large blue glazed pot containing a six-foot palm. 'Thanks, Marc,' he said as Marcus wordlessly handed him another capacious goblet. 'But what I really wanted to tell you was this: did you know there was some bird hiding in the shrubbery out front, spying on you, when I came in?'

'It was probably the weird teenager from three doors up,' said Marcus.

'No, that one I would have recognised, but this one wasn't short and fat. I didn't get more than a glimpse, just before the door closed, but she was well slim and she didn't look like a teenager. I'd never seen her before.'

'Why didn't you grab hold of her and ask her what the hell she was doing?'

'She was out the gate and scarpering up the road before I

219

realised what was happening. And I didn't fancy sprinting after her in these boots and leathers.'

'I can see that would have been uncomfortable for you,' said Marcus sarcastically.

'Who could it have been?' wondered Ayesha. 'And what on earth did she want? Do you think she's a burglar?'

'I don't know,' replied Marcus. 'But whoever it was had better not come back, or she'll regret it.'

'Supper ready yet?' asked Jefferson, bored with the subject.

'Ready in ten,' said Ayesha.

'I hope you've cooked some good red meat, and not another wokful of vegetables,' said Marcus, looking at the spatula in her hand.

'Steaks,' replied Ayesha, 'and I'm just going to put them under the grill.'

'Make sure mine's rare,' said Marcus.

'As if I'd forget!' And Ayesha returned to the kitchen, looking thoughtful.

'You don't think it could have been Roz's daughter, do you?' she said to Marcus later, when they were alone. 'I told you she was too curious for her own good.'

'Don't worry about her. She's not as bright as she thinks she is. She's only a novelist after all.'

# 22

On the phone to Jon, later that evening, Kate said: 'It would have fitted in so neatly if the Freemans' friend turned out to be one of the thugs who stole my mobile.'

'You think that would have changed Roz's opinion of them?'

'Yes. She'd see what sort of people they were.'

'I think she'd have felt sympathy for them: such a nice couple, pity their son turned out so badly.'

'I suppose you could be right.'

'What are you going to do tomorrow?'

'I haven't made up my mind yet.'

'Just don't go breaking into their house, expecting to find evidence of their evil crimes.'

'Hey! That's a good idea. I hadn't thought of that one. You'd bail me out if I got caught, wouldn't you? You could even act as a character witness in court.'

'Kate—'

'OK. Only joking. I thought I might go down to the library and check the electoral register, see who lives in that house. Three Freemans? Or maybe a different surname altogether.'

'You have the address?'

'Yes, of course.'

'Doesn't the new register come out in the New Year?'

'I think you're right. And they won't be in the last one if they only came to live in Oxford in the spring. I'm not having much luck on my side, am I?'

'And don't forget that people can opt out of having their names in the public edition of the register.'

'How do I get my hands on a copy of the full register?'

'You'd have to get yourself elected as a councillor, I believe.'

'I don't think I have the time for that.'

'Try looking on the city library's website. If they haven't opted out, you might be able to find the information you need.'

'It doesn't sound too hopeful, though. I can't imagine the Freemans leaving their details lying around for everyone to inspect.'

'A lot of people think that way. I'm not on the full register. What about you?'

'I ticked the secrecy box too.'

'Forget the electoral register then. Have you got any other ideas?'

'As a matter of fact, I have.' Kate proceeded to tell Jon about her scheme to take photographs of the Freemans.

'I have the memory card from the camera,' she finished, 'but I haven't downloaded the pictures on to my PC yet. I'll do it this evening. I said I'd return the memory card to Roz as soon as possible.'

'So she's holding on to your camera? That's what comes of being so devious.'

At least he appeared to have forgiven her for not being there for him. They were back on their old footing.

When Jon had rung off, she switched on her computer. She connected the card reader to the USB port and then pushed the card from the digital camera into the slot. A couple of clicks of the mouse and she had the photographs copied on to her desktop.

Before removing the card from the reader, she deleted all the images from it, then she opened the file and watched as the pictures paraded across her screen. Yes, it really was a neat little camera, that one. Every picture clear and sharp, and Roz had managed to catch two startled-looking Freemans at various angles as well as in close-up and full-length. Tomorrow she would edit them and print them out.

The next morning she was as good as her word to Roz, jogging over to East Oxford through the morning mist to post the data card and a covering note through her letterbox.

Later, when the post eventually arrived, she found that Avril, too, had done what she had promised and had forwarded the threatening letter. She was just examining its envelope when there was a knock at the back door and Brad's head appeared.

'Am I in time for coffee?'

'Come on in, Brad, and take a seat.'

He had timed his visit well. The coffee was just ready and she fetched out a second mug, then found a packet of chocolate digestives in the cupboard.

'How's it going?' he asked her. 'I was afraid you might be pining for Susanna, so I came round to cheer you up.'

Kate had the impression that Brad was the one who needed the comfort. She pushed the biscuits across the table. 'Try one of these,' she said.

'I'm interrupting you, aren't I?' he said.

'No. It's coffee time and I was just opening my post. In fact, Brad, you can give me your opinion of this letter.'

She moved her chair round so that they could both look at the envelope.

'I'd just got as far as staring at the envelope. Here, you take a look at it.'

Envelope and letter were blue – quite an intense blue – and made of thin paper, though not quite as thin as airmail paper. Avril had slit the top with a paper knife, as Kate might have expected.

'It was posted in London,' Brad remarked. 'Though it's too blurred to read the district or the date.'

'Yes. And what do you think of this font?' she asked.

'It looks foreign, in spite of the postmark,' he said promptly.

'It's something about the squareness of the characters and the wider spacing between them, isn't it?'

'Certainly it doesn't look English.'

'Could it be Spanish, do you think?' she asked.

'I've no idea. What makes you think that?'

'The letter inside was sent to a friend of my mother's and was intended to frighten her into paying out sums of money to the sender.'

'Can I read it?' Brad helped himself to a second chocolate biscuit and bit into it thoughtfully.

'Of course.'

'Only, Kate, do you mind my asking why you're taking so much trouble over this letter? It's not addressed to you, is it?'

'A long story, Brad. I haven't read the letter myself yet, but I know that Avril – who's a sensible woman – was upset by it. Roz, my mother, has been getting letters from the same source, apparently, but she won't let me see them, which is why I wanted to get hold of this one. I've been told that these scams often originate in the Iberian peninsula – that's why I wondered if it looked Spanish to you.'

Kate lifted the letter out carefully, using her fingertips, as though its touch might contaminate her. She and Brad read it through, and then, starting again at the beginning, they read it again, aloud.

'I urge you to note well what I have to say. I see a dark shadow standing close to you . . .'

'I want to tell you more about the danger you are in. I want no money. This service is absolutely free . . .'

'There is something more,' Kate said. 'I haven't told anyone about it, but I've received a couple of threatening emails and I just wondered if they came from the same people as the letters.'

'This is terrible! Have you told the police about them?'

'No. They're probably just a joke. I don't think the police would be interested.'

'You don't think the fact that you were mugged had anything to do with them?'

'I can't see how it could have done.'

'And Susanna?'

Kate was silent.

'I'll pour us another coffee,' said Brad.

When he had done so, Kate said, 'Tell me what you make of the letter.'

'Well, there is an address at least. North London.'

'That's an accommodation address, one of those places where you hire a mailbox and they lock your post in it for you to collect,' said Kate. 'They thrive because they don't answer questions from nosy people like me.'

'I suppose you're right. But there's a signature, too.'

'Tall, thin and spidery. And quite illegible.'

'It doesn't ask for money directly, does it?' Brad drained his coffee. She would offer him some more in a minute. She didn't want him to leave: she was finding that it helped her to have someone to discuss the problem with.

'No. Just a polite request for a contribution towards their expenses. So once again I don't think the police could do anything about it.'

'I can't imagine that they get many people sending off cheques. I wouldn't think it's worth the trouble they're taking.'

'That depends how many they send out. Suppose it's a few million every month, and a few thousand women send a large cheque – or several cheques, if it comes to that. They're making enormous sums every month.'

'Even with your sketchy arithmetic you could be right.'

'What else strikes you?' asked Kate.

'It's written by a foreigner – someone with good English, but who isn't a native speaker.'

'It's just too correct, a bit stiff, isn't it?'

'What about your emails? Were they like this?'

'No. The more I look at it, the more convinced I am that they're from two different people.'

'Can I see the emails?'

'No, not at the moment. I'm having problems with my computer,' she improvised. She found she was as unwilling as Roz to have anyone else see what had been written to her. She didn't know why this should be, but it felt as uncomfortable as asking someone to look through her dirty laundry basket.

'Fair enough,' said Brad, who had probably guessed how she was feeling.

'If there's one thing I can recognise, it's writing style. The emails are written by a native English speaker.'

'And the letter isn't, I agree.'

'And it's vaguer in its predictions than my messages, which were open to various interpretations, but certainly more precise than this.'

'So they did mention the mugging and Susanna's death?'

'Not in so many words, but it was easy to read them like that after the event. Getting back to this letter, I'm only amazed that someone like Avril – sensible, practical Avril – was worried by it. But maybe that was only after her mother's grave was vandalised – and I believe that was another coincidence. I read in the local paper that the police were

226

questioning a gang of twelve- and thirteen-year-olds who were caught spray-painting headstones in another grave-yard, and I gather it wasn't the first time.'

'Little horrors!'

'It's surprising how many otherwise sensible people are superstitious, isn't it? It's as though we want to believe in the supernatural and are taken in by the flimsiest of evidence.'

Kate stood up and collected their mugs. 'Shall I make another pot of coffee? I could certainly do with another cup myself. And I've probably got more biscuits in the cupboard too.'

'Have we really eaten a whole packet already?'

'Apparently,' she laughed. 'It's the tension. Biscuits are a great cure for stress.'

'Are you sure I'm not holding you up?'

'No. You're being very helpful. Please stay, as long as I'm not keeping you from your own work.' And she switched on the kettle and spooned ground coffee into the press.

'Work's a bit thin at the moment – and I'm tired of watching daytime television.'

'I'm sorry about that. I hope it picks up again soon.'

'So do I. I have some savings, but I don't want to be a kept man!'

Kate heard the pain behind the flippant remark. 'Have another chocolate biscuit.'

They kept up the small talk until Kate had poured the coffee and they were both seated at the table, chocolate biscuits in hand.

'Have I told you about Ayesha and Marcus Freeman?' she asked.

'I don't think so.'

'They're new friends of Roz's and I think they're a very bad influence on her. And I don't think their motives are pure and unselfish, either.'

'You're making them sound like the letter-writer.'

'I would just love to find out that they'd done something like this, but I can't really see any connection.'

'But you're lumping the letters and the emails in together. If they don't come from the same source, then it follows that they weren't sent for the same reason. Avril's letter is designed to extract money from her. Why do you think someone sent you the emails?'

'To frighten me?'

'Why should anyone want to do that?'

'To distract me. Because I'm doing something that threatens them.'

'And, knowing you, this would be something you're pursuing with unusual persistence.'

'So you think I'm pig-headed and obstinate too?'

'I wouldn't put it quite like that,' said Brad diplomatically. 'But what have you been getting up to recently? I thought you were working on the new book. Didn't you tell me you were going off on research trips?'

'Some of the research was into the Freemans' background,' she admitted. 'I'm so sure that they're up to no good that I wanted to find proof that I could show to Roz and convince her she should throw them out of her house.'

Brad looked at her as if she were a wayward child. 'But that's not going to work, is it? If your mother wants to have these people as her friends, she's not going to be influenced by anything you find out about them – even supposing there's anything to find. As a friend of yours, I can only advise you to give up, Kate.'

'I don't want to go into the detail, Brad, but I can't give up. Basically, I'm worried that Roz is ill – really ill – and the Freemans are persuading her to stay away from the doctor.'

228

'I'm not that keen on doctors myself,' said Brad. 'There's nothing like a large dose of vitamin C to set you on your feet again, I always think.'

'I don't think it would work in this case.'

'You're talking *serious* serious?'

'I am.'

'Well, in that case you have to ask yourself what's in it for them.'

'Money?'

'In that case, two more questions. First, how would they get their hands on your mother's money? I imagine she has every intention of leaving it to you.'

'With Roz one can never tell.'

'Well, the second question is: how would they stop you from persuading her to throw them out?'

'They'd try to frighten me off?'

'Or at least keep you so busy that you have no time to look at what else they're doing. Whether you can prove it or not, why don't you assume that your emails are coming from the Freemans, and that they've done something they don't want you to find out about and are trying to distract your attention.'

'Ignore the emails?'

'Exactly.'

'I wonder where they got the know-how. I don't know how to spoof an email address. Do you?'

'No. But I expect a passing fourteen-year-old could tell you.'

'Jefferson,' said Kate.

'I'm sorry?'

'Another long story, but I think he might be their son. They've never mentioned having such a thing, though I believe they did have one who died. Jefferson is rather older than fourteen, but younger than me, and possibly you.'

'Has any of this chat been of any use, do you think?' asked Brad, looking regretfully into his empty coffee mug and chasing chocolate crumbs around the table with a forefinger.

'I do believe it has,' said Kate.

'I think I'd better be leaving. And I think it's time you wrote a few pages of your novel.'

'Yeah, yeah – you're nagging like Estelle. Goodbye, Brad. And thanks.'

Kate returned to her computer, but not to write the next chapter of her book. She opened the folder where she had downloaded the images from the camera, and looked at the first one.

'They're brilliant,' she told Roz on the phone. 'After playing around with the cropping tool and red-eye—'

'Spare me the details!'

'Well, what it comes down to is that I've printed out really good photos of Marcus and Ayesha taken from different angles. Some are close-ups of their faces, and some are full-length, which gives a good general impression of what they look like.'

'So if anyone's going to recognise them, these are the photos to do it for you?'

'Yes.' It dawned on her that they were talking about two close friends of her mother's, and that Roz was naturally less keen than she was on the success of this project.

'Equally,' said Roz, 'if you show them to someone who thinks he knows my friends under a different name, and he doesn't recognise them, then that would be conclusive too.'

'Yes, certainly.'

'And if that happens, you will let me know, and you will make an effort to like them, and you will stop trying to persuade me to give them up.'

'Very well. And by the way, Roz, did you find the memory card on your doormat this morning?'

'I should have mentioned it before. Thank you, Kate. You must have been out before dawn to deliver it.'

'Just about,' said Kate.

'It's back in its slot and I'm all ready to practise my new-found skills with my lovely camera. Such a thoughtful present! Thank you so much.'

Kate hadn't contacted Jack Ivory again. It had been a forlorn hope, after all, that he had anything useful left to tell her. He and Marcus had known one another at college more than thirty years ago, and then there had been the friendship between Laura and the Freemans. That was all.

It was all the more surprising to her then that Jack bothered to contact her again.

Early that evening, as usual, Marcus and Ayesha Freeman called on Roz Ivory. Ayesha went to the kitchen to make them all a pot of herb tea while Marcus took the chair next to the sofa where Roz was reclining.

'I was wondering whether you had thought any more about settling some of your property into a trust fund?' he asked her gently.

'I have considered it,' she began.

'Oh, splendid!' interrupted Marcus. 'I'm sure you've made a very wise decision. Ayesha!'

'Yes, dear?' Ayesha entered with the tray of cups.

'Dear Roz has made the very wise decision to put some of her property into a trust fund.'

'I'm not sure that I've actually decided on anything yet,' protested Roz.

'I'll get our friend, the lawyer we told you about, to call in

231

to talk to you about the details. He'll explain it all to you far better than I can. I'll bring him round tomorrow,' said Marcus.

'Now, do drink up your camomile tea while it's hot, dear,' said Ayesha.

# 23

The email that Jack Ivory had sent to Kate was quite short:

> Such good news! I do believe I've found the link we were both hoping for. As it happens, I am passing close to Oxford tomorrow on my way to Winchester. Would it be possible for me to visit you then, say at 3.30 in the afternoon?

Kate's attention had been so firmly focused on the Freemans that she felt a pang of disappointment at his message. The Ivory family! No mention of Ayesha and Marcus. No clue to where they had been living before they were in Hove, or even where they originally came from. Just at this moment she really didn't care about her paternal grandparents and whether they were related to Jack Ivory's first cousins, or whoever it was.

Still, looking on the positive side, she might learn something about her elusive father from Jack, even if he had nothing to add on the subject of the Freemans. Roz had always been evasive on the subject – or perhaps it was that she was bored – and it was, after all, Kate's right to know about her forebears, even if names and dates on a piece of paper told her no more about the man who was her father than the little she already knew.

She looked again at the message: it was dated the previous evening. So it was this very day that he wanted to visit her. She sent off a reply:

Fine, Jack. Look forward to seeing you this afternoon.

Then, as an afterthought, she added her address and brief directions on how to get there. She hoped that he'd receive her message before leaving home.

Later that morning it occurred to her to phone her mother.

'Roz, I know that you're tired of the subject of family history – and particularly ours – but you must remember the names of Dad's parents.' She hardly ever referred to him as 'Dad' and she didn't know what had made her do so now. 'You must have met them. Weren't they at your wedding? Didn't you ever go round to their place for Sunday lunch?'

'I suppose they must have been at the wedding. Surely I gave you a copy of the photographs, and the other pictures that I had of your father? I kept none of them myself – I simply didn't have the room when I was globe-trotting.'

'I think I still have them. I must have: I know I've never thrown them away. I put them all in a box somewhere. You know how these things get mislaid when you move house, though. I suppose I really should have stuck them in an album.' Kate was gabbling, worried that somehow they had disappeared, melted away during the years since Roz had started on her travels, carelessly lost during one of her periodic turn-outs, or overlooked by the removal men.

'Well? So what were their names?' she asked.

'He wasn't another John, certainly. He was called something like Derek or Dennis. It began with a D, anyway.'

'David? Desmond? Daniel, perhaps?'

'Now you're confusing me, Kate.'

'And what about his wife? Your mother-in-law, if you remember.'

'Was she called Mary?'

'How should I know!'

'I think she was. I can't remember a thing about her

234

except that at our wedding she was wearing an enormous blue hat hung about with green cabbages.'

'That's no help at all, and anyway, I don't believe you. Goodbye, Mother. Go away and play with your new toy. And you can stop pretending you don't know how to use it too.'

She did finally remember where she had put the box of photographs, though. It wasn't long since she had unpacked the last of her belongings after her move from Fridesley, and the box was sitting on a shelf in her workroom, clearly marked 'Old Photographs' on the side as well as on the lid. She had grown used to the sight of it, so that now she barely noticed it, and its lid had stayed firmly closed, protecting her from memories which she preferred to leave in hibernation.

She brought the box into the kitchen, placed it on the table and lifted out the photos one by one. She laid the ones which featured her father in a square in front of her, like a tarot reading, and looked carefully at each in turn. She could see that she did take after him. She must now be about the age he was when he died, or even a year or two older. They had the same oval face and strong bone structure, with a thin nose and well-marked eyebrows. But there was something in their expressions that was quite different. She didn't think their personalities would have been similar. Her father, John Ivory, looked gentler than his daughter, less determined – in spite of the fact that her mother maintained Kate had inherited her stubbornness from him. She could imagine that Roz would easily have dominated this man, whereas Kate gave her a better run for her money.

Next she looked at the wedding photos. There was one of the bride, on her own, in a fitted silk suit and a wide-brimmed hat. Kate remembered that Roz had once told her that the hat was scarlet, and had laughed, because the effect of the colour had been startling with her red hair. She looked elegant rather than demure, certainly – no satin and tulle for her – the black-and-white photograph hiding the clash of red on red.

Then there was a picture of the couple at the church door, John in a dark suit looking bemused, Roz turned slightly away from him, smiling brilliantly at something – or someone – outside the picture. In her high heels she was as tall as her new husband.

And lastly there was the family group. Those must be Roz's parents, whom she hardly mentioned – an elderly couple, and strangers to Kate since they had died before she was born. They had married late, Roz had said, and were surprised when they produced a daughter at all, since her mother by then was well into her forties, her father more than ten years older. That stooping man with the balding head was Kate's grandfather, but there was no stir of recognition: he remained a stranger. And her grandmother was just another carefully dressed, ageing middle-class woman who had spent her life looking after her house and her husband with no thought for herself – until there was no self left to wonder about.

And on the other side of John stood another ordinary couple, pleasant-looking, conventional. John's mother was wearing a hat with roses round the brim, as Roz had said, but in Kate's opinion they resembled Brussels sprouts rather than cabbages. Roz, in her wide-brimmed hat, stood out from the group, looking as though she didn't quite belong and might decide to fly away at any moment.

She turned the photo over. Someone had pencilled in the words *John and Rosemary's wedding* across the centre, *Douglas and Mary Ivory* at the bottom on the right, *Robert and Margaret Holmes* in the bottom left-hand corner.

So, his name was Douglas. And Roz had remembered

her mother-in-law's name correctly after all. Kate had found what she was looking for.

Before putting the box away, she leafed through the rest of the contents: dog-eared black-and-white snapshots on the whole, many of them of a very young Kate doing all the things that children are urged to do when their father is holding a camera.

But then came a photograph, in colour this time, six inches by four, mounted on stiff board, that she had never seen before. It was another formal wedding picture, though the wedding itself looked to have been more flamboyant than her parents' ceremony. It had to be a wedding photo because the woman was holding a loose bunch of red and gold flowers and wearing a long scarf, tied bandanna-style round her head, and the groom was in a suit, though with a dark collarless shirt. Both were displaying shiny new wedding rings. The bride was recognisably Roz, twenty years or more on from her first wedding, but looking somehow younger, or at least more carefree. The groom was unfamiliar, a dark-haired, dark-eyed man – Spanish or Italian, perhaps. Too good-looking and not entirely reliable was how Kate would have described him. Just her mother's kind of man, in fact, and her heart sank at the thought.

There had been no mention of a second husband since Roz had returned to England, and Kate wondered where he was now, and whether there were any more of her mother's husbands scattered across the globe. No wonder Roz didn't want to talk about the past, and John Ivory's family. Maybe she had so many sets of in-laws in various continents that she hadn't a hope of remembering their names.

Kate turned the picture over. This time the handwriting was Roz's own: *Rosemary and António Filipe Soares da Silva*. Roz never willingly called herself Rosemary, to Kate's knowledge, but her husband's impressive list of names must have persuaded her to go for the longer option on this occasion. Roz da Silva – or was it Roz Soares da Silva? She could see that Ivory was simpler for everyday use, but the more exotic surname suited her mother. Underneath the names she had written *San Francisco, 12th June 1987*.

Kate glanced up at the clock on the kitchen wall. The hours had slipped by and now she just had time for a swift sandwich and a mug of coffee before Jack Ivory came knocking at her door. She returned all the pictures to their box and left it on the worktop, next to her short row of cookery books. If Jack had time, she might show him the photographs of her father and grandfather and ask him if he saw a family resemblance to anyone in his own family.

Jack arrived on time, his portfolio under his arm. She suggested that it might be convenient if he spread the family tree out on the kitchen table rather than balancing it on his knee in the sitting room.

'Can I make you a coffee or some tea before we begin?' she asked.

'No, really, it's very kind of you, but I haven't long to spare this afternoon, I'm afraid.'

He opened the portfolio and produced the now-familiar sheet of paper with its sketchy family tree, only this time she saw that there were more names in the centre of the bottom half.

'Working from the approximate dates of your parents' and grandparents' marriages, I managed to track these down. Look.' And he pointed to Roz and John Ivory. 'So, what do you think about these?' And he proudly indicated the space above John's head where his parents now had their names and dates recorded.

Kate looked hard, thinking she must have mistaken the

spot on the tree, but there they were: James Richard and Florence May (née Cheeseman), with their dates, and below them their son, John Ivory, married to Rosemary, with Kate dangling from a twig beneath them.

'And I'm quite sure James was a cousin of my father's. I have to seek corroboration, of course, but I'm pretty certain that it's the case. I just knew we were cousins, Kate, and now I've nearly proved it.'

'I can't believe it,' said Kate truthfully. 'It will take me a while to get used to having a whole new set of relations. Are you sure you wouldn't like that cup of tea?'

'Well, perhaps we should be celebrating, and tea would be quite appropriate.'

Kate wondered whether to break it to him that he'd got her grandparents wrong, but it seemed unkind after all his hard work, so she put the kettle on instead.

Just as she was pouring boiling water on to the tea bags, Kate's phone started to ring from somewhere on the floor above.

'I'm not sure where I left it. That's the trouble with the cordless: I'll have to go looking for it. Help yourself to tea and biscuits while I answer it, please, Jack.'

She found the phone in her bedroom and reached it just before the answering machine cut in. She looked at the screen: it was Roz.

'Hello?'

'Kate. Just a quick query. Do you remember what capacity memory card you'd put in the camera you gave me?'

'Of course: 256 megs.'

'That's what I thought. When I turned the camera on just now, the number of photos I could take had decreased quite sharply, so I checked the card. The strange thing is that it seems to have shrunk from 256 megs down to 64.'

Kate thought quickly. 'Who's visited you since first thing this morning?'

'I really can't say anything at present, and I have to go now, I'm afraid. Goodbye, Kate.'

Kate was left staring at the receiver, then she slowly descended the stairs. As she did so she heard the beep of a mobile phone being switched off. So she wasn't the only one to have received a phone call.

'Everything all right?' Jack asked. 'You look somewhat bemused.'

'An odd call from . . . my agent,' she said, her eyes on the space next to the bookshelf where she had left the box of photographs.

He smiled at her reply, and Kate felt an odd lurch in the region of her stomach. 'Perhaps she's coming up with a big American deal for you,' he suggested.

'That would be nice if it happened. But I mustn't keep you here chatting. I'll pour out the tea; I expect you'll be wanting to get off to Salisbury soon,' she said brightly.

'Winchester,' he corrected quietly, still smiling.

If the Freemans had looked at the SD card and found it blank, they would know by now that Roz had either deleted or passed on the images she had taken the previous evening, and if it was the latter, the most likely recipient would be her daughter – that nosy, interfering person who kept getting in their way. And then – surprise, surprise! – there was Jack Ivory on her doorstep. Jack Ivory, who had been a friend of Marcus Freeman's for more than thirty years and who just happened to turn up as she started to ask questions about Marcus and Ayesha.

What a fool she was to have taken him at face value! She should have seen long ago that he was part of the Freemans' team, acting on Marcus's orders.

He must have come here this afternoon to destroy the

pictures of the Freemans – which meant that they were just as important as she had thought. But her computer and the photographs were in her workroom, and she had been in the same room with him until a few minutes ago and would have heard him if he had left the kitchen to search for her computer, so he couldn't have stolen them, or even deleted them, without her noticing.

Why had he given up? It could only be because of the phone call he had made while she was talking to Roz. His smile told her that he knew the photographs were now irrelevant.

'You're right, though,' he said, watching her face with the same amused expression. 'Once I've drunk my tea, I really should leave.'

'James and Florence,' she said musingly. 'I'm surprised that Roz forgot their names, but then she's never been enthusiastic about family ties.'

She wondered whether she could convince him that Roz, inexperienced as she was with the workings of a digital camera, had deleted the photos by mistake. It was easily done, after all. But there was something too knowing about his expression for her to risk it.

She followed him out to his car and watched as he drove to the end of the street. Winchester is south of Oxford, and it would be logical for him to turn right, towards the southern bypass. But Jack's left indicator was flashing. He was going towards London, or, more likely, to the Freemans' house. There was only one thing to do.

Kate flew back indoors and fetched her bag and car keys from the kitchen. As she did so she confirmed her impression that the box of old photographs – so clearly marked with its contents – had been moved some way to the right of where she had left it.

'Damn!' No wonder he was looking amused. He'd had

enough time to riffle through and find the wedding photo with the names of John Ivory's parents on the back, especially since she'd left it conveniently near the top. She ran for the car. She just wanted confirmation that Jack Ivory was the toad she thought he was.

# 24

The engine started immediately and Kate followed in Jack's wake towards Walton Street. She had already worked out in her head a less-than-obvious route to the Freemans' house, just in case Jack looked in his rearview mirror and saw a familiar vehicle in hot pursuit, so now she zigzagged north and east, driving well over the speed limit and hoping that she hadn't mistaken the location of the speed cameras, until finally, twenty yards from her target, she pulled into a row of half a dozen other grey cars, where she trusted that the equally grey Peugeot would be inconspicuous.

There was no friendly darkness to hide her now, but at least the pavements were empty: children had already arrived back from school and were settling down to their homework, but fathers were not yet driving in from work. She got out of the car and ran to the Freemans' gate. If she was quick, she could hide in the shrubbery before Jack Ivory arrived. And she was sure that he would arrive. Before he left her house he must have known that she realised he had invented the connection between their families.

The laurel bush was not quite as dense as it had appeared the other night, but it provided good enough cover if no one was expecting her to be there, she reckoned.

And she was only just in time. Less than a minute later, as she crouched in the long grass, the bright blue Honda that she had last seen outside her own front door turned into the drive and pulled up beside Marcus's BMW. As Jack approached the Freemans' door it opened to reveal Marcus standing there.

'Marco!'

'Bill! Come on in. How did it go?'

But Kate didn't hear how 'Jack Ivory' had got on, for the door had closed behind the two men, cutting her off from their conversation.

Bill. So even his name was a lie. He must have found out that John was a common name among the Ivorys and chosen Jack to be just a little different.

She stood up and brushed dust and leaves from her jeans, preparing to make her escape. But then she froze. A familiar motorbike engine was approaching and she fell to her knees in the laurel bush again just as Jefferson turned showily into the drive and pulled up between the Honda and the BMW. Removing his helmet, he too entered the house. Kate counted three cars and one motorbike. As long as they weren't expecting guests, she was safe to leave, and she did so at speed.

Whether Jefferson was related to the Freemans or not, he was certainly spending a lot of time at their house.

It was barely five when she arrived back at her house in Cleveland Road. She dumped her jacket on the banister rail and ran to find her phone. As it happened, the number she needed was stored in the directory so she had no need to waste time in looking for it.

'Leicester College.'

'The library, please.'

There was a pause, then, after a single ring, a calm male voice said, 'Leicester College library.'

'Is that Kevin Newton?'

'Kevin took early retirement last year. You're speaking to the new librarian.'

Well, thank goodness for that, thought Kate, remembering just how obstructive Kevin had been when she had sought information from him a few years ago. 'My name is Kate Ivory—' she began, but was interrupted.

'The author of the exciting historicals?'

'Well, yes.' Kate felt a warm glow of satisfaction at being recognised.

'My name is Ben Knutson – that's with a K, by the way – and my wife is a great fan of yours. So what can I do to help?'

'Ben, what time does the library close this evening?'

'Not until ten o'clock as it's term time.'

'I'm in rather urgent need of information about an old member of Leicester and I was hoping I could take a look in your archive.'

'You're in luck. I happen to be the college archivist as well as the librarian, and I'm on duty myself this evening. Why don't you give me the details of the man you're looking for – it is a man, I assume? We were men-only until '75, of course – and his date of matriculation, if you know it.'

Kate gave him the two names and a range of probable dates, and he suggested she should call in after six and he would show her what he had found.

'Marcus's name might be Marco,' she added. 'I've heard him called that. Or I suppose it could be Mark. Sorry to be so vague.'

'Don't worry. I'll look up all the variations.'

When she had rung off, Kate went to find a hardback copy of her most recent book and signed the title page. She would ask Ben for his wife's name and add a friendly personal message.

Then she dialled again. With luck she would catch Roz at home before the Freemans descended on her. But she listened to the ringing tone for nearly a minute before giving

245

up. Was Roz all right? Had she collapsed and was now lying unconscious on the floor? She would drive to Leicester College by way of the Cowley Road, just to check.

It was a dull, grey day and dusk had come early. Many of the houses in the street had lights shining in their front rooms, but Roz's place was all in darkness. The curtains were open, Kate saw, so she must have been up and around during the day. She looked for Roz's car and spotted it ten yards away, so her mother should be at home.

She rang the bell and then banged on the door. No reply, and there was a stillness about the house that indicated that it was empty. Please don't let her go off with the Freemans, she breathed. Common sense told her that they were still entertaining 'Jack Ivory', but they could have phoned Roz before Kate did and invited her over to their place. She stared despairingly at the darkened windows.

'Hello, Kate. What are you doing here?'

It was Roz, standing on the pavement behind her, holding a couple of plastic bags full of shopping.

'Oh, thank goodness for that!' She found that there were tears filling her eyes, and she hoped her mother couldn't see them in the gloom.

'You are in a state. You'd better come in.' And Roz walked past her, fished first in one pocket then the other for her keys, found them, opened the door and walked through to the kitchen.

'I only popped down to the shops for a couple of things I'd forgotten when I was out earlier,' she said mildly. 'Whatever is the matter?'

'Sit down a moment. I want to tell you about the Freemans.'

'Not again! I thought we'd agreed to drop that subject.'

Kate noticed sadly that Roz's kitchen was looking quite dingy. There was washing-up waiting to be done and splashes of grease on the hob; the vase of flowers on the windowsill drooped sadly and their leaves were turning brown. Even as Kate watched, a petal detached itself and drifted to the floor. She turned her attention back to her mother.

'This is something new I have to tell you about. Jack Ivory called in this afternoon to tell me about some connection he'd found between our respective grandparents. He had their names and dates, all very convincing – except that they were wrong.'

'How do you know?' Roz sat down suddenly at the table and put her hand up to her forehead.

'What's wrong?'

'Just a touch of dizziness. I wasn't feeling hungry at lunchtime and missed a meal. A silly mistake – pass me over a banana or an apple or something from one of those bags.'

Kate did as she was told and noticed that her mother ate very slowly, in spite of saying she was hungry, and seemed to have difficulty in swallowing.

'What was it you were saying about your grandparents?' Roz said with an effort.

'I looked out the photos of your wedding and someone had pencilled in the names on the back. He called them James and Florence, but they were really Douglas and Mary.' She wanted to say something about how ill Roz looked – worse than the last time she had seen her, certainly – but she didn't dare. Her mother was quite capable of ordering her out of the house.

'He made a mistake, that's all,' said Roz.

'He came round to destroy the pictures you took of the Freemans, I'm sure. He didn't stay long enough to do that, but while I was out of the room answering the phone he found the same wedding photo, so he knew that I knew he'd made up the names and dates.'

'How complicated,' said Roz noncommittally.

'So I drove to the Freemans' and got there just before him. When Marcus opened the door he addressed him as Bill!'

'You're telling me you were hiding in a rose bush?'

'Laurel, actually. Look, Roz. These people are not who and what they say they are. And that has to be for a reason. Please, don't let them into your house again. Just for once, be a little cautious. This evening I'll be checking on something else they told me and I'll get back to you as soon as possible. But in the meantime, don't trust them.'

'Very well, just to please you, and only for the next three days, I'll tell them not to come round.'

'But you're the one who told me about the memory card in the camera! You must know that they stole it from you and replaced it with another.'

'I don't remember that,' Roz said, looking puzzled. 'Are you sure? And I can hardly confront them and accuse them of stealing, now can I?'

Roz was being as stubborn as ever, though Kate was afraid that she was becoming increasingly confused and forgetful. But underneath it all, surely her certainty about the Freemans was fading and she was slowly changing her opinion. Better not to push her advantage, even though she was afraid that Roz's illness was progressing so fast she might be too late to save her mother's health.

'I have to be going now,' she said. 'I'm seeing a librarian in a quarter of an hour. But there is just one other thing I wanted to ask you about.'

'More family history?'

'Of a sort. Who is António Filipe?' She'd forgotten the rest of his name. Maybe Roz had, too, if she was as careless about her husbands as Kate feared. But her mother answered:

'Soares da Silva?'

248

'That's the one.'

'He was my husband.'

Did the past tense mean that she had divorced him? Or was he dead?

'A very good-looking man, from his photo,' said Kate.

'I suppose he was.' Kate waited for Roz to expand the statement, but she sat in silence, frowning at her hands.

'Where did you meet?'

'In Portugal originally, then later in California.'

'Well,' said Kate eventually, giving up her attempt to draw her mother out, 'I'd better be going then.'

# 25

In the boardroom in Oporto there were only three men present at the meeting this time: António da Silva, Carlos Costa and Jorge.

'Thank you for your report, Jorge,' said da Silva. 'The practical details that you have provided concerning the lives of the Freeman couple will be invaluable to us when we move into the second part of our campaign against them.'

'Combined with the data that Pires and Oliviera have turned up, this information gives us a very full picture of who they are and what they have been doing,' said Carlos. 'Thank you, Jorge. And you can, of course, expect the usual bonus in your pay packet.'

'We'll speak again when we have planned the next phase in which you have a part,' said da Silva.

And Jorge, quite correctly, took that to indicate that his presence was no longer required.

'I'm visiting the librarian,' Kate told the porter as she paused by the glass window in the lodge of Leicester College. The lodge had been intended as the impressive entrance to an old and venerable institution, but somehow, after its recent refurbishment, it recalled only the ticket office of a minor London Underground station.

The porter nodded her through and she walked around a series of quads, past ancient staircases, through into a patch of grass shaded by an ancient beech, and up a flight of concrete steps to the library. The old part of the library included an elegant eighteenth-century reading room; the rest consisted of a prize-winning twentieth-century glass-and-steel structure which gave Kate vertigo when she thought of walking up the open-tread staircase to the top of the tower. Luckily for her, the librarian's office was in the old part of the building and on the ground floor.

As she pushed open the glass doors she saw immediately that changes had been made since her last visit. Then, every surface had been covered with warning notices, ensuring that Kevin Newton was rarely bothered by a student requesting access to one of his carefully shelved books. Now the only notice she could see was one welcoming her to the library, giving the name of the librarian and indicating the opening hours.

She knocked on the office door. Almost at once it was opened a couple of inches by a diminutive female figure who poked a cautious nose out of the narrow gap and inspected Kate through beady brown eyes. So, not everything had changed. This was the Hamster, a little older and greyer than before, but just as unhelpful, apparently.

'Open the door properly, Barbara, and allow our visitor to enter the office,' called the amused voice of Ben Knutson from within.

Kate entered. The Hamster still barricaded herself in with green-and-white carrier bags full of shopping, but these were now confined to a corner of the room and there was a clear passage from the door to the librarian's desk.

'Kate Ivory? Come on in and take a seat. Barbara, why don't you go and make us both a cup of coffee?'

'I'm off-duty in nine minutes' time,' she said, pleased to be obstructive.

'That gives you plenty of time to boil a kettle then, doesn't it?' came the swift reply from Knutson, delivered in a pleasant tone of voice that was difficult to argue with.

When the Hamster had snuffled out of the room, he said, 'That was an interesting enquiry of yours, Kate.'

'You've found the two men for me?'

'Not exactly. You know that we now have a database of all our old members, at least back as far as the eighteenth century – we're waiting for another grant to enable us to transfer the rest of the records on to the computer. Well, that makes it easy enough to trace someone's ancestor by undertaking a simple search – and that's what many people who write to me in my role as archivist are interested in.'

'And what did you find?'

'I'm afraid that we have never had an undergraduate named Ivory with the forename Jack – or John, or John Donald if it comes to that.'

'I'm not entirely surprised,' said Kate. 'I think he claimed to be a relation only so that he could make my acquaintance.'

'He must be a very keen fan of yours!'

'Unfortunately not. His intentions were more sinister than just obtaining a signed copy of one of my novels, I fear. How did you get on with Marcus Freeman? Did you get a result for him?'

'No, none for him either, at least not among our under-graduates – and I tried all the variations on his first name that you suggested. However, I did check the names you gave me against the general college database too, just on the off-chance.'

'And?' asked Kate eagerly.

'It was rather odd, really. I scored hits with both of them, but not exactly in the way you were expecting.'

'I can't wait. What did you find?'

'The first one to come up was Jack Ivory. You know that we let our student accommodation in the long vacation to tourists? We're just a superior B and B really during the summer.'

253

'I had heard that some colleges did that.'

'Well, one Jack Ivory booked a room for five days in late September – it was during the last week when we take in outsiders, in fact. After that the rooms are cleaned, and painted if necessary, and made ready for the new influx of undergraduates in October.'

'And yet he told me he was staying here in early October, in one of your guest rooms. I thought at the time that you probably needed every inch of space you could lay your hands on when the new undergraduates arrived.'

'Since it was so recent I went along to the bursar's office – they're the ones who handle these short-term lettings – and enquired whether anyone remembered him. And someone did. He had made a great fuss, apparently, insisting that if anyone phoned or called at the lodge for him they must be asked to leave a message instead of being told that he was no longer here. And he left a forwarding address so that any post that arrived could be sent on to him. And he did in fact ring several times to check whether any telephone messages had been left at the lodge. He treated this place as though he was an old and valued member of the Fellowship rather than someone using a B and B for a few days.'

'Did the bursary do what he asked?'

'They're a very polite crowd in there, so yes, they did.'

'It was quite a clever move on his part. When he told me he was staying in his old college, and they took messages, and he received post addressed here, I automatically assumed he was respectable, and that he must be the person he said he was. And also, he'd done enough research to convince me that we must be related.'

'Well, at least he didn't steal any of our silver spoons, it appears.'

'I'm glad to hear it.'

At this moment they were interrupted by the return of the Hamster, who brought each of them a mug of coffee, heavily sugared, and then retired to her corner, breathing gustily. She gathered up her carrier bags, stared pointedly at the clock as the second hand made its slow way up to the vertical, and then bustled out of the room.

'Thank you, Barbara,' called Ben. 'I'll see you in the morning. Good night.' But there was no reply from the shuffling figure. At least one member of the staff was intent on upholding the old, unfriendly traditions of Leicester College library, it appeared.

'Now, tell me about Marcus Freeman,' asked Kate.

'I found a Mark Freeman in the college at the time you suggested, but not as an undergraduate. He was on the maintenance staff.'

'What!'

'Well, he was quite young at the time and had just completed an apprenticeship, it would appear. Do you think it could be the same man?'

'But he seems so . . .'

'There's no reason why he shouldn't have been success-ful, you know,' suggested Ben. 'And if you think he appeared educated and sophisticated, well, he could have learnt something from his surroundings, both architectural and human – and why shouldn't he?'

'You're right. I shouldn't make assumptions about people: I assumed that Jack Ivory was honest because he'd been to Oxford. And Marcus Freeman is rich and said he'd been at Oxford, so I assumed he was educated here. It didn't occur to me that he was a plumber.'

'Electrician,' said Ben.

'Same difference. And the two of them weren't lying, were they? They both had been here, but not in the sense I understood. Though I do believe Jack told me how they both rowed for the college and that Marcus was only expected to get a 2.2 though he did in fact do better.'

'A lot better, from your description of him!'

'But no letters after his name – and I'm sure that's what he really wanted me to believe. How long was Mark Freeman here?' If it turned out that he'd worked at Leicester for thirty years, it was unlikely that this was the Marcus she had met.

'Nearly two years.'

'So it could be him, but again, no one's likely to remember him.'

'I'm afraid not. Though Alec Wright's a possibility. He came here as a lad and has remained ever since: he must be over sixty by now. Whether he remembers Mark Freeman or not is another matter.'

'Could you give me a contact number for him?'

'I can't do that. But you should find him in the college between eight and four tomorrow.'

Kate made a note of the name and the time. 'Thanks a lot. This is really helpful.'

'The question is, why should these two pretend to be what they're not?'

'To swindle my mother out of her hard-earned cash.'

'I do hope they've failed.'

'So do I. But I don't like to think of the satisfied smile on Jack Ivory's face this afternoon.'

'Is there anything else you need to know? I'm going to have to leave you and return to compiling a report on missing books quite soon.'

'I don't suppose you have photographs of the staff going back all those years?'

'Again, no. Though you could check in the history of the college. I think the latest volume goes up to about 1989. I have a copy on the shelf over there and you can look at it in the reading room if you like, though I can't allow it to leave the library, of course.'

Kate handed over the signed copy of her latest book, adding a short greeting to Knutson's wife. Then she thanked Ben profusely and retired to an inconspicuous carrel to look through the college history.

Luckily the author, a former vice-warden, had included a large number of photographs. Kate found portraits of wardens she had met in the past, only with more profuse, darker hair and smaller waistlines. There were triumphant rowing eights and a couple of victorious tennis players. There was a view of the new library building, its expanse of glass reflecting back the summer sky. And then there was a group photo of the college servants – did they still use that term? she wondered – butler, chef, waiters, gardeners and, at the back, three or four men who could well be the maintenance staff. The date was 1971, so Mark Freeman might be one of the figures in the back row. But the black-and-white reproduction was fuzzy. Faces were indistinct and wearing the impassive expressions common on these occasions.

Kate looked for someone of the right age and height. One man was much too short, but there were two other possibles, each with his face shadowed by the peak of his cap. Kate held the photo close to the reading lamp above her desk and wished she'd brought a magnifying glass with her.

It was a pity that Marcus had no obvious identifying marks on his face: a long scar would have been useful, or even a large mole. One of the young men did have regular features and a straight nose, and there was something about the mouth that looked familiar. But she'd be pushing it if she positively identified the figure in the photograph as Marcus Freeman.

She returned the book to Ben in the library office, thanked him and said goodbye. Even if she convinced Roz that she was right in believing that the young electrician working at Leicester College in the early seventies was her friend Marcus Freeman, she had the feeling that Roz would only shrug her shoulders and say, 'So what?'

'I might not convince Roz, but I'm getting more and more convinced myself that Marcus and Ayesha Freeman are con artists,' she said to Jon when he rang her later that evening.

'What is it exactly that you've found out?'

'Marcus Freeman, successful retired businessman, guru and charlatan—'

'Let's stick with the retired businessman for the moment.'

'And guru,' insisted Kate. 'That's what he is to Roz.'

'OK. If you say so. What else?'

'He started life as a maintenance man at Leicester College, staying there for two years before moving on. Later he claimed to have been an undergraduate at Leicester, and a friend of Jack Ivory's – who was also not a member of Leicester, but merely stayed there for a few days as a tourist in September. They backed up each other's stories and I believed them.'

'Maybe Marcus was just testing out your snobbery rating.'

'*Moi*, snobbish?'

'Perhaps he thought so – erroneously, obviously.'

'Thank you. And then we have his friend, Jack Ivory – whom he addresses as "Bill".'

'I've often wished that people would call me Fred. We all get these odd whims, don't we? Perhaps they're just living out a fantasy.'

'You're not taking me seriously, Jon.'

'OK. Where's the serious bit?'

'The two women who were burnt to death. The way that Marcus Freeman was there both times.'

'The fires were judged to be accidental, not arson.'

'You've checked?'

'Yes. And there's no proof that the Freemans profited from the women's deaths, so you can't get him on that, either. It's a pity we have no proof that Harding and Freeman are the same man: that might have helped the case for investigating him. You say he's a con artist. Why would he con old women who have no money to leave him? You see why I'm finding it difficult to persuade anyone to do anything as a matter of urgency?'

'Roz has money, invested in property.'

'But he hasn't stolen any of it yet, has he? As far as I can make out, all he's done so far is stop her from drinking too much alcohol and try to make her eat a healthier diet.'

'There was nothing wrong with her diet. She enjoyed a glass of wine occasionally, but so what?'

'I need something concrete.'

'I'm doing my best,' said Kate unhappily.

'Why don't we carry on this conversation when I'm down in Oxford next week?'

'You are? When?'

'Tuesday. It's my second interview, remember?'

'Of course. I'll write it down in large letters in my diary. What time will you be through?'

'About five, I should think. So we could go out to dinner somewhere. You choose.'

'There's a pub in Beckley you haven't been to yet. I'll book us in there.'

Kate was thoughtful when she came off the phone. Jon had sounded flippant before when she had talked about Roz, but he must have been taking her seriously after all. In spite of concentrating on finding a new job, he had taken the trouble to check her story. He must be more worried about Roz than she had thought. And since he worked with the police and gathered criminal intelligence, he must be interested in getting criminals off the streets and into prison.

Early the next morning Kate again presented herself at the lodge of Leicester College.

'I'd like to speak to one of your maintenance staff, Alec Wright.'

'You'd better try the bursary. The bursar's assistant deals with maintenance matters. There should be someone in at nine o'clock, so you haven't long to wait. Do you know your way?'

'I think so.'

She walked slowly round the front quad towards the archway in the opposite corner. The old buildings were draped in Virginia creeper that had turned every autumn shade from citrus yellow to deepest burgundy red. As she reached the corner, the sun came out from behind the clouds and lit the hanging foliage with points of flame so that the whole quadrangle looked as though it was consumed in fire.

I wish I'd brought my camera, thought Kate, and shivered, because there was something disturbing about the beauty of the scene. But then the sun retired behind another cloud and the blazing creeper was extinguished in an instant. Nothing to worry about, just the leaves turning, as they did every year.

As she entered the next quadrangle she glimpsed a grey-haired man in blue overalls entering a stairway on her right. She ran to catch up with him. Sure enough, in the hallway, under the staircase, she found him standing at an open cupboard door, inspecting the fuses.

'Alec Wright?' she asked.

He turned shrewd dark eyes, set in a weathered face, to look at her. 'Yes?'

'I was wondering whether you remembered a young electrician from thirty-five years ago. His name was Mark Freeman.'

'I might do. Why do you want to know?'

How much to tell him? If he'd liked the man, he wouldn't want to hear Kate's suspicions. On the other hand, he didn't look as though he'd have much time for a smoothie like Marcus, and if she didn't give him some sort of reason, he wouldn't answer at all.

'It's a long story, but I'm trying to save my mother from being ripped off by a man called Marcus Freeman. I think that he worked here for a couple of years around 1970 under the name of Mark rather than Marcus, and I want to find out more about him and show her that he's not all that he seems.'

'There's a photo of all of us in the college history book. Have you taken a look at it?'

'Yes. It's difficult to be sure that it's the same person after all these years, but it certainly could be. What was your Mark Freeman like?'

'Over six foot. Dark hair. All the girls thought he was good-looking, though he was too glib for my taste. And he was good at his job, of course.'

'I can imagine that. And the description fits, though his hair is silver-grey now. When you say "girls", do you mean students?'

'The college was all-male back in those days, and there were half a dozen men to every girl in the university, they say. But I reckon that some of them didn't mind playing around with a lad like Mark. Probably made them feel they were living dangerously.'

'And were they?'

Alec Wright laughed. 'You could be right, at that. He had the morals of a tom cat if you were to believe all his stories.

Look, I'd better be getting on, or there'll be no hot water on
this staircase before dinner time.'

'Do you think you could look at a couple of photos for
me? See if you recognise him.'

Kate pulled the prints she had made from Roz's camera
out of her bag and handed them across.

'This one, with the grey hair?'

'Yes. And here's one taken from a different angle.'

'Right. It could be. It could well be,' he said, examining
each one in turn. 'He's looking a bit smarter here than he
did when I knew him. Done all right for himself by the look
of it.'

'Are you sure it's the same man?'

'Not a hundred per cent, but it certainly could be the
Mark Freeman I knew.'

'Can you remember anything else about him? Do you
know where he came from?'

'He was Welsh. Couldn't you hear it in his voice?'

'It's gone, mostly. Do you know whereabouts in Wales?'

'Yes. I do, as a matter of fact, because when I was a kid
we used to spend a week in a caravan on the Gower Peninsula
every summer. Swansea or thereabouts, that's where he came
from.'

Footsteps approached the doorway and someone called,
'You there, Alec?'

'I'll have to go,' he said.

'Take this,' said Kate, retrieving the photos and handing
over her card. 'If you remember anything else you can give
me a ring.'

'I'm on my way,' Eric called to the man outside.

'Goodbye, and thanks a lot,' said Kate, following him out
and then turning in the opposite direction, back towards the
lodge.

\* \* \*

262

As she crossed St Giles's and walked past the Ashmolean Museum, Kate though over what she had learnt. Just confirmation of what she had suspected, really. And what about tracing Marcus – or Mark – Freeman back to Wales? Even knowing that he came from the Swansea area, she wasn't much further forward. Freeman might not be as common there as Jones or Davies, but she could bet there would be a few hundred of them nevertheless.

It was time to get on with her novel, she decided, as she walked through her front door. She had already parried one enquiry from Estelle that week. She would find herself delivering her manuscript late if she went on like this.

Despite feeling that it would lead nowhere, she penned a note to Eric Brayne, enclosing the best photo she had taken of his cat, Nelson. She added one of the pictures of Marcus and Ayesha, too, asking him to tell her whether these were Monica and Ned Harding. She knew that Mrs Morson had said he could be away for weeks, but Nelson might have got tired of travelling and they could be back in Hove by now.

There was only one remote possibility she might try out now, she thought, as she sat at her computer. She connected to the internet, called up the yellow pages and looked for electricians in the Swansea area, preferably called Freeman. Surely there were dynasties of electricians, just as there were of musicians, or even of writers?

In fact, to Kate's surprise, in the whole of Wales there was only one electrician called Freeman listed. And since the address was in Swansea, she thought it might well be worth her while to telephone him. Though what she was going to say when she reached him, she hadn't quite worked out.

# 26

'Freeman's Electrics,' said a female voice whose accent originated in the London area rather than South Wales. In the background, Kate could hear the sound of a small child demanding attention, and a churning sound that could well be a washing machine in mid-cycle.

'Is that Mrs Freeman?' she guessed.

'Yes, it is. Were you wanting Geoff?'

'As a matter of fact, I was trying to get hold of Mark Freeman. You wouldn't know where he's living, would you?'

'Mark Freeman? You mean Geoff's Uncle Mark?'

'That's the one. He moved to Oxford over thirty years ago. And then he was in Kent until recently. I was wondering whether you were still in touch with him?'

'No, not really. Him and Geoff's dad fell out years ago. What was it you wanted him for?'

This was a tricky one. Even if Mark wasn't the favourite son in the Freeman family, Mrs Geoff Freeman probably wouldn't want to hear what Kate suspected him of.

'It's a question of family history,' she improvised. 'I was trying to track down relatives on my mother's side, and I thought Mark Freeman could help.'

'You don't sound Welsh,' said Mrs Freeman doubtfully.

'Neither does Sheila,' said Kate. She didn't think that the name Ayesha would go down very well with the Freemans of Swansea.

'Do you mean that wife of his?'

'Yes.'

'Well, I hope for your sake you're not related to her. She has a winning smile and a wicked heart, that one.'

'I couldn't have put it better myself,' said Kate.

'If you really want to get in touch with them, the person you need to speak to is Geoff's old nan, Mark's mother.'

'She's still alive?'

'She's getting on a bit, of course, but she's living in an old people's flat, down near the marina. The warden checks she's all right every day, and she can still manage on her own, in spite of everything.'

'She sounds wonderful.'

'She is, though she's unpredictable in her temper. Mind you, I don't think she and Mark have much to say to each other these days. He doesn't like to remember where he came from, that one. And she has an unforgiving nature.'

'Could you let me have her phone number?'

'She wouldn't like to be phoned up by a stranger,' said Mrs Freeman. 'No, I don't think that would be a good idea.'

'Would she mind if I turned up unannounced on her doorstep?'

'I don't think she'd like it if I gave out her address to all and sundry. I don't know who you are, do I? Did you give me your name and say where you were from? I don't think so.' The small child in the background was becoming more insistent and the cries for attention were very close to the phone. 'I'll hang up now. I have to give Rhys his dinner or he'll be tearing the room apart. I'm sorry I can't be of more help, but you'd do well to give those two a wide berth, I'd say.'

'Thanks for all your help,' said Kate. 'Goodbye.'

When she had hung up she returned to her computer. It was amazing what you could find on the internet, even if you were in possession of the minimum of facts. It took a few seconds to find Swansea's official website, and only a few more to find details of sheltered housing. She would drive down there, she decided, the following day. Swansea didn't look too far away on the map, and all she had to do was stick to the M4.

She might have to knock on a few doors, but she was sure she could find Marcus Freeman's mother if she tried.

'I'm off to South Wales tomorrow,' she told her mother on the phone later that afternoon. 'Just doing a spot of research on the new book.'

'I'm glad you're turning your mind to your work again,' said Roz. 'I thought you'd given it up entirely in favour of tracking down the Freemans' secret lives.'

'Of course not!' said Kate, just a little too quickly to fool her mother. 'I wondered whether you'd like me to pop round this evening? Is there anything I can pick up for you from the shops?'

'How kind and thoughtful,' said Roz drily. 'I'm fine, Kate. I have everything I need. And I can't talk: I have to go out now. I have an appointment in fifteen minutes and I mustn't keep her waiting.'

There was a silence as Kate wondered where her mother was going, and whether she'd get her head bitten off if she asked.

'I'm off to see my GP,' said Roz, putting her out of her misery. 'I've been feeling off-colour for a little while now. Goodbye, Kate.'

Kate was left listening to the dialling tone in astonishment. She went into her workroom and switched on her computer but found that she couldn't concentrate on her novel. There was an email from Estelle:

Any sign of a completed MS yet, Kate? I'm off to San Francisco for a couple of weeks but I hope to be able to read it on my return.

Well, you'll be lucky, thought Kate, double-clicking on the recalcitrant chapter and staring moodily at the screen for another couple of minutes before returning to the kitchen for a mug of coffee and a chocolate biscuit.

At six o'clock she rang her mother.

'Roz? How are you? What did the doctor say?'

'You are being attentive today! One might almost think I was about to expire from some incurable disease.'

'Stop teasing and tell me what she said.'

'Nothing very exciting. That I was obviously run down, but she couldn't tell the cause without doing tests. I visited the nurse, who took an inordinate amount of blood, and told me to make another appointment to see the doctor in about ten days, when the results would be back. Detailed enough for you?'

'And she had no idea what was wrong?'

'I expect she could guess at various possibilities, but she wouldn't scare the punters before it was absolutely necessary.'

'Ten days seems like a long time.'

'They'll phone me if they have news any sooner.'

'And you'll let me know when they do?'

'If you insist.'

After she'd rung off, it occurred to Kate that, in spite of her off-hand manner, Roz was probably glad to have a daughter around to lean on if there was bad news. And although she would find it hard to wait ten days for the test results, she thought how much worse the delay must be for her mother.

Next morning Kate was up before sunrise. For a while after speaking to Roz she had wondered whether the journey to Wales was still necessary. Her mother was seeing a doctor, she would soon be getting some sort of treatment for whatever was wrong with her. But would the Freemans give up trying to get their hands on her money? She couldn't see it. They were probably planning their counter-measures already. She needed to have her own arguments ready to persuade Roz that she shouldn't listen to them. And anyway, she admitted to herself, she had reached the point where she wanted to find out about Marcus and Ayesha for her own sake – and she'd get on with writing her novel when she returned from Wales.

She filled a bag with a flask of coffee, a couple of apples and a cheese sandwich for the inevitable times when she would feel hungry and find that she was fifty miles from a service station. Then she gave some thought to what she would wear. She wanted to look respectable, but not too smart, as she didn't want to scare the old lady who found her on her doorstep. When she had dressed, she looked in the mirror and found that she looked like a librarian, or maybe a social worker, so she'd probably got it about right.

It was a chilly morning, and misty, but when she listened to the radio there were no warnings of fog on the motorway. She set off towards the A34 and Newbury, picking up the M4 at Chieveley. As she drove, she thought over what she would say to the older Mrs Freeman.

And what would she be like? Tall and imposing like her son, perhaps.

Maybe Kate could play the family history card again. It had worked for Jack Ivory, after all, and if Mrs Geoff Freeman mentioned her to her husband's grandmother, then the stories would dovetail. On the other hand, she would be found out as an impostor almost immediately. She hadn't done her homework the way Jack Ivory had, and she had no phoney family tree to show the old lady, either.

How old would she be, anyway? Marcus – or Mark, as she'd now have to call him – must have been born in about

1950 or '51. And supposing his mother had been twenty-five or so then, she must be somewhere near eighty by now. And formidable, with an uncertain temper, according to Mrs Geoff. Maybe she should pretend to be a social worker after all.

The mist had disappeared, but a light drizzle was falling now, covering the windshield with a greasy spray. Time for a coffee, she thought, and pulled into the Leigh Delamere service station. She added a muffin to her order: she would save her own supplies for later in the day.

She hoped that the coffee would revive some of her creative brain cells, but no good ideas were coming to her. She experimented to see the effect of raising her blood sugar level with a blueberry muffin, but that didn't work either. She climbed back into her car no further forward, and aimed for the toll bridge separating her from Wales. By the time she reached the outskirts of Swansea and left her car in the Park and Ride, she had decided to play it by ear. Inside the bus station she bought a tourist map of the town to give her some idea where she was going.

When she got off the bus in the town centre she was only too glad of the chance to walk after the hours spent in her car. She found on the map that the marina was, not unexpectedly, on the seafront, in an area that had once been docks. First of all, though, she walked down towards the beach.

The tide was out and she had several miles of wet sand nearly to herself. Only a distant dog-owner threw sticks and watched his animal race up and down the strand. The wind was fresh out here and blew the light rain into her face in sudden gusts. She walked half a mile in one direction then reluctantly returned to her starting point. Oxygen, she thought. That's what her brain had needed.

She toured the marina basin with its rows of expensive-looking boats, overlooked by equally expensive modern blocks of flats. Music blared out of open windows, followed by loud conversation. Kate didn't think it likely that the very elderly Mrs Freeman would be living in one of these flats. She walked on, past the theatre, exploring the streets just behind the seafront.

This was more like it. She found herself surrounded by solid red-brick flats, built around dark courtyards. A small notice informed her that these belonged to a local housing association, so she assumed that she had found the right place. Now all she had to do was find the one where Mrs Freeman lived – and there must be several hundred flats in this street, possibly more if she took one of the narrow side turnings. She looked around for a small corner shop, but she was too close to the town centre and there was no shop to be seen.

If Mrs Freeman was in her eighties, she could well be on the ground floor, Kate reasoned. It was also possible that residents had their names against their doorbells. She would have to go searching every entrance doorway and hope that she found what she was looking for before some observant resident reported her to the police as a suspicious character.

She entered the first courtyard. She found plenty of names, but no Freeman. And then, as she moved through an archway into another courtyard, she had a piece of luck: a small sign in the opposite corner directed her to the warden's flat. Of course, Mrs Geoff Freeman had mentioned that there was someone to keep an eye on the old lady, and if this was the case, then it followed that the warden would know where to find her.

She rang the bell. The warden was younger than she was expecting, and through the open door Kate could see into a pleasant hallway and sitting room painted a pale, light-reflecting colour. A small child was playing with a wooden puzzle on the floor.

'I can see you're busy,' said Kate, 'but I was wondering if you could tell me where I would find Mrs Freeman.'

'And you are?'

Kate fished out another of her business cards. Her supply was running low: she'd better print out another batch when she got back to Oxford. 'My name's Kate Ivory,' she said, thinking it best not to launch into an improbable story about why she wanted to see Mrs Freeman. It was a pity this small child was playing so very quietly in the background. If only it would distract its mother's attention, she might give Kate the information she wanted without worrying that she might be completely unknown to the person she sought.

'Is she expecting you?'

'No. But as you see, I've come quite a long way and I was hoping I could speak to Mrs Freeman before I drove back to Oxford.'

'Mummy!' called the child politely. 'This piece won't fit.'

'I'm just coming, Beth. I'll be with you in a minute. Now, Miss Ivory, if you walk across to the archway on your left over there, Mrs Freeman is in the building immediately opposite you. Go in through the door in the centre. She's on the first floor. If you press the bell, she should let you in. But I'm sure you're aware that she doesn't always welcome company.'

'Thank you so much.' It all sounded simple except that very last bit.

'Perhaps I should come with you,' said the warden doubtfully. But at that moment there was a loud cry from the child and the clattering of a wooden puzzle as it scattered across the floor.

'Don't worry. I'll find the way,' said Kate, as the child's cries grew more desperate.

The warden smiled in relief and turned quickly towards the child, closing the door behind her. In a moment Kate had crossed the courtyard and followed the directions to Mrs Freeman's flat.

# 27

The outside door to the flats was unlocked, and Kate walked upstairs to the first floor. There were two doors here and a card next to the bell on one of them read FREEMAN. Kate took a deep breath and rang. She heard footsteps – slow and shuffling – approaching the door, seeming to take a very long time to reach it. Then there was a rattle and click and the door opened a few inches, held by a strong chain. A suspicious blue eye stared at Kate through the narrow gap.

'Yes?' The voice was muffled.

Kate proffered the last of her cards, pushing it through the gap in the door. 'I was hoping that I could come in and talk to you.'

The card disappeared, presumably to undergo Mrs Freeman's scrutiny. There was a mumbling sound from the darkness beyond the door, as though she was chewing the card up and swallowing it. Kate waited.

'What do you want to talk about?' said the voice eventually.

'Your son, Mark, and his wife, Sheila.'

'Are they friends of yours?'

'Not exactly. Friends of my mother's, I'd have to call them. They're not really my type, I'm afraid.'

'What's your star sign?'

Kate's heart sank. 'I don't know.' Perhaps she should have said the first one that came into her head, but she had never been interested in astrology and she would probably have got it wrong.

There was a 'hmph' from behind the door which Kate couldn't interpret, then Mrs Freeman said, 'Very well.'

Kate wondered whether she had passed whatever test she was being given. Maybe she would have been sent away if she'd known her star sign. It was difficult to tell.

'Wait there.' The voice was still indistinct and Kate was having trouble understanding what Mrs Freeman was saying. It sounded as though she was speaking through a mouth full of rusty nails.

There came a rattling sound, and the chain was unhooked, the door was opened and Mrs Freeman stood revealed, the window behind her pouring its light on to the old woman's face and form.

She was of middle height, though as she was stooped and twisted it was difficult to be sure. Kate tried hard not to stare, but wished that the warden had warned her what to expect.

The white hair had been lost on one side of her head, the exposed scalp taut and shining and burning an angry pink. All down her face on the left side were scars, apparently the result of serious burns. The skin was puckered, pulled and twisted, yellow in places, red in others, and Kate winced at the thought of the pain and fear that must have accompanied the ruin of Mrs Freeman's face. One eye was gone, the lid pulled downwards, shielding the empty socket from view. There was no eyebrow over the wreck of her left eye.

Her left hand, too, was affected, the scarred skin disappearing into the long sleeve of her dark-coloured dress. She was leaning on a walking-stick, which made Kate realise that there must be more damage, more scarring to the parts of her body that were hidden by her heavy clothes.

'I suppose you'd better come in,' said Mrs Freeman reluctantly, and led the way along the mustard-yellow carpet, her footsteps lumbering and ponderous. 'Mind the steps,' she said, indicating the short stepladder with the broad treads that she had presumably used to open the door. No wonder she wasn't keen on visitors – it must be quite a performance to unbolt and unlock the front door.

The room that Kate entered was pleasant enough, in a 1950s way. Mrs Freeman had at least avoided the Festival of Britain style, and although dark and decorous, the furniture did look comfortable.

'Sit down over there.' The old woman indicated an armchair placed facing a window, so that she would have a good view of Kate's face. 'Would you like a cup of tea? Or have you not had your lunch yet? Can I find you something to eat?'

'Oh, no. I'm fine,' said Kate, unwilling to watch Mrs Freeman painfully making her way to the kitchen.

'That's good. As you can see, I don't find it easy to get about these days.'

'I'm very grateful that you've invited me into your flat like this. I can understand why you'd wish to keep me out – I'm a stranger, after all – but I'm curious to know why you decided to hear what I had to say.'

Mrs Freeman laughed, a strange, distorted sound that had nothing of humour in it.

'You've met my son and his wife?'

'Yes.'

'And you didn't take to them?'

Kate paused, then told the truth: 'No. I'm afraid I didn't.'

'Well, that's why I invited you into my home.' And she laughed the same dry, rusty laugh as before. Kate waited for her to explain.

'It was his fault, you know.'

'What was?'

'This. All this.' And she gestured with her good right hand at her face, her left hand and finally at her walking-stick.

'How did it happen?'

'In a fire. Can't you tell?'

'I did wonder.'

'I didn't think you were so mealy-mouthed. You seem the sort of girl who speaks the truth as she sees it.'

'I do try. But I don't always succeed, I'm afraid.'

'Did you know that he started out as an electrician?'

'Someone did mention it.'

'You couldn't tell by looking at him now, could you? But that's what he was, just like his brother. We're not fancy people, we've never lived the way he and that wife of his are living now. Good, plain tradesmen, that's what we are. Good at our job, working with our hands, and reliable. Who can expect anything more – or less, if it comes to that?'

'I would have thought that he'd be good at anything he took up. Are you telling me that he was an incompetent electrician?'

'I'm telling you that he met that evil woman, the one you mentioned, Sheila Williams.'

'Where did they meet?'

'In Oxford, when he took that job at the college.'

'Was she a student?'

'Her? No, she worked in Woolworth's. And it's a pity she didn't stay there, in my opinion. At least it was an honest job. But she always had ideas about the life she wanted.'

'And Mark went along with her?'

'He was easily led.'

Kate couldn't believe that the Marcus Freeman she had met ever did anything he didn't want to, but maybe she was underestimating Ayesha. 'And what happened next? They got married, I suppose.'

'Eventually, but not for some years. I believe Sheila saw how much money they could make and she wanted to be sure of her half of it – and that's when they made it legal.'

'I don't understand how they got from there to where they are now.' From what Mrs Freeman had said, it wasn't by working as an electrician or a shop assistant.

'Wickedness. That's what it was.' The stretched eyelid was quivering, and Kate wondered whether she should encourage Mrs Freeman to talk about what had happened or give up now and go home, leaving her in peace.

'Go on. Please,' she said. She had come so far, and she was doing it for Roz, she reminded herself.

'I lived in my own place before I moved to this flat. Nothing very grand – a terraced house in one of those streets that's packed full of noisy students these days, with their purple doors and painted flowers on the walls. But it belonged to me after my husband died, and it was all paid for, too. Mark and Paul – that's his brother – were always on at me to get it modernised. Said the electrics needed a complete overhaul and it was dangerous living in a place with old-fashioned wiring like that. Brittle insulation, frayed wires, they said. They'd do it for me and it wouldn't cost a penny. Well, of course I said yes, though I insisted on paying them for their materials. They were good boys in those days.'

Mrs Freeman put up a hand to touch her head where the skin was stretched and shiny, and the hair had never grown back.

'Are you sure—' began Kate.

'Someone has to stop them. I'm his mother, so I can't do it. But someone has to. What they've done in the past is wrong, but what they're planning now, that is evil. There's no other word for it.'

Kate waited quietly until she was ready to continue.

'Now Paul, he was subcontracted to work on a job up at

the university, and he couldn't turn that down to come and work for free for his mother. That's what I told him, "You go on and earn good money, Paul. I can wait." But Mark took a few days off from his job – he'd left the college and moved on. He was working somewhere in the Midlands by then. He said the boss didn't mind, he was owed some holiday, but I'm not so sure about it now. I don't think he'd been with the firm long enough to be taking days off.'

'They've been good sons to you,' said Kate.

'They were good enough boys,' said Mrs Freeman. 'But they'd been on at me – at least Mark had, I think Paul just went along with what his brother wanted – to sell the old house and move into one of these flats. It was after their dad died that they got this idea of selling up and investing the money in the two of them. In their futures, they said, and the grandchildren. They said I was rattling around like a pebble in a tin can. The cheek of it! Mark kept telling me I wasn't as young as I used to be and I should be living somewhere where they could keep an eye on me. I wasn't old, I told him! Not like I am now. But he wanted his share of the money from the house to set himself up in business. It was what his father would have done if he'd been alive, he said, though Joe had never mentioned a word about it to me. And in any case, I wasn't ready to be shipped off to a place full of lonely old widows and silly old men, I told him.'

'Looks like a very nice place to me,' said Kate, taking in the high ceiling and the broad sash windows.

'Well, maybe. But I was going to move in my own good time, not just when it suited him and his Sheila. Once they saw that my mind was made up, that was when they told me that if I was going to stay, then they had to do some work on the old place, and like a fool I agreed.

' "Come and stay with us while the work's done," Paul said. "We can put the boys in together in Darren's room and you can have Geoff's. His room's only small, and you'll have to share it with his posters of footballers, but it's not for long, is it? And it'll be even more uncomfortable in your place when we've got the floorboards up and the power's switched off at the mains."

'Well, since it was only for a few days while Mark got on with the rewiring, I agreed, and I moved over into Paul's house on the Wednesday afternoon so that Mark could get straight on with the work on Thursday morning. Sounds quite ordinary, doesn't it? I had no idea what was going to happen.'

The old woman stopped for a minute, kneading her scarred hand, as though collecting her memories together. Then she continued.

'It was that Wednesday evening, just as we were settled in front of the telly, that I realised I'd left my knitting behind. Stupid of me, but I don't like sitting idle of an evening, so I walked home to pick it up. Paul offered to drive me there, but it was only a twenty-minute walk and I like to stretch my legs when I can.

'I could tell there was something wrong as soon as I got inside. There was a funny smell, like fish – an oily fish, mackerel or herring, say. I picked up my knitting from the front room where I'd left it, and then I went upstairs to see what was wrong. And I soon found it, up there in my bedroom.

'Next to the wardrobe there was an electric socket on the skirting board, where I plugged in all the stuff I needed. Paul said it was a death trap, that they'd replace it with proper modern circuits, one socket for each piece of equipment. But it had always been good enough for me and his father, we'd never had any trouble with it, and I thought he was just making a fuss, trying to get me to get rid of the old house, the way he had before.

'I'd plugged in my electric bar fire, and the iron, and my bedside lamp, and the radio, of course, because I liked to listen to that while I was lying in bed at night when my husband had passed on. But I know I hadn't left the switch on. Well, that would have been a waste of electricity, wouldn't it? And I haven't got money to throw away like that.'

Kate pictured the wall socket bristling with cracked plugs and shredded wires. It was an accident waiting to happen, and it was a pity that her sons hadn't done something about it before.

'I saw immediately that everything was on, and there was smoke pouring out of the skirting board. That's where the funny smell was coming from. I'd have noticed the bedside light from outside, but the curtains were pulled close shut and you couldn't see even a glimmer through them.'

'I hope you didn't wait to investigate,' said Kate.

'I wasn't going to lose all my precious belongings,' said Mrs Freeman. 'I took my jewel box from the top drawer of the chest. There were a couple of carrier bags in the bottom of the wardrobe, so I stuffed in my best shoes, and my navy costume, then I went downstairs and rescued my photograph albums and my Post Office savings book, and the insurance policy, of course.'

'Then you escaped?'

'Then I remembered that Joe – that was my husband – kept the suitcase underneath the bed. There were plenty of things that I needed to take with me if the house was going to catch fire, and it hadn't yet, you know, so I thought I still had plenty of time. Those little presents that the children make for your birthday. The hat I'd bought for Paul's wedding and only worn the once.' She paused and looked at Kate. 'You think I'm an old fool, don't you?'

'I think anyone would attempt to rescue their life's

collected memories if they could,' said Kate carefully, wondering what she would try to rescue from her own burning house now that Susanna wasn't there. The memory key with all her work stored on it, she supposed. Her DKNY coat, perhaps. And the box of photographs sitting on her kitchen shelf. She couldn't think of anything else worth risking her life for.

Mrs Freeman was sitting slumped in her chair as though she no longer had the energy to hold herself upright.

'Can I make you a cup of tea?' asked Kate, worried.

'I don't like strangers poking about in my kitchen,' snapped Mrs Freeman, drawing herself upright again, ready to continue. 'Where was I?'

'You were going upstairs to fetch the suitcase from under the bed.'

'Ah, yes. That was a mistake, I admit. The trouble was that the socket was right next to the wardrobe, and that piece of furniture had belonged to my own mother. It was seasoned wood, and dry as tinder, not to mention the layers of varnish that my Joe had applied.

'When I got back to the bedroom the smoke from the skirting board was filling the whole of the upstairs, and I started to cough. Still, I thought, it's only smoke, like from a bonfire. It makes your eyes sting a bit but it doesn't do you any harm.'

No, thought Kate, not like a bonfire. This smoke was full of noxious fumes and Mrs Freeman was lucky still to be sitting here alive, in spite of her scars.

'And then I saw the flame, just like a golden flower at first, then bursting and spreading. It can't have been more than three seconds before the whole wardrobe was a mass of flames. You don't know how fast it moves until you see it.

'Stupidly, I still tried to reach the suitcase, but it was no good. My dress was on fire by then. All down this side,' she said, indicating. 'And my sleeve, too. It was time to run, but I was having trouble breathing. I don't know what would have happened if it hadn't been for the neighbours.'

'They saw the flames?'

'They saw that I'd left the front door open when I came in. I was worrying about the funny smell, you see, and I'd forgotten to close it.'

'Thank goodness for that.'

'They bundled me out of the house and called an ambulance. I lost everything in the end, of course. Anything that wasn't burnt in the flames or blackened by the smoke was ruined by the water from the firemen's hoses.'

'There must have been a report on the fire. What did it say?'

'That it was my fault. I was a forgetful old lady – me! – and I'd overloaded the socket and then left it switched on when I went to my son's place. As if I'd do such a thing! And they said the wiring was in a dreadful state. Well, I knew that. It's why the boys were replacing it all with something modern. They wrote it down as an accident, and when I came out of hospital, a couple of months later, they rehoused me in this flat. Said it proved that I needed someone to keep an eye on me now that I was getting so forgetful.'

'So the house was sold after all?'

'Yes. The structure was sound enough. It was the bedroom that was gutted, and I expect the place needed to be redecorated throughout. But the boys would have done that, and the rewiring, of course. I expect it looked good as new by the time they put it on the market.'

'And the insurance company paid out, no problem?'

'Yes. And it was then that I remembered that Mark had been asking me about it only a couple of weeks before the fire. He pretended it was all in my interest, but I know now it was in his. And that Sheila put him up to it, you can be sure.'

'But he can't have wanted to hurt you, not your own son.'

'Maybe he didn't. He thought I'd be at Paul's that evening, I'll say that for him. And he was supposed to be arriving really early on the Thursday morning, getting a train down from Birmingham. And that's what he maintained he did.'

Mrs Freeman paused for effect.

'Well?' prompted Kate.

'I wasn't unconscious, not completely, when they put me on a stretcher and took me out to the ambulance. I could still see, even if I only had one good eye left to me. And I saw him. I saw his white face and his eyes staring at me out of the darkness. He was in next door's garden, away from the lights. I reckon I was the only one as recognised him. And I'll never forget the expression of horror on his face. He knew then what he'd done all right.'

'You're sure it was him?'

'Would I make a mistake about my own son?'

Marcus in his fifties was a man you noticed, and looked at. As a man of, say, thirty, he must have been even more noticeable.

'He knew I'd seen him, but we never spoke of it. Perhaps he thought I'd forgotten about it during the weeks in hospital. They wanted me to go back for what they called cosmetic surgery, to hide the scars and rebuild what was left of my face, but I wasn't having it. I bear witness to the evil done to me by that woman and my son. And I remember his wickedness every time I look in the mirror.'

Kate shivered. 'It was a long time ago, wasn't it?'

'Maybe. But he and that woman haven't stopped. That was the start of it for them. I don't suppose he ever meant me to get hurt. He just wanted me to move out into a flat so that he could have the money to start his own business.

285

"Why don't you go in with Paul?" I asked him, but that wasn't good enough for him and that woman. Where will it ever end?'

'They're trying to steal some property from my mother at the moment,' said Kate. 'She's ill – I don't know what's wrong with her, but it's obviously serious. And those two have persuaded her for months now not to go to see her doctor. I think they hope she'll die and they'll walk off with her money.'

'If she gets better, it's then you've got to watch out for her.'

'Yes, I'm starting to see that.'

'And you've got to stop them. I'd do it myself, but I'm getting old and tired. And when it comes down to it he is still my son. I couldn't go to the police about him, could I?'

'It's not as though you've any evidence, I imagine,' said Kate.

'It's not the past I'm talking about,' said Mrs Freeman impatiently. 'It's what they're planning now. They're going to hurt my Paul.'

And at this point it became evident to Kate that Mrs Freeman wasn't interested in Roz, or any of the elderly women who had died in fires over the past years. She was on a mission to stop Mark and Ayesha for Paul's sake. And since she was no longer able to do it herself, she had fixed on Kate Ivory to do it for her.

'I don't understand how it was that they profited from their crimes,' said Kate. 'They didn't get anyone to change their will in their favour, did they? That would have caused immediate suspicion, I would have thought.'

'That was her doing. She got a job working for a solicitor, and it was there that she got the idea. Apparently the man she worked for spent all his time helping rich people to avoid paying tax when they died. Don't ask me the details, I didn't understand it, but they would set up a trust so that all their property was given away while they were still alive and no tax was due to the government when they died. Wicked, thieving people. But it meant that Mark and Sheila didn't need to persuade anyone to change their will: they'd already creamed off all the property and any money there was into a trust fund they'd persuaded some rich old fool to set up.'

'And they were the trustees?'

'They had a friend, a respectable-looking man called Wilton, and I know he was in it somewhere. They'd explain how the old woman could be sure that her money was going where it would do most good by writing a letter to say what should be done with it. But it would have looked too fishy if Mark and Sheila were the trustees, I suppose.'

'Did they tell you about this?' The name Wilton was ringing a bell at the back of Kate's mind, but she didn't have time to chase up the reference as Mrs Freeman was speaking.

'They wouldn't have dared. No, they tried it out on an old friend of mine, and I couldn't forgive that. I suppose you could call it their practice run.'

'Did they get away with it that first time?'

'No. Luckily for her, her son had gone away to college and become a solicitor himself instead of going into the steelworks. He looked into it for her, and when Mark and Sheila heard about it they got the wind up and cried off before any harm was done. I expect they did their homework a bit better after that.'

'And they went on to succeed with others?'

'They wouldn't tell me about it, but I could see they were getting a lot of money from somewhere. Of course, he got his start when he and Paul got their share of the house money. I should never have listened to them, but Mark can be very persuasive when he puts his mind to it.'

And after years of practice he could still charm the proverbial birds from the trees. Kate could see him spending his windfall on expensive clothes and a flash car, and probably renting a flat in a respectable area, to get himself into the right circles. And where would he meet rich widows? Why, at the local church, most likely.

'I've noticed he has a convincing line of talk,' said Kate.

'But now he's going too far.' Mrs Freeman was leaning forward, glaring at Kate with her one eye. 'When it comes to cheating his own flesh and blood, he's got to be stopped.'

'How exactly does he plan to hurt Paul?'

'He's always been a heavy smoker and now it's catching up with him. Emphysema, they say it is. He's not a rich man, but he lives on his own now that Hazel's passed on, and he doesn't spend much on himself. And then there's the house, of course. Even here in Swansea the prices are going up – not as daft as they are in England, but still, even a little house like his is worth something these days. And Paul's not going to make old bones, you can see that.'

'And Mark thinks he might inherit something from his brother one day?'

'But it should go to Geoff and Emma, and little Rhys, shouldn't it? And Paul's in no condition to stand up to Mark. It's all wrong, I've told him so. And then there's Sheila, telling him to give up his medicines, and not to bother seeing the doctor. She has some potion or other she's feeding him, and telling him that it's all a question of thinking positively, when anyone can see the poor man can hardly breathe without his oxygen.'

'I'm sorry. It must be very difficult for you.'

'It isn't as though she believes in what she's saying. You can see it's all an act. She'd be down at the doctor's faster than anyone if she was feeling a bit off-colour, and yet she's trying to stop Paul from getting any treatment.'

'She's doing the same thing to my mother.'

'They're not getting it all their own way, mind you. Geoff's a simple man, but he's not so simple he couldn't see what Mark was doing. He's been warning his father against Mark, and telling his uncle to keep away from him too. We haven't seen him around so much these past weeks, but you can bet he'll be back, and singing from the same old hymn sheet. Paul will tire of it all one of these days, and I don't know what will happen then.'

'I know just what you're talking about.'

'You've got to stop them!'

'How can I do that? I can't convince anyone that they really are dangerous.'

'I can't go to the police. I couldn't do that to my own son. But you could tell him that the game's up. That it's not just his mother who knows what he's been doing. You're on to him as well, you can say. He wouldn't dare carry on after that.'

Kate wasn't at all sure about that, but Mrs Freeman was breathing fast and picking agitatedly at her skirt, so she didn't contradict her.

'I suppose I'd better be getting back to Oxford now,' she said.

'But you won't forget what I've told you?'

'No, of course not.' She had a lot to think about on the journey home.

'I only told you all about Marcus and Sheila so that you could stop them from fleecing Paul and swindling Geoff and his family. I'm not a one to gossip otherwise, you know.'

Kate could well believe it. She didn't think that Mrs Freeman was one to socialise much, let alone gossip.

The old woman was leaning forward, her face close to Kate's. Her hands were clenched in her lap, the veins knotted, the scars livid on her left hand. 'You're a determined girl, I can see that. You won't stand any nonsense from Mark and Sheila. You go and tell them what you've learnt from his mam, and that they have to keep away from Paul with their daft ideas.'

'I'll see what I can do,' said Kate, promising nothing.

Mrs Freeman rose carefully to her feet and reached for her stick. Kate's card lay before her on a low table.

'Funny that you're called Ivory. It was my name before I was married. You and I could be related.' She stared hard at Kate's face. 'Not that I can see any likeness.'

No, thought Kate, though perhaps they shared a certain determination to get their own way. 'I'm afraid I know very little about my father's family,' she said, which was even truer now that she knew that Jack Ivory was an impostor.

Mrs Freeman walked Kate to the front door and stood there, watching her as she descended the staircase.

# 28

Outside in the street, Kate felt in need of another brisk walk and some fresh sea air after the close atmosphere in Mrs Freeman's flat. It wasn't just the fact that the heating was turned on and the windows were sealed shut, but the intensity of the old woman's hatred of her daughter-in-law and her distrust of her own son were adding to the poisonous feel of the place.

It had stopped raining, the sky was washed a pale, clear blue and a breeze was blowing off the sea. The tide had turned and the beach was narrower than it had been when she was here earlier, but she could still stand and drink in the view: the wide sweep of the bay stretching away on either side of her, the distant mountains, the greyish-blue sea.

This was a place that gave you a feeling of infinite possibilities, she thought. Did Marcus come here when he was a boy and dream of the life he would have when he was a man? Was this the place that started him out on his life of crime? The wind forced the hair back from her face and tugged at the ends of the scarf she had tucked into the neck of her jacket. Her hands were cold in spite of the brisk pace she was maintaining.

It wasn't all in her imagination: Marcus had nearly killed his own mother and attempted to defraud one of her friends. She could no longer fool herself that Roz would be all right now that she was seeing a doctor. Marcus and Ayesha had probably already laid the plan that would take her money and her life.

She returned to her car and drove a little further along the coast, thinking all the time about how she could convince anyone of Marcus and Ayesha's wickedness. If anyone asked Mrs Freeman to repeat what she had said about them, the old woman would obviously deny everything. As she had said, Marcus was her son.

Late in the afternoon Kate turned towards the motorway and home.

Back in Oxford, Kate reminded herself that as far as she knew, the Freemans had not yet stolen any of Roz's money. She was safe, at least until they had their hands on her property.

But who would believe her story? If only she could prove that the Freemans were also the Hardings.

Tomorrow she would ring Anne Morson and find out when her brother-in-law was expected home from his travels. Her letter would be waiting for him when he arrived back at his flat, and the photographs should prove one way or the other whether his Hardings were her Freemans. The fact that she had included the portrait of Nelson – printed out on glossy A4 photographic paper – meant that he would contact her, if only to say thank you. And if he wasn't yet back in Hove, she would persuade Anne Morson to provide a contact address or phone number for him.

She wondered how many other identities the Freemans had taken on over the years, and how many other old ladies had been conned out of their money. They had to be stopped, and at the moment it seemed that she was the only person interested in doing so.

Next morning things started to fall apart.

It began with an email from Neil Orson:

Kate, I wonder whether I could ask you for a firm date for the delivery of your new MS? No pressure, of course, but I need to plan ahead.

She hadn't written more than a few hundred words these past couple of weeks. She'd better see how much needed to be done and work out a schedule for getting it completed. What had he said before about a deadline? The end of November, she thought. She checked. Yes, that was it. She sent him an email promising that the manuscript would be delivered on the 29th. Then she divided the remaining work by the number of days left to finish it and realised that she really had to sit down and get on with some writing.

She worked for two hours before she was interrupted by a telephone call.

'Kate? It's Roz.'

Kate was surprised. Her mother wasn't someone who spent much time on the phone chatting to her friends, or to her daughter.

'Hi.' She didn't ask Roz how she was in case she took offence.

'I wonder whether I could pop round at lunch time. Don't bother about food – I don't want to interrupt your work. It's just that there's something I want to discuss with you.'

'One o'clock all right for you?' Kate asked.

'Fine. See you then.'

Then, looking in her diary, Kate saw that Jon was due for his second interview the following day. She'd better book them in to the pub she had suggested, and this evening she could arrange when and where they were to meet. She found the phone directory and made a couple of calls. Somehow twenty minutes had passed before she could return to her work.

She made herself a mug of coffee and took it back to her

desk. Time for at least one more hour's work before looking in the fridge to see what she could give Roz for lunch.

As she sat staring at her blank screen, trying to come up with some witty dialogue, a niggling thought came into her head and wouldn't go away: why had Jack Ivory not made more of an effort to destroy the photographs that Roz had taken on the evening of her supposed birthday?

Was it because he and the Freemans were giving up and moving on? Perhaps they had decided to concentrate on Marcus's brother, Paul. But everything she had learnt about Marcus showed that he didn't give up until he had achieved what he had set out to do. Then why were the photographs no longer relevant?

Roz arrived in a taxi, apparently not feeling up to the walk from East Oxford.

'And I couldn't face the drive through the traffic in the town centre,' she said. She looked more fragile than ever.

'Come and sit in the kitchen and watch me make an omelette,' said Kate, who had already put out a bowl of salad and a board ready for the baguette warming in the oven. 'Would you like a drink?'

'Oddly enough, I'd rather like a mug of herb tea,' said Roz.

'I have apple and cinnamon,' said Kate, putting on the kettle.

Once she had dished up and they had started to eat, she asked, 'So, what was it you wanted to talk about?'

'I think I may have done something rather stupid.'

Kate laughed. 'Only one thing? I thought it was a speciality of yours!'

'This one is rather expensive.'

Kate sat and waited. She had a nasty feeling that she already knew what her mother was going to say.

'You know that I haven't been feeling too well these last

few weeks. Well, Marcus and Ayesha have talked me into something that I don't think I would have done if I had been feeling stronger.'

'A discretionary trust?'

'How did you know?'

'They've done it before.' She didn't say that the settlor usually ended up dead shortly afterwards.

'They were very convincing about the inheritance tax benefits and explained that I could leave a letter saying how I wanted the money spent once I was no longer here.'

'Who are the trustees?'

'One of them is an investment advisor that Marcus has dealt with before, called William Wilton.'

'Have you met him?'

'No.'

'I think you might have done, only he was calling himself Jack Ivory on that occasion. I heard Marcus addressing him as "Bill" the other day. And his sister is Laura Wilton, only he told me that was her married name. It's too much of a coincidence for it to be someone else, don't you think?'

'Laura Wilton is the name of the other trustee, and I was told that she is his wife.'

Now it was Kate's turn to be surprised. But as she thought about it, it made sense. 'I wonder whether they've been the trustees before. But that's not important now. We have to get your money out of this trust. How much did you put in?'

'I have . . . had . . . a house that I was letting, one of the properties that Avril and I have developed. I bought out her half of it and it's been bringing me in a nice little income.'

'So you didn't have a mortgage on it?'

'Not on that one, no.'

'We have to get it back.'

'I don't think we can. I think I've lost it.'

'I'm sure they think so. I believe one of them phoned Jack Ivory while he was at my place to tell him that the job was nearly over and that his part in it was done. Don't let them get away with it! Go and see a solicitor.'

'I will do. When I'm feeling a bit better. The silly thing is, I thought I was doing something sensible. The beneficiary of this trust was supposed to be you, not Marcus Freeman. "The descendants of Henry Ivory".'

'Marcus's mother was an Ivory before she married. I bet her father was called Henry.'

'How on earth did you know that?'

'She told me. But it's a long story, so we'll leave it for the present. I think the fact that you're an Ivory too was a bit of luck for them. They can't have planned it that way.'

'No, but they used it once they'd discovered the coincidence. I wonder what they'll do now. I suppose they'll just disappear, taking my property with them. Or they'll transfer it into another fund somewhere in the middle of the Pacific.'

'I could ask Jon about it, if you like.'

'I doubt there's anything he can do either. I've been stupid, that's all.'

'They are very persuasive people. And I don't suppose they mentioned a son, did they?'

'They had a boy called Justin, but he was born with a serious heart defect and died a year or so ago.'

'I'm not sure I believe in Justin. He might be an invention, you know. I was wondering about a man named Jefferson – that's his first name, by the way. He's about twenty and I think he really is their son.'

'They've never mentioned him to me.'

'More salad?'

'No thanks.'

'I think it all started with those letters, threatening dire consequences if you didn't send money to an accommodation address.'

'They weren't exactly threatening, more like predictions. And they only suggested contributing to expenses. What did they have to do with Marcus and Ayesha? They didn't write them, did they?'

'I don't think so. But did you show them yours?'

'I did, as a matter of fact.'

'I think they cashed in on someone else's scam. They made the nasty things happen, and in such a way that they fitted in with the predictions. And they convinced you that they were protecting you from evil influences. Admit it, you are inclined to be a little superstitious.'

'I do admit that not all reality in this world is visible to the material eye.'

'You've been listening to Ayesha! Or rather, Sheila. And you do know that his name is Mark, don't you?'

'Well, you can't blame them for wanting something more glamorous.'

'I feel like blaming them for everything. You know that they sent me threatening emails, don't you? I think they based them on your letters, but they didn't get the style right, so it was obvious they came from a different source. They wanted me to worry about something other than you and your friends. So they had me mugged near the towpath.'

'You didn't tell me about that!'

'I didn't want to worry you and anyway, I wasn't really hurt.'

'You think they were the muggers?'

'I think that Jefferson found three likely youths and set them to follow me when I was out on a morning run. I told them I went running on my own, remember? They chose a misty morning when no one could see what they were doing.

I'm quite predictable, I suppose. I wouldn't be hard to follow.'

'Possibly. The connection is a little tenuous.'

'Not if you'd seen the message. And then the next time, they killed my cat. I'll never forgive them for that.'

'I'm really sorry about that. I know how upset you are, but again, you have no proof, have you?'

'We can't prove anything against them!' shouted Kate in frustration.

'I'll visit a solicitor,' said Roz soothingly. 'Maybe there is something to be done about the discretionary trust, as you suggest.'

'I bet he's too clever to leave a paper trail,' said Kate gloomily.

'I've brought some of your favourite almond croissants from the Maison Blanc. Here, have one of them with your apple tea. It will calm you down.'

'Any news yet from your doctor?'

'No. It's a bit early for that yet.'

'I wonder who "Jack Ivory" really is?'

'I thought you said he was Bill Wilton, married to Laura.'

'How did he know so much about the Ivorys?'

'He didn't know much, though, did he? Only as much as he could find by spending an evening Googling.'

'I thought I was finding out something about my family at last.'

'If you really want to know, you could do the research yourself.'

'I suppose so. When I have the time. I really must finish this novel I'm supposed to be writing. I've told Neil Orson I'll deliver it on the twenty-ninth of November.'

'Then you'd better get back to work. I'll ring for a taxi.'

'I'll run you home.'

'No, you get on with your book, Kate. I'm not exactly broke yet, you know.'

When she had put her jacket on, she paused by the front door.

'Just one more thing, Kate.'

'Yes?'

'You don't know a good, practical architect, do you? You know the sort I mean: someone who can help us with our next conversion, and who doesn't charge the earth. No, I don't suppose—'

'Yes. As a matter of fact I do. Remember my cat-loving neighbour, Brad? He just happens to be an architect, and he mentioned that this was the kind of work he was looking for. You can knock on his front door if you like. He works from home, so he should be in.'

'I might just do that. And thanks for not being furious with me for losing your inheritance.'

'You will be careful, won't you, Roz? They've invested months of their time in stealing your money and I can't see them giving up now. Promise me you'll keep them out of your house.'

'They still have a key,' admitted Roz.

'Then get your locks changed. Would you like me to arrange it?'

'No. I'll get on to it first thing.'

Kate left it there. Roz was sounding tired and she didn't want to nag. She'd check again tomorrow.

Late that afternoon, Kate rang Jon. He didn't answer the phone and she decided he was probably preparing for his second interview tomorrow. She was tempted to put the phone down without leaving a message, but found herself pouring out the conversation she'd had with Roz. Although there was no encouraging voice at the other end, she felt strangely comforted that she had shared the load. She realised she was looking forward to seeing Jon tomorrow.

* * *

Next morning brought a note from Eric Brayne thanking Kate profusely for the photograph of Nelson. He would have it properly framed and give it pride of place among his other family portraits. Almost as an afterthought, he added that he had looked carefully at the picture of Marcus and Ayesha, but he couldn't be absolutely sure that they were the Ned and Monica of his acquaintance. There was a similarity, certainly, but nothing he could swear to in a court of law.

Kate's heart sank. She realised she had been relying on his identifying the Freemans as the Hardings. It was a disappointment, but perhaps not so bad now that Roz herself had seen through the pair. She would talk to Jon about them, and perhaps someone, in some dim department somewhere in Whitehall, would open a file on them, or put their names and alleged crimes into a database on a computer. One day they would be brought to book for what they had done.

'How did it go?' she asked Jon as soon as they had both arrived at the pub.

'I'm quietly confident,' he said with a smile. 'They'll be letting me know within the next two days whether I've been successful. And if I do get it, I'll give three months' notice and then I'll be living on your doorstep by the early spring.'

'In Oxford we call that late winter,' said Kate.

'Since the unit's breaking up anyway, they might let me go a bit earlier.'

'The New Year? That sounds appropriate.'

'What would you like to drink? I think we should celebrate now, just in case.'

'I can't imagine you'd be confident about the outcome unless you thought you had it in the bag.'

'How about a bottle of pinot gris?'

'Better make it half a bottle as we're both driving.'

When their first course arrived, Kate said, 'I'm sorry about that rambling message I left on your phone yesterday. It's just that I hate feeling so powerless to stop the Freemans and Wiltons from preying on other vulnerable women.'

'That's all right. I'm sorry I wasn't around to pick up the telephone. But please, Kate, don't think of confronting them with their crimes. These are dangerous people.'

Kate ignored the warning. 'And I don't see why they should get away with all they've done to Roz, either. They were supposed to be her friends!'

'Can't you leave it to the professionals now?'

'And then there are the Wiltons, Bill and Laura. Where do they fit into it?'

'I can help you over Laura and Bill Wilton,' said Jon. 'After I picked up your message yesterday, I made a few calls and did a little research of my own. It appears that they were both actors at one time – in fact that's how they met. It was too late to ring you and tell you last night, and I knew I was seeing you today.'

'I've can't remember seeing them in anything on the box.'

'I don't think they've been more than extras on television. But they are professionals, and they've worked in provincial theatre. I think they enjoyed playing the parts that Marcus Freeman wrote for them, and from what you've said, they were both very convincing.'

'It wasn't kind.'

'No. You're right, kindness certainly didn't come into it.'

'There were one or two things I should have picked up on.'

'Like what?'

'He said that he had itchy feet and wanted to go travelling, but he must have been in his thirties then, not his teens or twenties.'

301

'He was probably in a touring company.'

'I hadn't thought of that. And then there was the way he kept saying he didn't want to gossip about Marcus behind his back – yet all he said about him was that he was an upright, moral man. Why should he feel bad about saying that?'

'Are he and Laura much alike?'

'Superficially. But then, married couples often are, I've noticed. And they had different accents, but that happens to real siblings too, doesn't it, especially if one of them has been to Oxford.'

'Anyone could have been taken in, Kate. Don't feel bad about it.'

When they had finished their meal and returned to the car park, Jon paused before getting into his car.

'Will you be pleased if I get the job?'

'Yes. Very pleased.'

# 29

Kate drove home in a more cheerful mood. Jon had cared enough to find out about the Wiltons for her. He had had to return to London, but they would see one another in a few days' time. And perhaps in the New Year they would be living so close to each other that they would be able to meet every night of the week if they wished. She knew that Jon would like them to buy a place together, but she was very fond of her house in Jericho and would need some persuading to move out of it.

'Together we could get a really lovely house,' he had said. 'If we pooled our resources, that is. It could be big enough for you to have your own private area. A large garden, too – I'd cut the grass, you wouldn't have to worry about that. We wouldn't be tripping over one another all the time, I promise you, Kate. You could do as much solitary thinking as you wanted.'

She could have pointed out that Oxford was nearly as far from the sea as it was possible to get in an island like Britain, and what was he going to do about his beloved boat? But she left him to think of that for himself.

'Iffley,' she said thoughtfully. 'It's like a village on the outskirts of the city. And there's a very nice pub out there, I believe. And it's on the river, of course.'

She'd always fancied a rose garden. Old-fashioned scented roses. Clematis and honeysuckle. And a hammock. And one of those summerhouses that turned on its axis to catch the sun throughout the day.

303

* * *

Although it was late by then, the phone rang a few minutes after Kate arrived home.

'Kate? It's Roz.' She sounded livelier than Kate had heard her for a long time.

'How are you?'

'That's what I'm ringing about. I'm glad I've caught you at last. I know it's late, but I just had to tell you.'

'Go on!'

'My GP phoned with my test results. I'm suffering from some nasty form of anaemia, but they can treat it. I'll be back to my old self in no time.'

'Thank God for that!'

'You were afraid I had something terminal, weren't you?'

'Yes. I can admit it now: I was scared stiff it was leukaemia.'

'The symptoms are similar, I believe. But it's all right, Kate. I have to go down to the surgery tomorrow and she'll start me on a course of treatment straightaway.'

'I'm so relieved.' Kate could hardly speak. It was irrational, she knew, but she was practically in tears at her mother's news.

'Shall I call in after you've seen the doctor tomorrow?'

'Could you leave it till later? I have one or two things I have to do.'

It was half past ten when Kate decided she would call in on her mother. She was driving down the Cowley Road when she heard the first of the fire engines.

As she drew nearer to the turning for Roz's house, the sirens grew louder. She turned left. Roz lived a couple of hundred yards down this street, but she had to pull in and leave her car on a yellow line, for the road ahead was closed.

'Roz!' she shouted. 'Are you all right?' It was ridiculous. There was no way that her mother could hear her.

But now she was remembering Marcus's mother, old Mrs Freeman, and the way her scalp shone pink where the hair would never grow again. Was this to be Roz's fate, too?

Calm down, Kate, she told herself. You don't know yet that it's Roz's house that's on fire. But she did, she did.

First the mugging. Then Susanna's death. Now Roz. It all made some kind of insane sense.

The Freemans had persuaded Roz to sign the documents that gave them control of her property, and now they were going to kill her since she hadn't obliged them by dying of leukaemia. It must have been a great disappointment to them when Roz had phoned with her good news. 'Not leukaemia,' she would have told them. 'Only a very nasty form of anaemia. But curable.'

Who had done it? Marcus? Jefferson?

She was pushing her way through the crowd of gaping bystanders now, moving closer to Roz's house, but it felt as though she was snared in one of those nightmares where you struggle to move, to run, to scream – and nothing happens. You are trapped, immobile, dumb, forever trying to escape. Running on the spot. Unable to advance.

'No, miss, you can't come through here.'

She woke up at last, eye to eye with a young police constable.

'It's my mother,' she gasped. 'She lives here. I have to find her.'

'No one is inside the house,' he assured her. 'No one,' he repeated, seeing that she wasn't taking in his words.

'She's there. They've killed her.'

'No one is dead.'

She stopped then. 'Are you sure? Number forty-two.'

'That's right. The householder has been taken to the JR—'

'I knew it!'

'Just to make sure she's all right. Really, she wasn't injured. She's going to be all right.'

'Can I see her?'

'I think you'd better try the hospital. There's nothing you can do here.'

'You're sure she wasn't injured?'

'No one was injured. She had a lucky escape.'

Kate turned round. Behind her she could hear the shouts and commands of the firefighters, the gush of water from hoses. All around was the glare of the emergency lighting that had been brought in.

But Roz was safe, he'd said.

Kate started to run. She reached her car and turned it around, fast, bumping the kerb front and rear, accelerating back the way she had come, turning right into the Cowley Road, ignoring the screech of braking cars and blaring horns. She didn't care. She just wanted to get to the JR and find out for herself what had happened to her mother.

'She's all right,' she told Jon an hour later, when she had left Roz dozing in a hospital bed. 'They're keeping her in for observation, that's all.'

'What happened? Can you tell me?'

'I can tell you exactly,' said Kate exultantly. 'Roz was waiting for them. She finally believed everything I told her about them and so she set a trap.'

'Oh my God! Didn't she realise how dangerous it was!'

'I expect she found it exciting. Anyway, she still had my camera, if you remember. She had the good sense to turn off the sound effect so that it was quite silent when she pressed the button.'

'And who did she catch?'

'Marcus and Jefferson, of course. They checked that she was asleep, and you know how awful she's looking, so it

306

wasn't difficult for her to pretend she was out for the next twelve hours.'

'Then she crept after them in her stockinged feet?'

'More or less, though I believe she was dressed in jeans and trainers under the duvet, ready for a quick escape.'

'If this is what she's like when she's ill, God preserve us when she's recovered her health.'

'She's a really good photographer, Jon. She used all the right settings and the photos are brilliant. Really clear.'

'So you've got the camera?'

'Yes, and I've downloaded the photos on to the computer, and copied them to a CD as well, just to be safe.'

'Email me a copy. I'll phone someone I know in Oxford and they can pick up the Freemans straight away. Just one thing before I rush off: I assume that as soon as the Freemans had gone, Roz did the sensible thing? She left the building and called the Fire Brigade from a neighbour's house?'

'Nearly right. She went looking for the family photographs first, and a couple of pieces of inexpensive jewellery – with sentimental value, naturally.'

'Oh my God!'

'It's all right. She was out of there in time.'

'Kate, do you realise just how fast a fire takes hold?'

'I do, as a matter of fact.'

'And I'll fill in the details later, but I have a piece of good news for you. I'm pretty sure that we can save Roz's money for her. The Freemans wouldn't have had time to complete the deed, let alone get it signed.'

'She'll be relieved when I tell her.'

'I'll talk to you later. I'm off to deal with the Freemans now.'

'Would you like me to give you their address?'

'Oh, thanks.'

# 30

When Ayesha answered the front doorbell she didn't recognise the young man who stood there. He was in his early twenties, she guessed, dark-haired, good-looking, with well-muscled forearms.

She particularly noticed this last because he was holding a gun. In fact, he was pointing it at her. She had no idea what sort of gun it was, but it looked dark and heavy and very, very real.

'You will make no noise,' he said, as she opened her mouth to scream. The gun's dark eye was raised a little so that she could stare straight into it. She closed her mouth.

'Good. Now, walk beside me into the living room. No, on this side,' and he indicated with his right hand, the one that was holding the gun. She couldn't take her eyes off it, though she noticed his accent, soft and with a tendency to pronounce the final 's' of a word as 'sh'.

'Do not be afraid. I will not harm you if you do what I tell you. Walk.'

And so she walked beside him, slowly and deliberately so that he wouldn't think she was going to do anything stupid, or warn the two men who were enjoying their first drink of the evening, sitting beside the open fire.

'Who is it?' called Marcus as their footsteps approached the door and Ayesha turned the handle so that she and the young man could enter.

'Do not be afraid. Do not cry out,' he said in his reasonable voice. 'Please remain seated where you are.'

309

'Who are you? What do you want?' Marcus was bluster-ing, but the young man remained calm.

'You do not need to know.'

Without taking his eyes from Marcus and Jefferson, he spoke to Ayesha. 'There is tape in my rucksack. Remove it, carefully.'

Ayesha hesitated.

'Please do as I tell you. As I have said, I will not harm you if you do what I say, but if you disobey me I will shoot one of those two.' He looked down at her. He was more than a foot taller than she was, and it was not only his forearms that were well muscled.

Ayesha removed a large roll of duct tape from his rucksack.

'You, Marcus, stand up and turn around.' Marcus did as he was told, silenced by the note of authority in the young man's voice. 'Now put your hands together behind your back. And you, Ayesha, will secure them at the wrists with the tape. Do not try to cheat, because I will check, and I am holding the gun.'

'I'll need scissors to cut the tape,' objected Ayesha.

'No, it is already cut to the right lengths. Unwind one at a time and do as you are told.'

There was a movement from Jefferson's chair and the gun swung round. Jefferson raised his hands in the air. 'Sorry,' he said.

'Keep your hands like that, where I can see,' said the young man.

When Ayesha had tied Marcus's wrists to his satisfaction, she was sent to bind Jefferson's wrists together behind his back as well.

'Now you will both turn round to look at me,' ordered the visitor.

'You can't do this to us,' said Marcus. 'The house is

alarmed. The police will be here in a minute.'

'I think not. I did not break in so there is no alarm. And yes, I can do this.' He turned back to Ayesha. 'I am tired of his talking. Put tape over his mouth.'

When Ayesha had obeyed, and gagged Jefferson as well, he made the two men kneel on the floor facing the far wall, took two dark canvas hoods from his backpack and slipped them over their heads.

'They'll suffocate!' objected Ayesha.

'I think they will not.' And he pulled her wrists behind her back, grasped them firmly in one hand, and twisted a length of tape around them. Then he sent her to kneel facing the wall with the other two, her head, like theirs, covered by a hood.

'Nearly finished,' he said cheerfully. And, taking a prepared length of rope, he tied Marcus's legs together, just above the knee, then did the same to Jefferson and Ayesha.

'You will stand up now,' he said to Marcus.

Marcus shook his head.

'Lean forward. Bend your feet.' And taking one elbow, he hauled Marcus upright. 'Now the son.' Jefferson staggered to his feet with the young man's help. 'And the mother.' He could lift Ayesha up with one hand.

'Now I will remove hoods and you will all walk to the car. We will be slow, but it is possible, you will find.'

The three gagged figures shuffled out through the front door. It was dark outside, they noticed, and their security lights were not working. Doubtless the efficient gunman had dealt with them before ringing the doorbell. In the space beyond Marcus's own car stood something long and low, an Audi maybe.

The young man opened the rear passenger door.

'One at a time,' he said. 'You will manage it, I think.'

It was tricky, tied at the knee, but each of them did

311

manage it, 'Arse first,' as the young man put it, bending over and sliding across the smooth leather seat one after the other. Ayesha was the last one inside. They sat there like three life-sized dolls, silenced by their gags, while their visitor once more placed the hoods over their heads.

'Heads on knees,' he ordered, neatly and quickly fitting a silencer on to the barrel of the gun. And then he shot them, Marcus first, Jefferson next, and finally Ayesha. Twice each, in the back of the neck.

He could have told them, before pulling the trigger for the first time, 'This is for Rosemary Ivory,' but he had no sense of drama, or even of closure, and so they died without ever knowing why.

The powerful engine started with barely a sound and the car glided out of the gate and slid smoothly into the road. Fifty yards on, Jorge turned on the headlights and drove towards the Banbury Road, taking the road towards the bypass.

He followed the A40 westwards to Witney, turning off and taking the narrow, potholed road towards one of the gravel pits. When he reached the secluded area he had chosen carefully two days earlier, he parked the car, got out, opened the boot and removed a spade.

The grave had been prepared, at night, twenty-four hours before. Now it was only a case of tipping in the bodies and shovelling back the soil. It was hard work on his own, but he was a fit young man.

He noticed a slight depression in the surface when he had finished, but even as he watched, the water seeped back into it. Around him were hillocks of earth and gravel and puddles of water. So similar were they that he could scarcely tell which was the one he had just created.

It was nearly over. He drove a mile along the track to where another car was parked, waiting for him. Da Gama had followed him in his own car when he had left it there early that morning, out of sight of the lorries that came to collect gravel, and had given him a lift back to Oxford. Da Gama hadn't known what the car was for, and neither had he asked.

Jorge drove to the edge of the gravel pit and stopped the engine. He didn't set the handbrake or leave the car in gear.

Thirty feet below him the surface of the water reflected back the light of the moon. Jorge pushed the heavy car until at last he overcame the inertia of its weight and it rolled slowly forwards, finally tipping over the edge into the void. A second later he heard the splash, and watched the ripples catch the light and finally settle as smooth as glass.